MOBILE 9

MOBILE 9

A Novel

BILL HAUGLAND

Véhicule Press

Published with the generous assistance of The Canada Council for the Arts, the Book Publishing Industry Development Program of the Department of Canadian Heritage and the Société de développement des entreprises culturelles du Québec (SODEC).

Cover design: David Drummond
Set in Adobe Minion and Helvetica Condensed by Simon Garamond
Printed by Marquis Book Printing Inc.

Copyright © Bill Haugland 2009

Dépôt légal, Bibliothèque nationale du Québec and the National Library of Canada, secpnd trimester 2009
All rights reserved.

LIBRARY AND ARCHIVES CANADA CATALOGUING IN PUBLICATION

Haugland, Bill

Mobile 9 / Bill Haugland.

ISBN 978-1-55065-255-0

I. Title. II. Title: Mobile nine.

PS8615.A785M63 2009   C813'.6   C2009-900677-4

Mobile 9 is strictly a work of fiction. Plot line and characters are a product of my imagination and are in no way intended to reflect on individuals, living or deceased. Certain events that actually occurred in 1969 are woven into the story for effect. I've taken license with the time frame of certain others, particularly in reference to organized crime in Montreal. Personalities, places and events in this regard are of my own invention and are merely a vehicle I've employed to move the narrative along.

Published by Véhicule Press, Montréal, Québec, Canada
www.vehiculepress.com

Distribution in Canada by LitDistCo
www.litdistco.ca

Distribution in U.S. by Independent Publishers Group
www.ipgbook.com

Printed in Canada on 100% post-consumer recycled paper.

To my wife Linda and my former colleagues and good friends Bill Draper, Tom Sharina and the late Bert Cannings. Fond memories of youthful days in the "news-biz."

Chapter One

TV cameraman Greg Peterson was exhausted. He'd put in a long shift, covering an overnight series of drug raids. He couldn't remember how many cups of coffee he'd swallowed. Yet he had a gut feeling the action was just beginning. Greg was usually right about gut feelings.

His perfectionism added to the pressure. The film had to be processed at the lab in downtown Montreal. Editing and scripting would come later in the day. Reporter Ty Davis would be under pressure to tell the story in fewer than a hundred seconds and neither he nor Ty would get any feedback on content before it went to air. The rule for reporters and cameramen was sink or swim. Get the story and succeed. Miss the shots or the point of the story, and live with the reputation.

So far, 1969 had been a year of escalating political turmoil in Quebec. Members of the Quebec Liberation Front, the FLQ, roamed the streets of Montreal. Bombs exploded. Manifestos espousing the need for Quebec to separate from the rest of Canada were delivered to media outlets. Greg enjoyed the challenge, but long hours and sleepless nights were sapping his energy and dulling his senses. He yawned, stretched his arms overhead and winced as a sharp pain traced its way across his right shoulder and down his spine.

The police sweep, dubbed *Opération Cantons de l'Est*, Operation Eastern Townships, began at 2 a.m. Five drug raids in the Townships resulted in twelve arrests. Greg had been tipped off at midnight by assignment editor Jason Moore.

"It's big!" Jason promised. "Cops say biggest bust in years." He sounded excited.

As he stepped out of the car back in Montreal, Greg squinted into the early morning sunshine. His head ached, and the August day wasn't helping. The humidity was high. It was already much too hot.

Montreal's Flash News won its viewer loyalty and ratings dominance by being first with breaking stories. Moore, nicknamed "Scoop," was on a first-name basis with most key players in the Montreal Police Department, the Quebec Provincial Police and the RCMP. They often gave him a heads-up on any major operation, so he could scramble his reporters and camera personnel.

Greg had shot plenty of sound-film in the Townships. He'd forgotten to load the Bell and Howell hand-held silent camera into his news mobile the day before, contrary to normal routine. Cameramen assigned a company vehicle were obliged to pack all the equipment that they might need for the next assignment. By the time Greg reached the Townships, the raid was in full swing. He'd gone with sound and the cumbersome shoulder-mount.

"Get that footage to the lab," Moore told him. "Cops called a press conference for later this morning. Drugs'll be on display for the media, so shoot sound if Davis shows up a little late. He'll meet you and bring the Bell and Howell. You got five hours. Go home. Get some sleep. RCMP headquarters at eleven, 10-4?"

Greg stared at the mobile radio for a few moments before responding.

"Yeah. Okay. 10-4."

He never could figure out why Moore insisted on the military code being used in all radio transmissions. "10-9" for "location." "10-6" for "repeat." "10-10" for "arrived at destination." "10-4" to end a sentence. Some reporters believed it stemmed from a secret desire to be a police officer. Moore, they said, hadn't met the height requirement, and played at being a police dispatcher.

Ty Davis knew better. He'd been in plenty of situations where static interference made radio contact with the station difficult, if not impossible. The code was most likely to be heard clearly. The emergency "10-5", for example, signalled the newsroom there was trouble. It was brief and avoided lengthy explanation. Moore knew where you were. As soon as he heard "10-5," he could call out the troops.

Ty lit a cigarette and stared at his typewriter. The overnight footage on the police raids had been processed and returned from the lab. There was plenty of wild sound as the cops kicked down doors, cuffed suspects and seized the drugs.

He glanced at the news director's office. The door was ajar. A faint blue cloud of cigar smoke wafted into the news department, momentarily clinging to the teletype machines. Clyde Bertram was in. Ty checked his watch. Nine-forty-five. Plenty of time to dig up some background on the police operation before the press conference. He pushed away from the typewriter, stood up and walked into Bertram's office.

The news director was on the phone, tipped back in his chair with his feet on his desk. The office reeked of cigar. Ty waited in the doorway until Bertram waved at him to sit down. He was a huge man with thinning red hair and a wisp of a mustache, carefully trimmed to turn up at the ends, a Salvador Dali wannabe. His midsection was so bulky, no belt would fit. Baggy trousers were held up by suspenders.

"Call you back, Don," he said. "Gotta go." He hung up the phone and laboriously moved his feet to the floor. Ty sat on one of the chairs in front of Clyde's desk.

"Waddya got, Ty?" He stuck the cigar into the corner of his mouth.

"Greg's been out most of the night. Bunch of police raids in the Townships. Drugs. Arrests. The whole nine yards."

Bertram puffed out a mouthful of smoke. "Heard about it from Moore. Got a price tag on the drugs?"

Ty shifted his weight in the chair. "We'll know about that from the cops in about an hour."

Bertram nodded and picked up his phone again.

"Okay, kid. Stick with it. Wrap the piece for the six o'clock."

Ty went back to his typewriter.

He resented being referred to as "the kid." He was in his late twenties. He'd been on the payroll for seven years and was married with two children. He paid his bills, worked hard at his job, and felt the "kid" reference was an insult. Ty considered himself a product of the times. Richard Nixon was in his second year as U.S. President. War raged in Vietnam and Americans were sharply divided on the need to spill blood in the name of democracy. Ty sometimes found it difficult not to inject anti-war sentiment into the on-air work. He and Greg saw eye-to-eye on matters of war and peace.

Sometimes he hated the job. Ty wished somebody would have the *cojones* to tell Bertram to shove his cigars where the sun don't shine. The news director constantly berated him for what he called his "hippie haircut." He invariably advised Moore to assign any story involving Vietnam to Ty and Greg. Then he'd call them both into his office, grin from ear to ear, blow fetid smoke into their faces and criticize their leftist politics. If Ty and Greg felt they'd lent a justifiable slant to the story, Bertram would argue they had no business editorializing. Then he'd rant on about the domino theory, a scenario that foresaw a Communist takeover of all of Southeast Asia. "Somebody's gotta stop 'em. Might as well be the U.S. of A."

Bertram made Ty edit out references to the plight of draft-dodgers who'd taken up residence in Montreal. His efforts to tackle issues involving the homeless and disenfranchised, including Americans who didn't believe in the war, would always be met with another round of bickering in Bertram's office. Draft-dodgers were the lowest of the low in the news director's opinion.

"Cut that pinko shit out."

Ty had his orders. No one could ever argue that the CKCF news department was a democracy. He leaned back in his chair and lit another cigarette. His typewriter stared up at him.

Greg couldn't sleep, stimulated by the black coffee and the high-speed trip down the Ten and back. The Eastern Townships Autoroute connected metropolitan Montreal with farmlands to the east of the city, meandering through a patchwork of communities on the South Shore of the St. Lawrence River.

The region was dotted by old seigneurial lands that bore the history of both English- and French-speaking Quebeckers. Numerous landmarks were named after Abenaki Indians, who had fought against the British in the French-Indian War. United Empire Loyalists who rejected the concept of a country called the United States had settled there at the end of the American Revolution.

Greg lay in bed, wondering if his footage had turned out okay. He lived with his mother in an upper three-bedroom duplex in

Montreal's blue-collar Park Extension district. She was retired from her personnel job at Bell telephone and spent most of her time trying to get Greg to eat more.

"You're too damn skinny," she scolded. "Eat. Eat."

Greg sat on the edge of his bed. His reflection in a full-length wall mirror next to his closet reminded him that his mother was probably right. He looked exhausted. His ribs protruded. Dark circles underlined his eyes.

"Ma," he shouted. He could hear her rattling dishes in the kitchen. "Ma!"

She came down the hall toward his bedroom.

"What godawful time did you get in?" she asked, leaning into the doorway. "I didn't even hear you."

Greg rubbed his eyes and smiled. "It's the job, Ma. Just the job. What're you gonna do?"

"Well, if you can't sleep"—she looked concerned—"I'll fix you some eggs."

Greg stood up. "Make that sunny side up," he grinned.

The news department is the core of a major-market television outlet. It generates more air time than any other local production, and the on-air personnel of CKCF were known throughout the city. Jason Moore often felt under-appreciated. After all, he was the reason guys like Ty Davis had something to report. He was the heart of the news-op, overseeing the wire services, dispatching the reporter-camera units, monitoring the police radio, establishing valuable contacts. Moore believed the assignment editor's job definition was to run the entire ship and then take most of the shit from Clyde Bertram when a story was missed or a reporter wasn't spoon-fed some vital detail. He was always in the eye of the storm.

Moore had a hunch about the Townships raids. He settled back in his chair and concentrated on blocking out the constant noise of the teletypes and the police and mobile radios. At least the phones weren't ringing.

Initial wire copy on *Opération Cantons de l'Est* indicated some sort of regional drug ring. The usual suspects. Local thugs operating out of farm houses and trailer parks. One of the police targets, however, was different. It was a strip joint outside Knowlton, one of the biggest towns in the region. Months before, a contact in the Quebec Provincial Police had told him that the Club Coquettes was more than it appeared to be. It was being watched for prostitution and drugs and, more importantly, as a possible money laundering center for the Montreal mob.

Moore's glassed-in work station provided a clear view of the entire news department. He spotted Ty Davis, back at his typewriter. He tapped on the glass to get the reporter's attention. "Ty, gotta sec?" Ty gestured with his hand. "Yeah, Jason. Be right there."

Ty had learned from one of his own contacts that the Mounties were putting a street value of more than three million dollars on the seized drugs. He closed his note pad and walked into Moore's cubicle.

"Cops're calling it one of the biggest coke busts in history," he said.

"Right. There's more to this than a home-grown drug ring."

The Wood Avenue headquarters of the Royal Canadian Mounted Police sat in the center of one of the most affluent residential neighborhoods in North America. The city of Westmount nestles against Mount Royal, the once volcanic heart of the island of Montreal. Westmount's personality is dictated by its British origins.

Ty walked up the stairs of the RCMP building. He had a heavy wooden tripod slung over his shoulder. In his left hand, he carried the silent camera Greg had forgotten the night before. "Press?" someone asked, after he awkwardly maneuvered the tripod through two sets of glass doors. Ty thought, "Bucking for sergeant," as he sized up the spit-and-polish appearance of the constable who greeted him.

"Right. Flash News for the eleven o'clock news conference."

The constable straightened his shoulders. Ty was sure the man was about to salute. He forced a straight face, as the Mountie turned and pointed to the left. "In there. Ask for Corporal Armand Gadbois." Ty nodded. "Thanks. Are the drugs laid out, by the way?"

The constable wheeled around to face him. "Drugs, cash and weapons." He spoke in a quieter tone, as though revealing a great secret. "Quite a haul."

"Alright then," Ty said. "Lights, camera, action!" The constable didn't appear amused. Ty swung the tripod back over his shoulder, smiled and walked towards an ante-room off the main lobby.

Members of the press were assembling in front of a podium that resembled a tree-stump on a bad-hair day—a tangle of cables led from wall-sockets and portable battery-packs to a riot of microphones that protruded from the podium like Medusa's serpentine locks. Radio and TV reporters who'd arrived early had set their mics in the center. Sound clips, picked up by the others, might prove tinny and hollow. Newspaper reporters had it easy. They carried only their steno-pads and a perennial attitude of superiority. Radio and television, they maintained, were the new kids on the block. Shallow, at best, in their efforts at responsible journalism.

"Ty," someone shouted. "Over here!" It was a tired-looking Greg Peterson. He had taken a cab to RCMP headquarters and had already staked out a section of floor-space to the left of the podium.

Ty pushed his way through the crowd, being careful not to clobber anyone with the heavy tripod. He set it down beside the cameraman.

"You look like shit," Greg said. He tossed back a mane of dark hair and stuck out his lower lip.

"Well," Ty replied with an effeminate air, "I just didn't have time to put on my makeup."

"But, as usual, you look so-o-o-o cute." Greg frequently teased the on-air personnel about their studio makeup.

Ty grinned at his friend. "G'morning to you too."

Corporal Armand Gadbois looked like a walking oil-drum as he entered from an adjoining office and walked to the podium. He strutted on legs that appeared too long and too spindly to support his upper body. He had a barrel-chest, no neck to speak of, and a meaty face that seemed directly attached to his shoulders. His arms were huge. He surveyed the room.

"At approximately zero-two-hundred hours this morning," he began, in a high-pitched nasal voice.

Ty winced and whispered into Greg's ear. "Great, he sounds like Peter Lorre doing a Donald Duck impression."

Greg chuckled. "Do you want any o' this?"

Ty shook his head. "He's not saying anything we don't already know. Let's wait for the Q & A."

* * *

It was something about the name. Jason Moore ran his hand over the top of his head. He was prematurely bald, a process that had begun in his mid-twenties. At thirty-three, he suffered from what some people referred to as "a wide part."

Jason spent the better part of the morning talking with his police contacts about the drug raids. One of them provided him with a list of the eight men and four women who were arrested. Nine were to be arraigned on trafficking charges before the end of the day. Lesser charges were being leveled at the other three. One of the names triggered a memory. Gino Viscuso. Where had he heard that name before? He decided to run it by Clyde Bertram.

The news-director was hovering over a teletype machine. He'd smoked his cigar down to a butt, which still occupied one corner of his mouth. Jason grabbed his notes on the police raids and walked out to the newsroom.

"Clyde," he said.

Bertram was reading some Canadian Press copy. "Yeah, Jason."

"Clyde, one of the guys arrested this morning near Knowlton," Moore glanced at his notes, "his name seems familiar, but I can't put a finger on it. Have you ever heard of Gino Viscuso?"

Bertram raised an eyebrow. "A soldier in the Salvatore Positano crime family. One of the radio operators knows about him, if it's the same Viscuso."

CKCF Radio shared space with CKCF Television, under the same corporate umbrella. The radio studios were down the corridor from the newsroom. Flash News reporters were often required to file radio reports on developing stories while covering for television. They held two microphones, one for radio and one for TV. Writers for television occupied one side of a long, boardroom-style table in the newsroom. Writers for radio worked the other side. There were eight typewriters on the left and eight on the right. When he wasn't in his office, Bertram often sat in a semi-circular slot at the head of the table, overseeing both news divisions. He took pride in a hands-on management approach, but writers were frequently intimidated by his presence. They called him "Big Daddy" behind his back. Bertram had heard the nickname and he liked it.

Moore walked to the radio studios. He pushed through a heavy metal door. It was like entering an air-locked space, foreign to the atmosphere in the rest of the building. Three soundproofed announcer-booths were on his left, each with its own metal door. Recording studios were to the right. A long, narrow corridor in the middle led to another heavy door and the station's master control. Moore pressed his shoulder into it. The on-duty operator, surrounded by audiotape decks and a sea of switches and controls on the master board, swiveled his chair around to greet him.

"How ya doin', Jason?" he asked.

He immediately turned the chair back towards a large window. Each on-air studio had its own window, looking back at master-control. In the central studio, morning-man Gerry Miller was giving a time-check, sounding perky and cheerful in the manner of all radio morning-men.

"CKCF time 11:45. Where are you going for lunch today?" His voice came over the control-room speakers.

Miller cued the operator, who pressed one of a myriad buttons. A reel-to-reel tape began rolling on his right and a smooth voice proclaimed the gastronomic virtues of Sam's Delicatessen in Old Montreal. "Your choice of desserts. Fully licensed," the commercial droned on.

"I'm looking for Joe Maurizio," Moore told the operator.

"Starts at three. Three to midnight."

Moore didn't want to wait that long.

"What about a home phone?"

The commercial came to a close and the operator cued Miller.

"Should be on the shift-schedule," he said. "On the wall behind you."

Moore located the list and made a note of Maurizio's telephone number. "Thanks."

"See y'around," the operator replied.

Victor Gordon's office was the Cadillac of offices at CKCF Radio and Television. Everything Victor owned was as big as he was small. He sat behind an over-sized mahogany desk. He drove a luxury car. His cigars of choice were at least an inch longer and much more expensive than Clyde Bertram's. Most of all, he liked his women big. The taller the better. Long legs. Big chests. Victor thought he deserved the best of everything. After all, he was the boss.

The president's office had three entrances. His secretary occupied an adjoining room. Her door fronted on the main corridor, which led to the sales division. A separate door opened directly into Gordon's office, but even divisional vice-presidents felt they had to go through the secretary to gain access to the boss. A third door led off the corridor into a boardroom, which was an extension of the president's office. Nobody went through the boardroom. It was an invitations-only kind of portal to the inner sanctum.

Victor Gordon was feeling pleased with himself. He'd managed to achieve a corporate *coup d'état* in sales, hand-picking a retail sales V.P. over the protests of a majority of the sales staff. He'd put down a potential palace revolt by carefully explaining to the salesmen that they had a choice, either accept the new vice president or take the proverbial door. It was how he conducted most of his business affairs.

"My way," Gordon said out loud, "or the highway."

After the RCMP news conference Mobile 7 wound through traffic. Greg Peterson was driving to the film-processing lab, and lunch-hour tie-ups were to be expected. Ty Davis sat in the passenger seat writing his on-camera intro and extro. They were often teamed-up for an entire shift.

The car radio was at high volume, tuned to the local rock station and Greg was singing along with a Bob Dylan hit. Greg was matching it decibel for decibel. He had an uncanny ability to copy Dylan's style, but Ty found the combination of the radio and the singalong distracting.

"Jesus! Can ya keep it down for a minute?"

Greg put on a hurt expression. "My singing offends you?"

Ty scowled. "Between you and Dylan, I'm not sure there's a pane of glass within a hundred yards that's still in one piece."

Greg turned off the radio. "Touchy, touchy. Must be your time of the month."

Ty smiled. "Actually, I'm just frustrated. That Corporal was useless. We'll be lucky to get fifteen seconds of sound."

"Lots of silent stuff though," Greg reminded him.

The Mounties had set up a display of seized drugs, weapons and cash on a long table. Greg had protested against Ty's assertion that he should do his on-camera standup in front of the table.

"Bo-o-oring," Greg said. "You do the talking. Let my camera do the walking."

They'd agreed to do the sound-piece after dropping the rest of the stuff at the lab.

"Cops're fulla' crap, though," Ty said as they approached University Street along Pine Avenue. "They claim this was the biggest coke bust in years, if not the biggest ever. What they're doing is a bit of a shell game. They focus the media on weapons, emphasizing the potential for violence. They get us to shoot plenty of footage of the cash, which is incidental. We're steered away from the actual quantity of the drugs." He paused, thinking it over. "In fact," he said suddenly, "I'm going to use that in my intro."

Greg turned right onto University and descended a steep hill into the city's downtown core.

"What are you going to use in the intro?" he asked.

"The truth," Ty replied. "Cops want us to believe they're making history with these raids, but how'd they come up with this three million dollar figure?"

Greg grinned. "You're the damn reporter. You tell me."

He glanced to his left. Two youths, standing at the University-Sherbrooke corner, had flipped him the finger. CKCF Television was widely known as the voice of Montreal's English-speaking community. The station's logo was clearly displayed on both sides of the car. French-speaking separatist militants frequently showed their disapproval, sometimes violently. Two cars had been attacked recently, and one of them was actually overturned. A McGill University student, riding along that day, had to be treated in hospital for a gash on his cheek.

"If you take all that cocaine," Ty continued, "and divide it into kilograms, you'll get one street value. What the cops did is divide it all into grams. Sold in bulk as kilos it doesn't add up the same. Sold as grams, a street dealer is gonna pull in one hell of a lot more bread. A thousand grams in a kilo. Individual street price for each gram. See what I mean?"

Greg nodded. "Fuckin' far out. See, that's why they pay you the big bucks."

* * *

Jason Moore was busy. The ten-to-seven shift began and he assigned a reporter-camera crew to the Mayor's office. City hall and Mayor Jean Drapeau were still reaping the political benefits of global attention that followed the Expo 67 world's fair. Drapeau's reputation for putting Montreal on the map was recognized in virtually all major capitals. The mayor, however, was viewed by the mainstream media as an autocrat. Moore, like all editors worth their salt, was determined to pin him down on several issues.

Jason finally had an opportunity to make a call to Joe Maurizio, the radio guy. For the moment, at least, the newsroom was quiet. The phone rang several times before Maurizio answered.

"Hello," he sounded not quite awake.

"Joe?" Jason asked.

"Yeah."

"Joe, it's Jason Moore at the station."

A pause.

"Yeah, Jason." Maurizio seemed surprised. "What can I do for television today?"

Moore was accustomed to sarcasm when dealing with radio types. It was always a friendly sort of rivalry between the two divisions, but there was an underlying sense of territory. Moore saw it as a kind of perennial pissing match, particularly among the radio and TV on-air personnel.

"Joe," Moore said, "Clyde Bertram mentioned that you might know something about a guy named Gino Viscuso."

There was a shuffling noise at the other end of the line. Maurizio came back on. "Yeah, that's right. It's the Italian connection."

Moore laughed. "You're all the same," he replied. "Seriously though, Joe, *how* do you know Viscuso, and what do you know about him?"

"The fights," Maurizio said. "Boxing. Every time one o' the Sands kids is in the ring, in an out-of-town fight on a Friday night, this guy calls me up. No idea how he got the direct line to master-control, but he calls me direct and asks how the fight's goin'. Seems most interested in Billy Sands."

Moore's general knowledge of sports was limited. He knew of the Sands family, however. Billy and his two brothers were notorious. All were fighters. All followed the Sands family tradition of ringside controversy and run-ins with the police. There was a history of tavern brawls and rumors of mob influence.

"What's Viscuso want to know?" Moore asked.

"That's it. How's the fight goin'? That's it."

Moore digested the information. "And he never calls unless one of the Sands brothers is on the card?"

"Nope. Like I say, he's got the hots for Billy Sands more'n the others."

Moore recalled that Billy had come up through the ranks quickly. The World Boxing Association even felt he had a shot at a middleweight championship bout.

"Okay. Thanks Joe," he said.

"You gonna tell me what it's all about?"

"Nah. We're television, y'know. Lots of secrets."

"Yeah. Screw you and the horse you rode in on."

Moore hung up. He was sure the Sands family had connections with organized crime in Montreal. Clyde Bertram had identified Gino Viscuso as a "soldier" in the Positano family. It followed that Viscuso's calls to CKCF radio were prompted by the mob. The Townships drug ring, like so many criminal activities, probably had its roots in Montreal. Now, he thought, all he had to do was wait until the courts kicked in. Then he might be able to link the entire operation to the Montreal Mafia.

Formal charges were brought against Gino Viscuso about four o'clock in the afternoon. Two hours before air-time, Clyde Bertram was consulting with Moore on the Davis piece.

"He's missed the point," Bertram told the assignment editor.

"This Townships thing has all the earmarks of a much bigger story. Davis is knocking the cops and ignoring the broader picture."

Moore pursed his lips. "In fairness, though, Clyde. He didn't know a whole hell of a lot about the mob angle. In fact, he didn't know anything about this Viscuso character."

Bertram looked angry. "Christ, why not?"

Moore's face reddened. "Well, Clyde, neither did we, until I got a hold of Maurizio. Viscuso wasn't even charged until late this afternoon."

"Yeah, yeah," Bertram snarled. "You should have kept him in the loop."

Moore pulled a pencil from behind his ear. "What about this?" He jotted some words on a note pad.

Bertram waited until he was finished and began to read it aloud. "Flash News has learned that a series of police raids in the Eastern Townships last night was connected to the Positano crime family in Montreal. How you gonna prove that?"

"Viscuso *is* one of the boys," Moore replied.

"You know that. I know that. But we can't say it on the air." He clucked his tongue. "Look. You say Viscuso has been arraigned?"

"That's right."

"Okay. What are the charges?"

"Trafficking is the main charge. Some other weapons-related stuff. Could be more coming."

Moore could see that Bertram was concerned about drawing a direct line between Viscuso and Salvatore Positano.

"How about this, then," he continued. "We simply get the anchor to say Flash News has learned there could be connections with organized crime in Montreal, and leave it at that?"

"That's the way to go," Bertram agreed. "Then you'll have to add in Davis's main focus about the RCMP overblowing the size and significance of the coke bust. Goddam kid drives me crazy. Give him the reins, he'd probably be calling the cops *pigs*."

Bertram pulled out a fresh cigar from a breast pocket.

"This thing is gonna have follow-ups. Give Davis and Peterson mobile units to take home tonight. Both of 'em. Separate cars. I want 'em front and center by seven tomorrow morning."

He bit off the end of the cigar and retreated into his office.

Chapter Two

A black limousine, followed by two cars, pulled up at Cabrini Hall in Montreal's Italian district. The hall was lit up and the sounds of a live band spilled into Jean Talon Street. Several people were out in front of the building, with drinks in hand. Others were just arriving and trying to find parking on the side streets. The limousine's tinted windows made it impossible to see who was inside. Four men climbed out of the cars and began walking towards the limo.

Two of them took up positions on the driver's side, two on the passenger side. The rear door swung open and Salvatore Positano stepped out. His bodyguards immediately closed ranks around him. The five men walked toward the hall.

"Sal!" someone shouted.

A portly, middle-aged man left the group at the entrance and raised his arms to embrace Positano.

"Sal. Good t' see yah."

They hugged, slapping each other on the back. Positano kissed the man on each cheek.

"You too, Massimo. You too. How's the family?"

The other men, who were gathered at the front doors of Cabrini Hall, stepped aside to let them through. A young man with slicked-back hair and an unbuttoned shirt that drew attention to a gold chain around his neck said " 'Lo, Sal." Positano just nodded and walked past him. Two of his bodyguards entered the hall first. Positano and the rotund Mafia *caporegime*, Massimo Gianfranco, went in together.

Ty Davis drove home slowly. He never quite knew what to expect when he got there. Usually Elizabeth was into her first martini, but that was when he came home at the supper hour. Now it was after nine. He swung Mobile 14 into the laneway next to his flat and plucked a microphone off the dashboard.

"Fourteen to News," he said.

There was a loud clicking sound as he released his finger from a transmission switch on the mic.

A female voice said "Go ahead, Fourteen."

It was Maggie Price, the lineup editor for the late news. Ty smiled. He liked Maggie.

"Hi, Mag. I'm 10-10 at my house."

"Long day," she responded.

"Too long. See you tomorrow, Mag. Have a good show."

He turned off the radio and the car engine and, as he walked out of the lane on to the sidewalk in front of his home, he couldn't help feeling a sense of pride. The flat he and Elizabeth rented was more than they could really afford, but the residential street in Montreal's west-end Notre Dame de Grace district, commonly known as N.D.G., was tree-lined and peaceful. The sun had set long ago, but a street lamp cast a gentle, golden glow into the immediate area around his front stairs. The leaves of a nearby tree rustled in the warm August evening.

An entire block of flats stretched between Terrebonne and Monkland Avenues. Each brick building housed four units, two upstairs and two on the ground floor. Inside, a foyer stood at the head of a long hallway. A huge living room off the hall featured a log-burning fireplace. Multi-paned windows fronted onto Oxford Avenue, and each pane of glass was artfully framed in bronze-colored metal.

A wooden archway, carved in the Victorian gingerbread style, led from the living- room into a full-sized dining room. Three large bedrooms were further down the hall, then a bathroom and a kitchen complete with breakfast nook and walk-in pantry. There was even a maid's room off the kitchen, but of course there was no money for a maid. It was the perfect location for their washing machine.

In happier days, he and Elizabeth had turned it into a sort of morning-room. Lots of green plants. A couple of comfortable chairs with a small table between them. The sun streamed through an east window. The two often shared their morning coffee in that room.

That was before. After their son, Robin, was born, Elizabeth slipped into postpartum depression. Her doctor prescribed mood-altering drugs. Ty's company insurance provided counseling. Nothing worked. Elizabeth began drinking.

At first, Ty thought she showed signs of recovery from the depression. After her first martini, she seemed happy and talkative; more like her old self. That was fine, until the after-dinner habit became two or three martinis. The talk turned bitter and angry. The relationship began to decline. Robin was now two years old. Their daughter, Catherine, was four and in pre-school. By nine o'clock at night, Elizabeth was usually drunk.

Greg Peterson was in a deep sleep when the phone on his bedside table began ringing. At first, the sound melded with a dream he was having. He was in high school. He was writing an exam he hadn't studied for, and the school bell was ringing.

"Pencils down," the teacher said. "Time's up."

She was wearing a purple dress that was blinking on and off like a strobe light. She looked like Mick Jagger.

Gradually, Greg emerged from the dream. His heart was pounding as he reached for the phone. His alarm clock said 4 a.m.

"H-hello," he said sleepily. It was Moore. His tone was serious.

"Sorry to wake you," Moore apologized. "Something's happened downtown."

Greg resisted an urge to snap at the assignment editor.

"Geez," he said instead. "Two nights in a row, Jason. A guy's gotta sleep sometime."

There was a pause on the line. "This isn't about a news story. Or let me put it a different way. Let's hope to hell it doesn't become one."

Greg was fully awake.

"What are you talking about? Y'know, it's four in the morning?"

"A woman has been attacked, Greg."

"Yah-h-h, so-o-o? This is worth getting me out of bed?"

"Out of a CKCF News mobile unit."

Greg threw back his covers and sat on the edge of the bed. "Holy shit!"

"Seems some guy went out on his balcony for a smoke, about one-thirty this morning. He spots the car, parked at the curb just below. A man is arguing with the woman on the sidewalk. He grabs her and lets loose with a roundhouse blow to the side of her head."

"Christ."

"There's more," Moore added. "She goes down. He kicks her in the stomach. Leaves her there. Gets into the news vehicle and takes off."

"Well, I'll be a son of a bitch. What I don't get is what all of this has to do with me."

For a moment, Moore was silent.

"It's Bertram," he said. "He wants you and Ty and anybody else who had access to a CKCF news mobile in a police lineup. Downtown in about three hours."

Greg was stunned.

"A police lineup! What the fuck for?"

"He woke me up twenty minutes ago, Greg. The main reason is both you guys have mobiles at home. The cops are going to dig that up anyway. Bertram also figures you and Ty are, uh, hop-heads."

"The hell is that?"

"Marijuana. Look, don't get me wrong. Clyde loves the way you two work together. He's happy, almost all the time, with your productivity and so on. But he thinks you're a coupla' hippies."

"Why? Because we both have long hair?"

"That and the fact that you both come off, well, anti-establishment. Peace and love and all that crap."

Greg felt his ears redden.

"Goddam' it, Jason. You mean, he figures that anybody who has a leftist philosophy or who might think the U.S. should get out of Vietnam, is capable of violently attacking a woman? Does that make any friggin' sense to you?"

"No, it doesn't. But he's the boss. He told me to call you and Ty, and that's what I'm doing." He cleared his throat. "Just so I know, Greg, you been home all night?"

"All evening. All night."

"Your mother can back that up?"

Greg thought for a moment. "Yeah," he said. "Yeah, she can, but you said this thing happened at about one-thirty this morning. She was asleep, Jason. And I was trying to sleep. Christ, I'm bloody exhausted."

"Okay. So if it came right down to it, she couldn't alibi you."

"Guess not. I just sneaked out of the house after she went to bed, drove all the way downtown, parked the car when I spotted a potential victim then beat the shit out of her."

"I know you didn't!" Moore emphasized. "But I had to ask."

Greg took a pack of cigarettes off his side table.

"Sure," he said. "Fuck you."

Chapter Three

Two horse-drawn *calèches* blocked the early morning traffic flow. The *calèche* drivers decided to stop side by side on eastbound Notre Dame Street, at the very moment Ty Davis was trying to make a left hand turn off St. Laurent. It was 6:40 a.m. The drivers were probably discussing their plans for the day, before the morning rush hour reached its peak. They waved their arms at each other, engaged in animated conversation. Neither they nor the horses paid attention to Ty and half a dozen other motorists who were honking their horns impatiently.

Ty figured he'd park Mobile 14 on the Champs de Mars behind city hall, and walk over to the Gosford Street entrance of Montreal police headquarters. He'd done it hundreds of times. Media vehicles were a common sight in the huge parking lot. There was no fee for the press.

One of the *calèches* finally pulled out of the way, allowing traffic to start moving again. Ty was thinking about the sleeping faces of his children. So innocent, so peaceful, as he'd prepared to leave home. Robin was still oblivious to the tension between Elizabeth and him. Catherine, despite her young age, was beginning to sense that something was wrong. Her pre-school teacher had called recently to complain that Catherine had bitten one of the other children. She was already starting to act out her own frustrations.

Old Montreal, once a walled-in fortress called Ville Marie, covered an area of less than half a square mile. It reflected a bygone era, caught timelessly between the St. Lawrence River and the city's modern core. Narrow, often cobbled, streets wormed their way through a collection of museums, parks, hotels, restaurants and businesses. Tourists flocked into the area from all over the world. Inside of two hours, it would be bustling with life. Lost in thought Ty drove past Notre Dame Basilica.

Greg Peterson walked past the cellblock at Montreal police headquarters. The anger he'd experienced with the 4 a.m. call had barely subsided. He knew Jason Moore was just following Bertram's orders, so the anger was mixed with guilt for telling the assignment editor to go fuck himself.

Greg paced back and forth outside a large door off the main lobby. A female officer told him to wait there while the lineup was organized. There was a hard, wooden bench along one wall, but sitting down seemed out of the question.

He had left a note for his mother, telling her only that he'd had an early call from the station. She was used to his comings and goings and he didn't want her to worry. He, on the other hand, *was* worried. Someone, driving a CKCF news mobile, had attacked a young woman. Was it random? Was there something more to it? The reality of the situation hadn't entirely sunk in.

Greg glanced at his watch just as Ty Davis sauntered up to him.

"Wanna put the cuffs on me now?" Ty grinned. "Or ya figure we should try to make a break for it?"

Greg smiled back. He needed some comic relief right about now.

"I don't get it. Why us?"

"Just lucky, I guess," Ty replied. "Besides us, though, I want to know who else had company cars at home last night. Bertram's welcome to think we're a couple of freaks, but—"

He was cut off in mid-sentence. Dick Tomlin, the overnight police reporter, was walking toward them.

"Hi guys. Ain't this fun?"

Dick was wearing a T-shirt that read "Tricky Dick," a reference to his own name, but in fact a caption for the cartoon drawing of Richard Nixon on the back of the shirt. Tricky Dick was shown flashing his double-handed "V" for victory, with his left foot firmly planted on the throat of a Vietcong guerrilla fighter. Tomlin didn't share an anti-war philosophy, but liked presenting a hip image.

He was in the last two hours of his midnight-to-nine shift. His job at CKCF Radio and Television was to monitor the police radios overnight, follow up on any developing local stories, clear and organize teletype wire-copy for the radio announcer who came in to prepare a 6 a.m. newscast, and call Clyde Bertram if something major occurred.

"Anything happening in Gotham City?" Ty asked.

Tomlin shrugged.

"Couple of fires, the usual shit."

"You here for the lineup?" Greg wanted to know.

Tomlin often visited the cop shop to check on stories and to develop his contacts.

"Yeah, yeah. Bertram's really pissed. Says everybody with a mobile unit, you guys, me and Keith Campbell all gotta be here."

Campbell, a radio full-timer, usually reported for work at five to prepare his first newscast.

Ty had a sudden thought.

"What about keys? Anybody take a car out during the night?"

Tomlin hesitated before answering. One of his duties was to keep track of all mobiles in use overnight. A pegboard, containing all the keys, hung on the wall in Jason Moore's office.

"No," he finally said. "Least, I don't think so." Another pause. "I, uh. I was on the road for awhile."

Something about the police reporter's eyes troubled Davis. Tomlin's eyes weren't meeting his own.

No one saw Maria Claudio. She knew her way around the building. Maria had no trouble locating the detective-sergeant she'd spoken to, after she'd picked herself up off the sidewalk. Her ear was bleeding after the beating. Her stomach hurt like hell. Maria knew where the police lineup would take place. She pushed through the right doors, carefully avoiding the one that would have opened on to the main hall. Maria had no intention of letting herself be seen by any of the CKCF personnel. She'd entered police headquarters by a side street. She'd been here many times before.

Detective-Sergeant Pierre Maillot stood up from his desk to greet her. "*Mademoiselle*, this way, *s'il vous plaît*."

He ushered Maria into a long, narrow room, lit only by a dim blue light.

"Number three, step forward please."

The voice came from two speakers to the right and left of a broad, one-way mirror. Ty Davis, Greg Peterson, Dick Tomlin, Keith Campbell and a CKCF technician known around the station as Brains stood side by side. Brains often took a news mobile home with him, to work on a two-way radio or some other technical problem. Two other men, probably cops, were also in the lineup. Greg was number three. He stepped forward.

"Turn to your left please," the voice said.

Greg glanced at Ty and followed the instruction. He was suddenly overcome with an urge to giggle. This whole thing seemed ridiculous and he was very, very tired.

"Alright. Face front and step back, number three."

Greg did so. For what seemed an eternity, the voice was silent. Then a door opened at one end of the lineup room. Detective-Sergeant Pierre Maillot stepped through.

"*Monsieur* Peterson, follow me." He gestured at the others. "The rest of you, *merci*. You can go."

Greg had lost the need to giggle. He felt a cold rush up his spinal column.

"We'll wait outside," Ty quickly told him. "Don't sweat it, man."

Greg followed the detective into a sprawling office space, containing twenty large desks. Only half were occupied at this early hour. Maillot pointed to a single chair next to his own.

"Have a seat, *monsieur*."

Greg noted the tone of voice was stern, almost unfriendly.

"What happened in there?" he asked.

Maillot sat down behind his desk and shuffled some papers.

"If you don't mind, *monsieur*. I'll ask the questions. The complainant has identified you as the one who attacked her this morning."

Greg's eyes widened in disbelief.

"That's crazy!"

"Perhaps," said Maillot. "Can you tell me where you were and what you were doing, between one and two o'clock?"

"Home. I was home, asleep."

The detective began taking notes.

"And you live in the north end?"

"Yes. Querbes Avenue in Park Extension."

More notes.

"Can anyone verify your whereabouts?"

Greg knew the question was inevitable.

"I live with my mother," he said.

"A widow?" Maillot looked directly into Greg's eyes.

"Yes."

"She can confirm you were on the premises?"

"She was asleep. She can confirm that I went to bed shortly after ten. She was watching television and I was very tired."

Maillot scribbled something down.

"But she can't say whether you left the house later," he said matter-of-factly.

Greg began to feel nauseous.

"At one-thirty in the morning," he began, in a voice that sounded thin and high-pitched, "she was asleep. I was asleep. Most people are asleep aren't they?"

"Not the man who attacked the young woman downtown."

"It wasn't me," Greg said desperately.

"We will see. That is all for now, *monsieur*."

Greg swallowed hard. "Well what happens next? Am I under arrest or something?"

Maillot smiled. "For the present, no. We will be in touch." He handed Greg a business card. "You can reach me at this number."

The interview was over.

"Son of a bitch."

Clyde Bertram paced back and forth in the office of CKCF's operations chief, Hal Nichols, who threw up his hands.

"I have no choice," he told the News Director. "This is a criminal matter. Peterson is facing possible criminal charges."

Bertram stopped in front of Nichols's desk and brought his fist down on it.

"Goddam it Hal, the kid is my best shooter. And the operative word here is possible." He paused for effect. "*Possible* criminal charges."

Nichols winced. He was never at ease in Bertram's company.

"I know that, Clyde, but the woman positively ID'd Peterson. It's a matter of company policy. I'll have to put him on suspension, without pay, until this thing is cleared up. I say again, I have no choice."

"You're a prick."

The operations chief scowled.

"Company policy, Clyde. I'll take it to Victor Gordon, but I'm sure he'll agree. If I keep Peterson on, it's my ass in the sling."

Bertram turned to leave.

"You *are* an ass," he said, stalking out the door.

Chapter Four

Polo's Restaurant and Bar, otherwise referred to by CKCF personnel as The Hole, was a city block away from the television station. It was a home away from home for Flash News; an extension of the work-day, away from interruptions and management oversight. Polo's was rumored to be owned by the mob. Salvatore Positano and his cohorts were often seen at table, scarfing down copious quantities of pasta, veal and fish.

Ty Davis, Greg Peterson and Jason Moore sat in a corner. Nick, the barkeep, had refilled their pitcher of beer. The three men were deep in hushed conversation. Greg was tearful.

"Fuck am I gonna do?" he threw out the question, not expecting an answer. "My mother depends on my paycheck."

Moore was writing something into a notepad.

"Stay focused, for one thing," he said. "Let's look at what we know."

He held his notes in the center of the table, so all three could see them.

"Number one, and most importantly, you were home when the attack took place." He looked at Greg. "But we can't prove it, because your mom was asleep."

"Right," Greg agreed.

"Number two. We know that mobile units 7 and 14 were with you and Ty. Dick Tomlin used Mobile 10 that night. Keith Campbell had number 8 at home and Brains was driving Mobile 6."

Greg and Ty nodded in unison. Moore tapped his notes with one finger.

"Fifteen cars in the fleet. Five are unmarked. No logo. That leaves five marked and five unmarked in the parking lot. There were ten sets of keys hanging in my office."

"Under the watchful eye of our beloved police reporter," Ty interjected.

Ty wasn't a fan of Dick Tomlin.

"When I asked him, the other day, whether anyone took a car out that night, he wasn't sure."

"And that," said Moore, "brings me to number three on the list. Whenever someone uses a company vehicle, it has to be signed out. No one signed for any of the cars, except for Tomlin when he made his rounds at the cop shops. According to the sheet, he signed out Mobile 10 at twenty-two minutes after he checked in at midnight."

Greg swallowed a mouthful of beer.

"Wait a minute. Who says Tomlin couldn't have beat up that woman? He was on the road. He was out there."

"One problem," Ty replied. "She says *you* did it."

Moore appeared frustrated.

"We're getting off track. Tomlin was uncertain when you asked him about anyone else taking a car off the lot. He was on his rounds between twelve twenty-two and two-thirty, when he returned to the station. I called him shortly after four, to tell him about the attack downtown and Bertram's orders that all you guys had to be in a police lineup."

Ty scratched his head and appeared confused.

"So, for better than two hours, anyone could have helped themselves to the keys."

"And we know someone did," Moore said, "and they didn't sign the car out."

Greg glanced at Moore's notes.

"Or, Tomlin's lying. Maybe he's covering for somebody."

"Point number four," Moore began writing. "Tomlin was out of the building until two-thirty. We'll have to talk with Maggie Price and everybody involved with the late news that night. We don't know whether all of them actually left the station, when the show was over. Could be someone was still in the building, when Tomlin pulled out at twelve twenty-two."

Ty had a thought.

"Let's assume Tomlin is on the up-'n'-up, that he isn't aware who might have borrowed those keys. We know the attacker was in a marked CKCF mobile. Maybe it wasn't somebody from news at all.

Maybe they were from some other department. They either knew about our system of signing in and out and ignored it, or they didn't know about it and just helped themselves to the keys."

"Yeah!" Greg exclaimed. "Maybe they took the keys earlier in the evening, when Maggie was down the hall getting coffee or something. The anchor doesn't report in 'til ten. Your office is wide open, Jason. Christ, it could have been anybody."

"Point number five," said Moore. "We have to start interviewing Maggie, members of the studio crew, the anchor, the control-room people. Anyone who was in the building, let's say, after the early news signed off and the night shifts began."

Ty groaned. "We should use a tape-recorder. This is gonna take awhile."

Chapter Five

The first few days of September hit like a sledgehammer. The heat and humidity lifted suddenly and gusty winds carried a cold front in from the north. Ty Davis turned off Terrebonne Avenue and drove slowly down Oxford toward home. The heater was on in Mobile 14. Greg Peterson had left town. He discussed the idea with Ty and Jason Moore. They agreed to carry on with their investigation while Greg "got his shit together," as he put it. He'd been badly shaken by the recent events and decided to visit his girlfriend in Ottawa for a few days.

Ty shivered in the night air as he climbed out of the car and emerged from the laneway next to his flat. It felt like late October. He dreaded the winter ahead.

"Daddy! Daddy!"

Ty was startled to see his daughter, Catherine, sitting on the front stairs. The four year old was wearing only her pyjamas. Tears ran down her face.

"Catherine!" Ty exclaimed. "What's the matter?"

He ran up the stairs and picked her up, holding her close to his chest.

"Mama fell down, and she won't get up."

Ty fished in a coat pocket for his house keys, then realized the front door was wide open. He carried Catherine into the foyer and set her down.

"Where, Catherine?" He glanced frantically into the living room. There was no sign of Elizabeth. "Where is Mama?"

The little girl pointed down the hallway.

"In the back. She fell down."

"Where is Robin?"

Catherine wiped at her eyes. She was still crying.

"He's having a bath," she said.

Ty felt a sharp pain in his chest. He rushed toward the bathroom where he found his two-year-old son sitting in the tub, cheerfully playing with a plastic boat. He continued down the hall.

"Where is Mama, Catherine?"

"Kitchen," she replied. "She's in the kitchen."

He found Elizabeth, lying on the floor. She didn't appear to be hurt.

"Liz," he said. "Liz." He prodded her shoulder, and she opened her eyes. "Liz. What the hell?"

She groaned, and Ty knew immediately what had happened. Her breath reeked of alcohol. Elizabeth had passed out on the kitchen floor.

Marg Peterson wasn't the paranoid type. She prided herself on a no-nonsense approach to life. During her years at the phone company, she never took shit from anybody. She wasn't about to start now.

The black car parked outside her duplex was beginning to get on her nerves. It showed up just after supper. Marg hadn't thought anything of it at the time, but that was several hours ago. Now, she was getting ready to turn in for the night, and it was still there.

That wasn't what worried her the most. There were two men in the black car and one of them had been staring at her windows through binoculars. That was strange. Marg didn't like it one bit.

She stood behind her living room drapes, peering into the street below. It didn't help that Greg wasn't home.

Her name was Susan Waldon. Her parents and most of her friends called her Sue. Greg Peterson, on the other hand, preferred Suzie. The Everly Brothers' song "Wake Up Little Suzie" became a running gag between them.

Greg had fallen asleep with his head in her lap. Susan Waldon, of Ottawa, Ontario, was concerned. He had been so upset as he told her about the woman being beaten up and about his suspension from CKCF Television. Greg's life was tied up in his work. He was always playing with cameras and camera equipment. She knew about his secret dream to own a studio in Old Montreal.

Greg often used Suzie as his model, dressing her in exotic gowns, posing her in multiple locations, snapping her picture whenever he had the chance. Several of the photos were on the walls of her apartment. One, in particular, was dear to her. They had been in Vermont, staying at a friend's cabin on a high hill overlooking Lake Champlain.

Greg waited until they were ready to go to bed that night. Suzie was wearing a long, silken nightgown. He convinced her to go outside and lean against a tree at the top of the hill. Suzie was shown, in the photograph, wistfully staring into the distance. Around the northern fringes of Missisquoi Bay, the lights of Venise en Québec appeared like so many fireflies, dotting the shoreline.

They made love that night, for the first time. Now, she stroked his long hair as he slept. She wondered what the future held for both of them.

Chapter Six

September 28, 1969 dawned cold. An Arctic front had dropped temperatures to freezing. Every news agency in Montreal was focused on a single story. The FLQ, the *Front de Libération du Québec*, had bombed the residence of Mayor Jean Drapeau. It was yet another shot in a shrill call for revolution. A manifesto underlined Quebec's right to self-determination. To that end, the *Felquistes* planted scores of bombs between 1963 and 1969. Riots were touched off. Blood was spilled. Quebec's very character was being radically transformed.

Against a backdrop of economic uncertainty and shifting population, there was a sense of growing division between French- and English-speaking residents. Federal, provincial and municipal politicians debated a so-called "French fact," while Quebec's majority Francophone population demanded control of the region's purse strings. Federalists and separatists were entrenched in opposing and increasingly angry camps.

Ty zipped up his windbreaker. The Drapeau family had received numerous threats from radical elements in the separatist movement. Police bomb-squad inspectors were frequent visitors to the Avenue des Plaines residence in Montreal's Rosemount district. No bomb had ever been found, until now.

Ty was engaged in conversation with a police reporter from one of the French-language newspapers. Réal Gendron had a wide readership. His reports on the city's underbelly earned him a loyal following, not only among local politicians and the police hierarchy, but by organized crime itself.

"So," Réal said, pointing to the Drapeau home, "this was going to happen, eh?"

Ty shrugged.

"Nobody hurt, though. Guess that's a blessing."

The two men stepped aside as a fire truck and an ambulance began to pull out. The five thousand block of Avenue des Plaines was still blocked off to all but emergency vehicles and news organizations.

"*C'est vrai*," Gendron agreed. "*Mais, tabarnac*, the FLQ sent a message, *n'est ce pas*?"

"Where was the bomb placed?" Ty asked.

Gendron grinned.

"In a toilet. In the back of it. The inspectors, they were here last week. They missed it."

"Jesus!"

Gendron's facial expression suddenly changed.

"*Alors*, you guys are having some troubles of your own?"

It was a question.

"Trouble?" Ty asked.

"*Mais oui*. Last month. Downtown. A CKCF car? A woman beaten up?"

Ty stiffened.

"You asking me, or telling me?"

No charges had been filed against Greg Peterson. The last thing Greg, or anyone at the station, needed was publicity.

"I 'ave my sources, eh? Don't worry. It's of no interest to me."

He stepped closer to Ty.

"I was aroun' that night. Foun' out about it because I was in the north end with the RCMP."

"RCMP?" Ty appeared concerned.

"Your guy beat up the woman," he added. "I was on surveillance with the cops. In a church on Jean Talon."

He paused.

"We were watching, eh? The RCMP took photographs. *Moi aussi*, of everybody going into and out of Cabrini Hall. The church is on an opposite corner."

"Why?" Ty asked. "What was going on at Cabrini Hall?"

Gendron grinned. The newspaper reporter seemed to enjoy divulging his inside information.

"Mafia. Big Mafia meeting. Positano, Gianfranco. Many others."

"I'll be damned. On that same night?"

Gendron nodded.

"Party didn't break up 'til early morning. One more thing." He edged even closer, talking directly into Ty's left ear. "The woman, who was attacked downtown?"

"What about her?"

"May be no connection with Jean Talon, but I ask around. Her name is Maria Claudio. She's a lawyer. Some of her clients are made members of the Positano crime family."

Jason Moore didn't believe in coincidences. A CKCF mobile unit downtown. A Mafia lawyer attacked, allegedly by a news employee who was driving the car. A mob party, simultaneously, in the north end. Moore opened his filing cabinet and pulled the August records. He withdrew a folder marked *Opération Cantons de L'Est.*

Moore wanted to know two things. Who was legal counsel at the arraignment of Gino Viscuso, after his arrest in the Townships drug raids? How, specifically, was Viscuso tied in with the Sands boxing family? He decided to check, once again, with radio master-control operator Joe Maurizio. It was after three in the afternoon. Moore walked down the corridor toward the radio studios. Maurizio was working the three-to-midnight.

"Well," he greeted Moore. "Once again, Flash News seeks out the lowly radio tech."

Moore watched, as the operator brought up the sound on a live traffic report. The rolling home show was in progress.

"You still getting calls about the fights on Friday nights?"

Maurizio shook his head.

"I wasn't for awhile. They stopped for a coupla weeks."

Moore made a mental note to do a follow-up on the August drug raids.

"You mean, they resumed?"

"Yeah. Yeah, they resumed. Same as usual. How's the fight going? How's Billy doing? etc., etc."

"Same guy calling?" Moore asked.

"Same guy. Gino Viscuso. By the way, Billy's training for a shot at the middleweight title, eh?"

Moore was writing in his file-folder.

"Oh yeah? Where's he training?"

The live traffic report came to a close. Maurizio rolled a commercial.

"Sands family gym. They got their own setup, somewhere out on the lakeshore."

"Okay," Moore smiled. "Thanks."

Maurizio shrugged.

"Still all cloak and dagger, eh? Not gonna tell me what this is all about?"

"You know us," Moore said. "Always looking for a scoop."

"Uh-huh," Maurizio made a smacking noise with his tongue. "The glamorous life of TV news."

It was a funny thing about Clyde Bertram. The more excited he became about a news story or corporate head butting, the more rapidly he puffed on his House of Lords cigar. As Moore told him the developments, Bertram's head was enveloped in a thickening cloud of smoke.

"I want to know more. Goddam it, I want to know everything about that mob hootenanny at Cabrini Hall."

He jabbed at the air.

"I want to know who was driving my fucking news car."

By now the atmosphere in Bertram's office was almost unbreathable.

"I want you to find out about this—" He tried unsuccessfully to remember the name Moore had mentioned, "this Mafia lawyer who got beaten up."

Bertram's face was beet red.

"And, I'm gonna tell that little snake, Hal Nichols, down in operations, that he's a prick. We never shoulda' suspended Greg Peterson."

Moore stood up.

"Wait a minute. Wait a minute," Bertram said. "From here on, you, Peterson and Davis make regular reports to me on this shit. I mean regular. It stays with me until we put the pieces together."

He managed a smile.

"Good work, Jason. Good work."

* * *

Greg was beginning to see double. He'd been drinking boilermakers, for several hours, at Polo's. The whiskey and beer were starting to wage war on his empty stomach.

"Nick," he waved at the bartender.

Nick was cleaning glasses, behind the bar.

" 'Nother one?" he asked.

Greg's head was swimming.

"No, I don't think so, Nick. Better get home to Mom's cooking, before ya have ta carry me outa here."

Nick's face appeared pinched. Humorless.

"Cash or tab?"

CKCF personnel, especially members of the news team, often ran tabs at The Hole.

"What're the damages?" Greg asked.

Nick checked the bill.

"Seventeen-fifty."

"Geez. I didn't wanna buy the place."

The barkeep remained poker-faced. Greg laid a twenty next to his empty shot-glass and climbed down off the barstool. His legs felt rubbery.

As he walked out onto Hutchison Avenue, the Park Extension district seemed unusually quiet. There was very little traffic on Jean Talon Street and only a few pedestrians. Greg realized he was unsteady on his feet. He weaved his way along the sidewalk. His mother's duplex was only a couple of blocks away.

He didn't notice the two men in conversation on the south corner of Jean Talon and Hutchison, or the fact that they'd interrupted their discourse and were matching his westerly pace along Jean Talon.

When he got to Querbes, he crossed and walked south. If Greg had been unaware of the two men before, he failed to notice now that they had completely disappeared from sight. He walked into the shadows on Querbes, out of the pools of light cast by street lamps and shop windows on Jean Talon.

He was suddenly confronted by a tall, broad-shouldered man, not three houses up from his home. Greg moved to one side to get around him, but the man blocked his way. A second man was suddenly behind him. The tall one began speaking, in a phlegmy voice.

42

"Like hitting women?" he asked.

Greg backed up, but the second man grabbed him from behind and held his arms.

"That wasn't me!" Greg exclaimed. His breath came in gasps, and an icy fear tightened his throat.

"Says you," the man in front replied. Then he punched Greg, hard, in the mid-section.

"I'm telling you," Greg said, desperately trying to breathe. "I never hit a woman in my life."

"After this," the man said, "you never will again."

He swung his elbow into Greg's cheekbone. Blackness swept in. He didn't realize he was falling, until the sidewalk connected with his shoulder. A pain knifed through his neck and back. He tried to pull his knees under him, but the second man kicked him in the stomach. Then one of them brought his boot down on Greg's hand. He heard the bones snap, just before he lost consciousness.

Chapter Seven

The open-air arcades at Jean Talon Market were boarded up for the winter. Farmers who brought their produce in from the countryside around Montreal were now concealed behind temporary walls. October weather was already closing in.

Ty Davis drove east along Jean Talon, toward the church where Réal Gendron and the RCMP had observed the goings-on at Cabrini Hall. The northern fringes of Montreal's Little Italy district, along Jean Talon and east of Henri Julien Avenue, were mostly commercial. His main targets were the residential streets, just to the south. Ty was sure that a Mafia gathering, the size of the late August event, couldn't have gone unnoticed by local residents.

He parked Mobile 14 just off Jean Talon. The church was Romanesque in style, and was bordered on the south by row upon row of adjoining duplexes. Ty wondered what sort of reception he might get when he started ringing doorbells. He pushed the record button on his tape recorder and placed the small device in his overcoat pocket. People had a way of clamming up if they knew they were being taped. He decided to violate journalistic ethics and not tell them.

A steep staircase led to four doors, fronting on to the street, at the first duplex behind the church. All the buildings on this side were boxy and constructed of red brick. The other side of the street featured grey stone facades. Ty figured the tenants there paid higher rent.

Just as he was about to ring the doorbell, he spotted a woman on the opposite sidewalk, leading her two dogs on long leashes. He made sure the tape recorder was still running, backtracked down the stairs and crossed the street. He didn't want to alarm the woman, so he walked slowly and casually approached her.

"Nice dogs," he said.

The woman appeared somewhat startled.

"Thank you," she replied.

Ty crouched down to pat the smaller dog, but it snarled and backed away.

"That's Pearl," the woman said. "She's very particular about people."

Ty noticed that the larger of the two dogs was sniffing at his hand.

"And this is Max. He loves everybody."

"Hello, Max." Ty scratched the animal behind one ear.

"Ma'am, my name is Ty Davis. I work for CKCF Television, and I'm doing a little survey in the neighborhood."

The woman yanked on one of the leashes. Pearl decided she'd had quite enough of this intrusion. She had other things to do, and was intent on getting on with her morning walk.

"Won't take long," Ty said. "Would you mind if I just asked a couple of questions?"

"What about?"

Ty smiled. Pearl had reached the full extension of her leash and was trying to squat on a tiny patch of browning grass. Max, on the other hand, was sitting obediently on the sidewalk. His tongue lolled out of his mouth and he seemed entirely content.

"A few nights ago there was a big party, just up the street, at Cabrini Hall. I'm asking people what they might have seen or heard that night."

The woman nodded. "It was the talk of the town. I'm Italian, you know."

"I didn't know."

"Well, I am." She pointed up the street, toward Jean Talon. "I was walking Max and Pearl. My neighbor told me about it. Big names up there at Cabrini. Big names."

"Like, who?" Ty asked.

"Salvatore Positano, for one. But you should know."

Ty wasn't sure what she meant. "What do you mean, I should know?"

The woman began walking away.

"It's none of my business, anyway. Nobody wants anything to do with that crowd."

"Just one more question," Ty began walking with her. "Why do you say I should know who was at this party, or meeting, or whatever it was?"

"Because," the woman stopped walking and Max promptly sat down. Pearl was biting at Ty's legs. "Because your television station was here. Just about where we're standing, there was a CKCF-TV news car parked right here."

Ty felt a tingle of excitement. It seems he'd struck gold on his first interview.

"Are you sure?"

"Course I'm sure. The letters were written right across the door."

Ty didn't know what to say. The woman continued.

"There was something else. Across the back of the trunk."

Ty felt this was too good to be true.

"A number?" he asked.

"Yeah, a number. It said News Mobile 9."

The Sands Family Gym in Ste. Anne de Bellevue near Montreal was housed in a former legion hall on the shores of Lac St. Louis. As a family enterprise, it served two purposes. It provided Billy and his brothers, Jimmy and Russell, with a cutting-edge training facility. The gym included a full-sized boxing ring. It was fitted with speed bags, heavy bags, head-gear, jump ropes, medicine-balls and related equipment. There were lockers and showers for regular members, and a weight-room for anyone interested in achieving the body beautiful. The gym was a profitable business.

The Sands family employed two full-time trainers and paid a monthly fee to a retired sports doctor. Boxing classes were scheduled daily. Deals were made with area high schools to organize and train students. Several phys-ed departments had developed their own programs, utilizing the Sands facility.

Jason Moore parked his '62 Volkswagen Bug on Lakeshore Road. His day off work was turning out to be more stressful than he'd bargained for. It started with an early morning phone call from Clyde Bertram. It seemed Greg Peterson was in the Montreal General Hospital, recovering from a beating.

Moore debated whether to postpone his trip to Ste. Anne's. Bertram said Greg had undergone surgery and would be groggy from the anesthetic. He convinced himself he'd be more helpful to Greg by keeping the appointment than by heading directly to the hospital.

His first impression of the Sands Gym was that it was poorly lighted and stank of stale sweat. He was there under false pretenses. One of the trainers, Carmen Acelino, agreed to be interviewed by CKCF Television. On the phone Moore led him to believe he was interested in Billy Sands and his possible run at the WBA middleweight title. Acelino no doubt thought Moore was a sports reporter. When he had offered to make Billy available, Moore simply told him that wasn't immediately necessary. He was after background.

A large man wearing an oversized suit coat and corduroy pants emerged from an office behind the boxing ring. He had a face like a bulldog, eyes nearly lost in the folds of his brow, and the cauliflower ears of a veteran fighter. Carmen Acelino maneuvered past a young man, pounding away at a speed bag, and extended a hand to Moore.

"You the TV guy?"

Moore shook his hand.

"Jason Moore," he replied, smiling pleasantly. Acelino's hand completely enveloped his own. "Want to talk to you about Billy. About his, uh, training."

The big man appeared puzzled.

"You new? We usually get Mark Carter or Walt Taylor out here."

Carter and Taylor were two of the three sports staffers at CKCF.

"I'm just a stringer," Jason lied. "A freelancer. Mark and Walt'll be following up on this, down the road. I'm just putting some details together."

Acelino shrugged. "Whaddya wanna know?"

"Well," said Moore, "what sort of regimen have you got Billy on? How ready do you think he is for a shot at the title?"

Acelino glanced around the gym, making a sweeping gesture with his arm.

"He's here workin' the heavy bag. Jumpin' rope. Sparring with me and doin' his thing every day. Oh yeah. He's ready."

Moore reached into his coat pocket.

"Mind if I use a tape recorder?"

"G'head."

Moore turned on the tape recorder and realized he was totally out of his element. He tried to think of a credible sports question.

"So, uh. This is just so Mark and Walt can listen." He held the recorder between them, like a microphone.

Acelino nodded. "Don't matter t'me."

"It's been suggested by some people that Billy might have come up too fast; that maybe the champ'll put him away in the early rounds."

"Nah. My boy can handle Tubbs."

Moore realized he didn't even know the champ's name. He faked it.

"But Tubbs has a hell of a rep' for getting the job done."

Acelino showed some yellowing teeth.

"Jackie Tubbs is good. But he's nearly ten years older'n Billy. He's ready t'go down. Specially if he's overconfident and doesn't train proper."

Moore was running out of ideas.

"So, uh, Billy's here at the gym every day?"

"Every day. Usually early morning. He hadda go somewhere this morning."

"I see." said Moore. "What about a venue for the fight?"

"Montreal Forum. Prob'ly late this month or early in November."

Moore tried to look impressed.

"That soon."

Acelino grinned. "Like I say, my boy's ready as he'll ever be."

"But the date's not pinned down?"

"It's being negotiated with the Tubbs people. It's a sure thing, though, and Tubbs is in for a surprise."

"Glad to hear it, By the way, before I forget, one of our radio operators, Joe Maurizio, wanted me to send his regards to Gino Viscuso."

He noted a marked change in Acelino's facial expression.

"Who?"

"Gino Viscuso," Moore replied. He noted the trainer's suddenly cautious tone. "The guy's pretty interested in Billy. Calls Maurizio all the time, when Billy's in the ring."

Acelino seemed to relax.

"Oh yeah, Gino."

Moore thought he could safely pursue the subject.

"He a promoter or something?"

"Nah. The Sands family knows him is all."

Moore pretended to suddenly recall something about Viscuso.

"Got himself into some trouble, recently, didn't he?"

Acelino shrugged.

"No big deal. He's got a good lawyer."

Moore switched off the tape recorder. He wanted to reassure Acelino he was only passively interested in Gino Viscuso.

"Right. Right. Yeah, what was her name?" He snapped his fingers, as though he couldn't quite remember. "Maurizio told me, but I don't remember."

"Maria," the big man replied. "Maria Claudio."

"That's it. Well, listen. Thank you. I'll give this tape to Walt Taylor. He may have more questions about Billy."

"Anytime," Acelino said.

He seemed to have no idea that Moore couldn't care less about Billy Sands.

Chapter Eight

Greg Peterson woke to a sharp ringing in his right ear. He gradually became aware that his right hand and arm were in a plaster cast up to the elbow. His head throbbed and he felt nauseous. The first thing he saw was a dim outline standing over him. Then his eyes began to focus.

"Suzie?"

Susan Waldon leaned into view.

"Greg. Oh, Greg what happened?"

"How'd you get here? How'd you know?"

He tried to sit up, but she put her hand on his chest.

"You have to lie down. You have a severe concussion. Your hand has been"—she wiped away a tear—"your hand has been mangled, and the doctor says you have two broken ribs."

Greg felt he might pass out. He obediently lay down again.

"Where am I?"

Suzie ran her fingers through his hair.

"You're in hospital, the Montreal General. Jason Moore called me this morning, and I came as fast as I could." She pulled a chair closer to his bed. "Who did this?"

Greg tried to recall what had happened and found it difficult to put his thoughts together.

"Don't know. Last thing I remember is sitting in The Hole drinking."

Suzie sat on the left side of the bed and held his good hand.

"This must have happened after you left the bar. Try to think back."

Greg frowned.

"Well, obviously, somebody doesn't think too highly of my

photography." He lifted his injured arm. "This is gonna put a crimp in my style."

Suzie smiled.

"Always joking. There's nothing funny about this, though."

"Too true," Greg agreed. He suddenly remembered his walk home from Polo's Bar and Restaurant. "Two men!"

Suzie raised an eyebrow.

"Two men what?"

"There were two men. Right near my mother's house. They—" he turned on his side in the hospital bed, ignoring the pain in his chest. "They stopped me from going home."

Suzie pursed her lips.

"They certainly did. Question is why?"

Greg's memory of the incident became clearer.

"They beat me up. One of them was huge, maybe six-five. He asked me if I liked hitting women."

"What?"

"Hitting women. This was payback, because of what that woman told the cops. They think I attacked her. I mean, she picked me out of the lineup."

He tried to get up again, but Suzie told him to lie back down.

"Didn't your mother say something about people watching her house?"

A cold sensation rolled through his body.

"My mother!" he exclaimed. "That's right! Suzie, they know where we live!"

Suzie patted his leg.

"She's all right. I called her, just after I got here. She's coming to the hospital. Said to tell you she loves you and to try not to worry."

Greg was about to respond, when a uniformed police officer entered the room.

"*Monsieur* Peterson?"

"That's me," Greg replied.

"Feel up to answering some questions?"

Greg smiled.

"Who me? Never felt better."

It was snowing heavily by the time Ty Davis wound up his shift and visited the Montreal General. He was genuinely concerned about

Greg. Not so much about the injuries. He'd get over those. Greg, however, had made a disturbing point.

"They know where I live. They're a threat to my mother, as well as me." Greg had recalled his mother's story about the black car parked across the street and the man with the binoculars.

Ty switched on his windshield wipers. The snow was melting on contact with the road but visibility was reduced to several car lengths. He reminded himself to buy some heavy-duty wipers. These weren't doing the job.

Susan Waldon, or Suzie as Greg liked to call her, had told him she decided to remain at the hospital until visiting hours were over. Greg's mother had invited her to stay at her home, for as long as she liked. Suzie telephoned her boss to let him know. He agreed to let her take some time off. Ty headed home. He turned off Sherbrooke Street onto Harvard Avenue. He decided to park Mobile 14 in his garage at the rear of the Oxford Avenue flat. The snow was beginning to accumulate on the ground, but he thought it was too early to begin the winter ritual of cleaning and scraping the car windows in the morning.

A block-long laneway ran behind the flats. There were four garages leading off the laneway, one for each tenant. Ty pulled into his space, reached up to bring the garage door down and climbed the stairs to the ground floor. The heavy wooden door at the top of the stairs was unlocked.

"Hello," Ty shouted, stepping into the hallway. "Elizabeth?"

There was no reply.

"'Liz, are you there?" Still nothing. "Kids, it's Dad. I'm home."

The flat seemed to be empty. Ty unbuttoned his overcoat, taking a moment to remove the tape recorder from his pocket. He placed it on the telephone table, just beyond the basement doorway, and walked into his bedroom. It wasn't unusual for Elizabeth to take Catherine and Robin to the grocery store or on some other errand on Monkland Avenue. It was out of the ordinary, however, for this to happen so late in the day. It was nearly 8 p.m. Ty doubted whether the grocery store was even open.

"Elizabeth?" Again, no response. He hurried through the various rooms, feeling more and more uneasy with each passing moment. It wasn't until he discovered the note from his wife that he sat down.

"*Dear Ty, you have to admit that this isn't working. We aren't working. I've thought long and hard about it, and I've decided to take the children and move out for a while. I believe you'll agree we need some time apart. I've notified Catherine's pre-school. I bought train tickets. We left this morning, for my folks in Boston. I'm sorry. I just couldn't bring myself to talk about this with you. I knew you'd try to convince me otherwise. I'll call you from Boston.*"

The note was signed, simply, "Elizabeth."

Ty found he could hardly breathe. Suddenly, he needed a drink.

It was a huge house even by Upper Westmount standards. South-facing windows provided breathtaking views of the city immediately below and the St. Lawrence River snaking its way past a haze-shrouded south shore. Snow-embroidered terraced gardens ran down the slopes of Mount Royal. A tennis court and swimming pool hugged the mountain at the rear of the house.

The building consisted of three levels. One entered the first floor just above the gardens and a paved half-moon driveway. The gigantic double-door entry was made of imported red wood, with a bird spreading its wings carved across its width. Two ebony-colored statues, in a Greco-Roman motif, stood at each side.

Salvatore Positano sat at the head of a long, highly polished table in his downstairs library. Books covered one entire wall of shelves. A ladder, on rollers, provided access to the highest among these, fully twelve feet from the floor. Classical works of art were carefully placed throughout the room, on glass-topped tables and in alcoves along the other three walls. Two Picassos were tastefully illuminated. A tapestry, depicting the Gulf of Taranto, hung above the mantel of a massive stone fireplace. A local decorator had been under strict orders to strive for understated elegance, while avoiding gaudiness and flamboyance.

Four men were seated at the table, two on each side. All were wondering why Positano had called the meeting. There was tension in the Montreal crime family, the *borgata*. They had felt it. They had heard rumors, but they didn't know the source. Positano leaned forward in his chair and began speaking.

"Frank Ragusa is sending an underboss from New York."

There was silence around the table.

"Two things. This guy will oversee all our operations. Drugs, gambling, bookmaking, prostitution." He sliced the air with one hand. "The works."

Still no one spoke.

"His name is Giovani Lorenzo. Goes by G. He reports directly to Ragusa. You still take orders from me. G will show respect, unless we fuck up."

Positano pounded the table with his fist.

"And we already did. What the fuck happened at Knowlton?"

He glared at a glassy-eyed man in a silk shirt. Tony Soccio was responsible for drug traffic into the U.S. from points in Quebec's Eastern Townships. He swallowed hard.

"Sal, we got a rat. Cops knew 'zactly where to go. That blow jus' came in from Marseilles. Cops knew it was coming. Knew where we had it stashed. We were gonna ship it to New York next day."

Positano sat back in the chair.

"Tony, Tony. That's your problem. We're out millions, and you're telling me you don't know who's tipping the man. You got a rat. You find the sonofabitch and you find him quick."

Soccio nodded in agreement.

"Got it covered, Sal."

"Got it covered. Hell you do. Bad enough I gotta deal with G. Ragusa gets hit in the pocket, it's my balls in the crusher."

Massimo Gianfranco rested his hands on his oversized belly. The *caporegime* was widely regarded as Positano's number two in Montreal.

"You said Ragusa's sending this G for two reasons. What else?"

"The Sicilians. We got 'em breathing up our ass about everything. Hotels, restaurants, real-estate. They been here only a few months and they want a cut of everything. Not just this legitimate stuff. Everything."

Gianfranco clipped the end off a cigar.

"They got no respect."

"But they got balls. And they got muscle. One of the reasons Ragusa is sending G is this is turning into a power struggle."

Positano stood up and pointed at Gianfranco.

"These bastards are set up solid in Venezuela now. That's a new power base. They could take out a contract on you, or me. Anyone in the *borgata*. No way that's okay by me. Has to be at least a five-year probationary period before they start tapping the bank."

No one at Positano's table could disagree.

Chapter Nine

The Green Room at CKCF Radio and Television was mainly used for staff meetings and the occasional party. It also served as a way station for guests of live on-air shows. Makeup could be applied. Coffee could be served. The guests could be made to feel comfortable and important.

Clyde Bertram made a list. Everyone on it gathered for what they believed would be a pep-talk about the Autumn Book, the TV ratings that allow a sales department to sell more air-time at higher fees. That was not the case. Bertram's list was based solely on Greg Peterson's dilemma, his job suspension and the company's position. The News Director's face and tone were extremely serious. Ty Davis, Jason Moore, Dick Tomlin, Keith Campbell, Brains the technician, and lineup editor Maggie Price, were seated. Bertram was standing, holding a clipboard and notes.

"We've been lucky so far. This story hasn't appeared in the rest of the media. You all know the circumstances. If you weren't told directly, the grapevine has probably filled you in on a late August incident downtown. Maggie, you're the only one here besides myself who wasn't in the resulting police lineup. Greg, as you no doubt have become aware, was picked out of that lineup by a young woman who claims she was severely beaten by someone driving a CKCF news mobile. And Greg, through no decision of my own, is on the official shit list until it's demonstrated he wasn't involved."

Bertram gauged reactions around the room.

"Some of you might not be aware of what we've learned since. We placed Mobile 9 at a Mafia party in the north end that night. We learned, through sources, that the victim of this so-called attack is a lawyer by the name of Maria Claudio. Again, through sources, it seems Claudio has dealings with the Positano crime family. Now, on the surface this would appear to be a slam dunk, but there is no proof that Claudio attended the Mafia party and no way to place Mobile 9 downtown."

Ty interjected.

"Clyde, there were ten sets of keys in Moore's office. Tomlin here was responsible for monitoring who had access. But no one signed out on Mobile 9."

"Which only contributes to the problem of proving anything. And that brings me to another point. From here on in, Dick, Jason's office and those keys are to be locked down when you go out on your rounds."

Tomlin went on the defensive.

"But who can say for sure that another set of keys wasn't taken earlier, that another mobile, besides number 9, wasn't out on the street?"

Bertram nodded.

"Exactly. No one can say. Maggie, you're the odd man out here. You weren't in the lineup. You were on the desk until the late news signed off. Is there anything you can remember?"

"I went to the ladies' a couple of times. I suppose there was occasion for someone to borrow keys while I was out of the newsroom. But that would have been long before Dick visited the cop shops, say before ten, when the anchor comes in."

"Okay. Let's look at that. Who would have been in the building?"

Maggie suddenly appeared to recall something.

"Usually nobody but the late reporter and me. The reporter was out on a story. I was alone in the newsroom. But, something was going on downstairs."

"Like what?"

"Like a management meeting. Something like that. Anyway, I had to go down to the studio around nine, because the early lineup editor had left his fountain pen on the anchor desk. He called and asked me to get it for him and leave it in his mail slot. I noticed the door was partially open and the lights were on in Vic Gordon's boardroom. I could hear voices, but I've no idea who was in there."

Bertram added the information to his notes. The mystery of the missing keys would have to remain a mystery for now.

The file on *Opération Cantons de l'Est* was growing. Jason walked back to his office from the Green Room meeting, feeling as if he were missing something. He stared at the file, not even knowing what he was looking for. He had underlined several points. The RCMP claimed more than three million dollars of cocaine was seized. Eight men and four women were arrested in the police sweep. Five separate raids. Three of the targets were farmhouses. One was a house trailer. One was the Club Coquettes near Knowlton.

Jason kept coming back to the name Gino Viscuso. He, among all those detained, appeared to be the only direct connection to organized crime in Montreal. He thought the seven other men and four women probably were hired to guard and then transport the drugs across the border into the United States. He'd already checked that out. Three of the men had commercial trucking licenses. Jason remembered two instances in the past, where heroin or cocaine had been hidden in hay bales or in secret compartments inside fuel tankers.

"Why the women?" he wondered.

CKCF had done a follow-up on the court proceedings. He sifted through the file. Seven of the men and only one of the women were arraigned on charges of possession with intent to traffic in cocaine across an international border. The other three women were charged with possession. Essentially, Jason concluded, they were considered found-ins. Wrong place at the wrong time.

Then it hit him. Two months had passed since *Opération Cantons de l'Est*. Eleven of the twelve people arrested had been formally charged. Sentencing dates had been set. According to the follow-up report, the only individual whose sentencing date had not been set was Gino Viscuso, and *he* was out on bail.

Jason felt a tingle of excitement. He distinctly remembered Billy Sands' trainer, Carmen Acelino, saying, "He's got a good lawyer." That lawyer, Jason thought, appeared to be the key to an eyer more complex puzzle.

A waxing moon hung in the sky as Ty Davis pulled into the laneway behind his home. It was encircled by an aura of bright light, likely a portent of wintry weather. Soon, it would be full, rising bright orange into a late-autumn evening. Ty realized that, equally soon, it would be Halloween. Neighborhood kids would be ringing doorbells asking for treats and threatening tricks if anyone dared hide in the shadows behind unlighted windows.

A heaviness of heart accompanied him up the stairs from the garage. It was the same every night. Home from a long day to an empty flat. He wouldn't see Catherine and Robin dressed up for Halloween this year. Ty hoped they'd get costumes and plenty of candy with Elizabeth's family in Boston.

He tossed the keys to Mobile 14 on the telephone table. For just a moment, he thought he heard a child's voice in one of the bedrooms and then realized it came from the upstairs flat. An old clock that had belonged to his grandfather chimed eight. It was an antique that now occupied a place of honor on their fireplace mantel.

His gramps told him he'd taken the thing apart to fix it, years ago. When it was all back together and working normally, there were three components left over. It had functioned just the same and still did. Gramps died when Ty was sixteen. The clock ticked on.

These sad recollections stuck with him as he opened a can of baked beans for supper. Ty remembered a disturbing series of nightmares. In one of them, he was looking into his grandfather's bedroom. It was nighttime. He was standing in the hallway. Everything seemed quite peaceful. The bedroom was tidy and his grandfather appeared to be asleep. In the dream, Ty remembered a phone ringing. He turned briefly toward the sound but when he turned again to look into the bedroom, it was horribly changed. A wall mirror was shattered. Glass fragments on the floor reflected tiny snapshot-like images of his own face. All the bureau drawers were open. Clothes hung out or were strewn about the room. Lime-colored window curtains were now black. His grandfather's bedding was tousled, and out of the twisted sheets and blankets extended two white arms.

Ty poured the beans on to a dinner plate, added some hot mustard to the mix and helped himself to three slices of wheat bread. The nightmare clung to him. He knew it was a reflection of his overall sadness, apparently triggered by the old clock on the mantel. His throat felt tight and he realized he was crying.

Montreal's Park Extension district was a neighborhood of demographic opposites. An entire segment of the population considered it a temporary jumping-off point for moves up the social ladder. Others were trapped by economic reality.

Park Ex, a little under two square kilometres of territory, housed more than three times the number of residents of other city districts. A large percentage were immigrants who largely kept to themselves. Their lives seemed fundamentally better than what they'd grown accustomed to in their home countries. As a result of perceived good fortune, poverty was handed down like used clothing through the generations.

There were few jobs to be had. Dimly lit streets fronted on one- and two-story brick buildings, erected in the middle of the 20th century. City contractors had underlined expansion, not esthetics.

Marg Peterson was born in Park Extension. When she married, her husband shared her sense of community. He worked as a stevedore on the Montreal waterfront after immigrating to Canada from Norway. Times were hard. There was no union to provide any income security. It was first come, first served for the men who lined up daily to load and unload scores of ships. Employers selected the lucky few who would take home a day's pay.

Bjorn Pederson, who later changed the family name to Peterson, was proud of his involvement in the organization of waterfront workgangs. In the late 'forties, employers dealt with illegal strikes and featherbedding, the practice of choosing which cargoes would be attended to and which not, based on weight.

Despite all his efforts, Pederson did not live to see any form of union protection. He managed, however, to salt away enough money to set up a private pension. He was proud of the home he provided for his wife and son. He died in 1948, when Greg was three years old.

Marg worked diligently at her job in personnel at the phone company, choosing to ignore the ever-present poverty that walked the streets of Park-Ex. Now a pensioner herself, this was where she chose to spend the rest of her life.

She drove her '58 Ford Fairlane slowly home from the Montreal General Hospital. Greg and his girlfriend Susan were in the back seat. She worried about the severe pain her son was experiencing in his crushed hand. His head was on Susan's shoulder as the battered old Ford came to a stop on Querbes Avenue.

"Now, Susan," Marg said. "Let me come around to help get Greg on to the sidewalk."

She pulled her keys out of the ignition and opened the driver's side door. Greg objected.

"Chrissake, ma, it's my hand that's messed up. Not my feet."

"Yes, but your broken ribs!"

"I'm fine, ma. Fine."

He disentangled himself from the back seat and climbed out of the car.

"Besides, Suzie's a good nurse."

He smiled at his girlfriend. She did not smile back.

"Listen to your mother, Greg. The doctor told you. If you move too fast or twist in the wrong direction, you can puncture a lung."

Greg waited on the sidewalk.

"Yeah, I know. But I'm all taped up. God, it's good to be home."

The three of them gradually made their way up the front stairs of Marg Peterson's duplex.

Chapter Ten

It was Victor Gordon's pride and joy. The twenty-seven-foot sailboat was one of only a hundred and seventy-five that were built by a Rhode Island manufacturer. The boat combined the comforts of a cruiser with the advantage of a modified full keel and spade rudder. It tracked well. It had excellent stability and maneuverability in the water and an uncontested reputation in the yachting world of being the first American racer-cruiser.

Gordon had named it *The Flash* after CKCF's flagship news program. He never raced it, but believed it lent him the appearance of being a true sportsman. Women, he thought, liked the outdoors type. There was a modern galley to starboard and a settee to port. He'd upgraded the instrumentation to include depth, speed and wind gauges. Gordon's favorite features, however, were the four sleeping berths. There had been numerous mixed parties aboard *The Flash*. He planned many more.

Every autumn, after the vessel was loaded on to a trailer at Lake of Two Mountains, Gordon had it hauled to the television station. It spent the winter in the employees' parking lot directly behind the building. This year's early snowfall obliged him to rig the canvases for protection against the weather, somewhat earlier than he planned.

He often sat in the cabin during the months of September and October, dreaming of summer winds. CKCF personnel, walking to their cars past candle-lit ports in the late evening, would speculate on which secretary was being given the Gordon boat tour. Female employees felt sorry for the president's wife. She was an invalid, having been left physically impaired by a stroke, and they surmised *The Flash* was more the boss's playpen than a family pleasure boat.

* * *

The two Harley-Davidsons pulled into the Club Coquettes in the late afternoon of October 10. Two men swung their legs off the bikes and walked toward the main entrance of the strip club near Knowlton. Business had been down since the August police raid. It was beginning to pick up again.

One of the two riders was short, heavy-set and muscular. The other could be described as tall and wiry. Both bikers wore Hells Angels insignias on the back of their sleeveless jean jackets. The tall one's jacket was covered with them.

The Hells formed the front line of a thriving criminal subculture. There were hundreds of members scattered across the world. The jacket patches were well known, but only to the biker gang itself. No one, not even the authorities, was sure of their significance. Most believed they were some sort of recognition for bloody acts on the battlefield. The Hells' battlefield was society in general.

Gang activities in Quebec and Ontario were under constant surveillance by both provincial and federal police forces. Montreal became a focal point for an ever-expanding territory that grew deep roots in the Irish West-End gang and the Mafia. Politicians referred to it as "the Montreal crime consortium."

Together, according to law enforcement researchers, the three groups manipulated the price of illegal drugs, laundered millions of dollars and lent out millions in loan-sharking operations. Sidelines were said to include gambling, prostitution, pornography, fraud and even contract killings. Studies concluded that the Hells conducted business, virtually unchallenged, along some of the busiest border crossings between Canada and the U.S.

The tall biker, known among his comrades as Razor, pushed through the front door of the Club Coquettes. His reputation for using a straight razor as a weapon of choice was widely known. Gang members knew that one of the patches he wore on his jacket indicated at least one kill to his credit. No one challenged his authority.

The second man, called Tank, followed Razor into the building. The atmosphere inside was smoke-filled and smelled of beer, cigarettes and cheap perfume. The bikers were greeted by a middle-aged man with slicked back hair and a scar running across his forehead and right eyebrow. Gino Viscuso held out his hand. Razor shook it.

"Nice day," Viscuso said.

"Yeah. Highways are bare. Snow's gone."

Tank walked over to the bar and ordered three beers. Viscuso gestured towards a nearby table.

"Here's the deal. Billy Sands is gonna take a run at the middleweight champ, Jackie Tubbs. Fight's gonna be at the Montreal Forum, later this month."

Razor watched Tank put the beers down on the table.

"So?" he asked.

"So, Sands is gonna win."

"How you know that?"

Viscuso took a swallow of beer.

" 'Cause you guys are insurance. Tubbs has a wife and a one-year-old son. They live in Jersey. Nice five-, six-hour hop on your bikes from Montreal."

He paused to let the information sink in. Razor sat back in his chair. A stripper was doing a pole dance on stage, mouthing the words of a song being played on the sound system. Her eyes stared blankly into the dimly lit room. Her bump and grind lacked enthusiasm.

"A little persuasion called for?" Razor wanted to know.

Viscuso appeared impatient.

"Tubbs is the champ. He'll have people around him most all the time. No rough stuff. Just the threat."

"You want him to throw the fight."

Viscuso nodded.

"Like I say, he's got a wife and kid. You tell him to start spreading the word around he's got a blunt injury to his right hand. Not bad enough to keep him out of the match, but enough to get people thinking he's goin' into it with a handicap. Tell him no disciplined training, only casual 'cause of the hand."

"What if he don't go for it."

Viscuso's eyebrow scar twisted into a scowl.

"If he don't," he said, "let him know, so's he can't possibly misunderstand, that you think he's got a great wife and kid. He wouldn't want anything to happen to them, would he?"

This was the kind of business Razor liked best.

"We have a clubhouse outside Atlantic City. I know two or three guys down there. We'll get the job done."

Tank just listened to the transaction. He was busy drinking beer and wondering how much the stripper would cost for a little back room attention.

Mafia finances were paradoxical. They were an exact reversal of the traditional payment from the top down. Moneys, instead, circulated upwards through the ranks from the lower echelons. Salvatore Positano was boss. Six *capos* served immediately under him. Each *capo* controlled a crew of at least ten soldiers, who acted as enforcers. Profits, generated by the mob's various and widely scattered enterprises, were collected by the soldiers. The enforcers paid the *capos*. The *capos* gave the boss his cut.

Positano was the heart. The body was much larger. The Montreal mob was part of a vast underworld empire. It was a subsidiary of the Frank Ragusa family of New York, and Ragusa took no chances. Huge sums of money were generated in Montreal. He depended on Positano, as Positano depended on his *capos* and their crews. Trust was hard earned and, more frequently, didn't exist at all.

Ragusa's underboss, Giovanni Lorenzo, was on his second Glenlivet, sitting in a dark leather chair in Positano's library. The single malt was going down smoothly. G made it clear he wanted to communicate, not dictate to the *borgata*.

Positano had his doubts. He was aware of a building conflict between the New York family, the Calabrian faction of which he was a part, and the Sicilians.

"They been here less than two years. They think they own the place."

G twirled the Glenlivet in his glass.

"Tell me about Rocco Panepinto."

He referred to one of the six *capos* in the Montreal *borgata*.

"He's Sicilian. His reputation was good. I made him *capo*. What can I say? Thought he'd ease in, know what I mean? Now, he's the fucking problem. He and his crew think they got a right to the bank."

"Problems can be solved."

Positano raised his hands.

"How? He's doin' the job. He's got a good crew. He's payin' up front. I got nothin' on 'im."

"Ragusa and I think you should expel the sonofabitch. He

imports his crew from Agrigento Province in Sicily. Don't seem to care we got our own methods of moving people up. They cut out a serious piece of business and operate like they don't have t'answer to anyone. Ragusa don't like it. He don't like it one bit."

Positano stood up and poured himself another scotch.

"You mean bust him? No more *caporegime*?"

G hesitated. Then he appeared troubled.

"You tell Panepinto his Sicilians take orders from you, not from him. You tell him he's no longer *caporegime*. He has the right to appeal. As *capo*, he can ask for mediation."

"There's another can o' worms," Positano said. "Could take months."

"You want this bastard out or not?"

"Yeah. Yeah. Course I do. When you wanna move on this?"

G showed some teeth.

"The Sicilians gotta prove themselves. Panepinto waits out a probationary period, maybe he gets to become *capo* again. For now, fuck 'im."

"What about his crew?"

"They get spread out among the other five *capos*. They don't like it, they can go back to fuckin' Sicily."

Positano was still uncertain.

"Panepinto can argue they're producing. They staked out a territory. Dry-cleaning, coupla restaurants. They're buyin' up real estate. It's money in the bank. Our bank."

It didn't seem to make any difference to Lorenzo.

"Not the point, Sal," he said. "Ragusa thinks it's only a matter of time before they try to take over. Could be big trouble. Could be your ass."

"So what now?"

G drained the last drop of Glenlivet from his glass.

A pattern of red played across his forehead, a reflection of the log fire burning in Positano's fireplace. He seemed almost demonic.

"Expel Panepinto sooner than later. Erase the problem, before it erases you."

Chapter Eleven

Sometimes you just get lucky. Jason Moore was on the telephone with a police contact. He put his lunch-hour aside to get some answers. Who is Maria Claudio? What is her connection to the Positano crime family? RCMP Corporal Normand Francoeur was coming up with some of the answers.

"She's part of the inner circle. Knows her way around a courtroom and when she gets the right judge, the prosecuting attorney is usually shit out of luck."

"How so?"

"Some o' these guys on the bench are aware of Claudio's background and are afraid to cross her. Others, and I won't get into names, are on the take."

Moore felt he was on the threshold of a major story.

"You mean kickbacks?"

"They're on Positano's payroll. Two of 'em are currently under investigation. No proof. That's the problem."

"How does it work?"

Francoeur carefully weighed his words. He liked Moore but he wasn't naive about the media.

"Mob wants a favor. They get it."

"Like what? Gimme a fer instance."

"Well, suppose we have a wiseguy dead to rights. He's committed a crime. He's arrested. He's arraigned, but the sentencing date keeps getting postponed."

Moore was getting goose bumps. His first thought was Gino Viscuso.

"So he's formally charged and winds up doing no time?"

"Sometimes no time at all. Sometimes a shorter sentence. It varies."

"Jesus. How does Claudio fit into this?"

"She greases the wheel. If it looks like the judge isn't playing along, she has the authority to up the ante."

"In other words," Moore said, "his worship goes home with a fatter wallet. What I don't get is where she gets the power."

"Do you have any idea who she is?"

"No, that's why I'm talkin' to you."

Francoeur didn't immediately reply.

"Give me your word, Jason. You never talked to me."

"You have my word."

Another pause.

"All right. You owe me big time. Maria Claudio is two things. She is not a gangster, but as I told you she's part of the inner circle. You might say she's like a *consigliere* to Salvatore Positano, functionally if not actually."

"*Consigliere?*"

"Advisor. The real McCoy is generally male and second or third in the mob pecking-order. Claudio has Positano's ear on all things legal but doesn't have the rank."

"But she's obviously powerful."

"You bet your ass. And here's the kicker. She is also first cousin to *caporegime*, Massimo Gianfranco."

Ty Davis lit a cigarette. He spent the morning on stakeout with the Montreal Police. They'd had an anonymous tip that a Royal Bank branch in the Cote des Neiges district would be robbed. It wasn't.

Ty sat for several hours in a small park about half a block from the bank. He had a portable two-way radio hidden in a shopping bag. Two cops were parked nearby in a jeep. They wore sports shirts, down-vests and jeans. It was deer hunting season in Quebec. The cops looked as if they were planning a trip to the Laurentians. In the end, Ty returned to the station without a story. The bogus hunters went back to headquarters without a suspect.

"Wasted morning?"

Ty squinted at Jason Moore through his cigarette smoke.

"You could say that. Three hours on a park bench."

The assignment-editor grinned.

"Those cigarettes'll kill ya, y'know."

"Sure. And sometimes the shortcut seems like a good idea."

Moore was still doing his version of a Cheshire cat.

"Got some news. Greg Peterson's gonna love this. Seems the gal he's supposed to have beaten up is a little better connected than we thought."

As he explained, he watched Davis's facial expression shift from bored to flabbergasted.

It was shortly after lunch when Suzie stood, bags in hand, at the front door of Marg Peterson's duplex. She and Greg were eye to eye. Marg was sipping tea in the kitchen, trying not to eavesdrop. A mixture of sleet and freezing rain pummeled the street outside.

"Well, Suzie," he winked, "couldn't've done it without ya."

She zipped her parka, glancing out the window with a mixture of nervousness and disgust at the weather.

"I wish I could stay, but duty calls."

Greg's voice became serious.

"It's the shits out there. You sure you couldn't stay one more night?"

"I'm sure. My boss has been pretty good about this. I promised I'd be at work tomorrow."

She set her bags down on the floor.

"Oh, Greg, I'm worried about you."

"Don't. Nothing to worry about."

He threw his arms around her. She hugged him back.

"You're kidding," she said. "First you're accused of a violent crime, then you're beaten within an inch of your life. Some thugs have been spying on your mother's house."

Suzie started to cry but Greg squelched the tears by kissing her full on the mouth. When he stepped back, she was wide-eyed and trying to smile.

"I love ya, y'know."

Greg began to feel a little unsteady on his feet. His broken ribs had healed well but the constant gnawing pain in his hand and arm wore him down.

"And I love you, Suzie. Thanks for everything. Drive carefully and call me when you get home."

"I will."

She picked up her bags and left.

Ty had an idea. He drove downtown when his shift ended and parked Mobile 14 on a side street next to the Windsor Hotel. Sports-director Walt Taylor clued him in on the whereabouts of a sports doctor who spent most of his evenings in the bar off the hotel lobby. Walt was sure Doctor Thomas Sinclair had worked with the Sands brothers at their gym in Ste. Anne de Bellevue.

"Ergo," Ty thought, "he might have run into Gino Viscuso or the elusive Maria Claudio."

The bar at the Windsor was long and luxurious. It was made of cherry wood and finished in a lustrous coating that highlighted its natural grain. Two businessmen sat at one end. A woman wearing a jacket and slacks was by herself. Ty couldn't help thinking of Elizabeth and her many hours of solitary drinking. Three-quarters of the way down the bar to his left, he spotted an older man. He was reading the sports pages of the *Montreal Star*. Ty approached.

"Doctor Sinclair?"

The man put his newspaper down on the bar.

"Yes?"

"Doctor Sinclair, my name is Ty Davis. I'm a reporter with CKCF Television."

"Yes?"

Ty wondered how far Sinclair was into his cups. He seemed kind of vague.

"I believe Walt Taylor knows you. He's the sports director at the station."

"Yes, I know Walt."

"Well he tells me you've had some dealings with the Sands boxing family out in Ste. Anne's."

"I have and I do. What can I do for you? What did you say your name was?"

"Ty. Ty Davis."

"Oh yes. I think I've seen you on the tube."

"Right. Anyway, I was wondering, Doctor Sinclair—"

"Call me Tom."

"All right, Tom. I was wondering. When you've been out at the Sands' Gym, have you ever run across either a Gino Viscuso or a young female lawyer by the name of Maria Claudio?"

Sinclair shook his head.

"No to Maria Claudio. Yes to Viscuso. A thoroughly unpleasant man."

"How do you mean?"

"Nasty sort. I think he's probably some kind of outlaw."

Ty flagged the barman and ordered a beer. He continued when he had it in hand.

"What makes you think that?"

"Looks like a mug. Big scar on his face. Dresses like Oil Can Harry. And the way he talks. Nearly every sentence with an expletive."

Ty took a swig of beer.

"Okay. So this is your impression, but is there anything he's said or done that would lead you to believe he's doing anything illegal?"

"Look," Sinclair said, "I'm contracted by the Sands family to look after Billy and his brothers when they're in the ring. I'm a good cut man. I also show up at the gym when some of the high school kids are there for training. Just in case somebody gets hurt. But I did overhear something."

"Like what?"

"Might've been nothing. One of the students took a good one on the nose. He was bleeding, so I had him over by the office. That is, Carmen Acelino's office. He's the gym's Jack-of-all-trades. He's also Billy's corner man."

Ty had heard about Acelino from Jason Moore.

"Yeah, I know about him. What did you overhear?"

Doctor Sinclair studied Ty's face.

"You making a TV report or something?"

"Nah. This is strictly off the record."

"Right. Well, Acelino and this Viscuso character were talking odds."

"Odds?"

"Yeah, like what're the odds on the various fights the Sands boys have lined up. I heard Acelino ask Viscuso what someone called Positano would think. That's when Viscuso seemed to lose his temper."

"Really?"

"He shouted. Said something like what Positano don't know won't hurt him."

Chapter Twelve

It was a matter of choice.

Frank Ragusa always wore his shirt collars up. It didn't make any difference whether he was turned out in a tailored suit. The collars were always up. He imported his ties, his shoes and his suits, but the wide variety of ties was a waste. He seldom wore any of them. The combination of a thick neck and a buttoned shirt drew too much attention to his double chin. He was an Elvis Presley fan and he thought the turned up collars made him look young and virile, like The King.

Despite a manner of dress many took to be a sign of weakness, nothing was further from the truth. Frank "The Shark" Ragusa ruled his territory with an iron hand. He was referred to in New York as "the chairman" and his ruthlessness and careful management of mob finances earned him wide respect.

Frank knew the odds. He was constantly aware of plots against his life, often schemes dreamed up within his own ranks. That was an unwritten rule of the mob. The boss could easily wind up on a slab at the morgue.

Today, The Shark wasn't concerned so much with his own immediate safety. He saw, however, a growing threat to his Montreal operations and his ultimate control over the profit-driven drug trade over the border. He thought about Rocco Panepinto, the Sicilian *capo*. He knew in his dark heart that Panepinto and his crew were a clear danger to Montreal boss Salvatore Positano. By extension, the Sicilian element was a Sword of Damocles hanging over the Calabrian faction.

Something had to be done. Underboss Giovani Lorenzo reported to him regularly. Panepinto, he'd said, demanded a hearing. G's plan to expel him as *caporegime* and assign his crew to the five other *capos* in Positano's family was being formally challenged.

Ragusa knew what that meant. He would send his representative to Montreal. Sicily would dispatch its own. A tribunal, reflecting the views of the New York family and the Agrigento-based mob, would reach a decision on the expulsion proposal. That decision would be binding on all concerned. The Shark felt the walls closing in.

It was a contradiction of terms to refer to East Orange, New Jersey as part of a Garden State. Pavement, not gardens, carpeted the city. Residents spent their days worried more about survival than esthetics. Despite some affluent areas across the state, East Orange was a backwater. Residential sections were in a state of decay. Many structures in the city's commercial district were derelict. Some were actually in danger of collapsing.

Unemployment, primarily among the city's African-American population, raged through the community. Opportunities beckoned in nearby New York City, but East Orange was no springboard to achievement. Children attended public schools under the jurisdiction of the East Orange School District, where education was a word in someone else's dictionary. Getting through the day was the underlying code. Learning to deal with reality was the goal. There was a high crime rate and student behavior reflected the ways of the street.

Jackie Tubbs, World Boxing Association middleweight champion, was born in East Orange. His prowess in the ring had brought him riches beyond any of his childhood dreams. Tubbs' father cleaned floors for a living. His mother died when he was ten. He lived with his father in a coldwater apartment on South Munn Avenue until his father's death when Jackie was eighteen.

Now, he had a wife, Arlene, and a one-year-old son, Jackie Jr. He'd bought and renovated the entire twelve-story building where he'd grown up, and was in the process of upgrading and renting. He thought of it as a retirement plan. Some of his closest friends and business partners already occupied several of the units.

Jackie Tubbs had thought of moving out of the area. He worried about the school system, but his son was still too young to make that an immediate concern. He and Arlene were comfortable in their decision to remain in East Orange for at least three more years.

The Tubbs' penthouse provided a straight-on view of the Manhattan skyline. New York City was less than a half-hour's drive. At night, that side of the tracks was, at least to Jackie, more of an entertainment than an attraction. He loved East Orange. It was his town, his childhood, the origins of his success as a young prizefighter. The truth was, he never really wanted to leave.

Mid-October weather teetered between the season to come and the season past. A cold rain slapped the faces of four bikers as they pulled into East Orange's Brick Church Station. Razor and his sidekick, Tank, had been in New Jersey for two days. They spent one of them recruiting two other Hells Angels from the gang clubhouse near Atlantic City. They passed the second day observing Jackie Tubbs' routine.

Razor was told before leaving Montreal that Tubbs did most of his training at a gym in Newark. Yesterday Tubbs had left his Cadillac Eldorado at the apartment building on South Munn Avenue. He and his entourage, it seemed, found it easier to take the train to Newark. They grabbed a cab to the station and Razor wanted to make sure it was part of a daily ritual. Access to Tubbs' wife and son depended on it.

Brick Church Station, originally the Second Presbyterian Church of Orange, sat just to the north of the rail terminal. The terminal was built later on. Planners duplicated the design of the 19th-century church, leaving the impression that the two structures were built simultaneously. Architecturally, they were almost twins.

Razor climbed off his Harley. The three other bikers followed him into the terminal. Razor gave them careful instructions.

"We watch. That's all we do. Like we don't have any fuckin' interest in Tubbs. Tank, you over there."

He pointed at a ticket outlet.

"Make it look like you're plannin' a trip. Like you're readin' up on ticket prices to Hoboken or somethin'. Rest of you, spread out. He should be comin' in soon."

Brick Church Station wasn't particularly busy at ten o'clock in the morning. Commuters heading for Newark or New York's Penn Station had already come and gone. Razor didn't want to attract attention to himself or his fellow bikers.

Shortly after ten, three men walked into the building through the Main Street entrance. Jackie Tubbs, his trainer and a bodyguard immediately headed for the ticket counter. The bodyguard looked as if he could mop the floor even with the muscular Tank, who stepped aside as the trio purchased return tickets to Newark. Razor was satisfied. This was in fact the Tubbs routine. Arlene Tubbs and Jackie, Jr. were now vulnerable. The middleweight champ and his entourage headed trackside. Razor, Tank and the Atlantic City duo headed for their bikes.

Mealtime with a one-year-old can be difficult. Arlene Tubbs, now twenty-six, had plenty of experience. She'd been the oldest of five children growing up in Newark. Her parents were absent most of the time, trying to scrape together enough money to put food on the table and pay the rent. It fell to Arlene to look after the little ones. She was no longer a surrogate. Jackie Jr. was her own baby and tending to his needs came naturally to her. She watched her son lift the spoon from his breakfast cereal and deliver it to his own mouth.

"Look at that," she told him. "You did so well. You're such a good boy."

Jackie beamed all over. He didn't really understand why his mother was so pleased. He just felt good all the time.

Arlene, her parents and siblings had lived through an era of upheaval in Newark's Central Ward. African-Americans in that part of town were New Jersey's disenfranchised. There were few jobs. Urban renewal was changing the face of the black community and was referred to by the residents as "negro removal." Blacks were relegated to the ranks of the hopeless. Newark's city fathers planned to cut the community in half with super-highways. Land was expropriated. Homes were demolished. Industries pulled out of the area and hundreds of tenant families were evicted. Unemployment among black males became an expected, albeit dreaded fact of life. Arlene's three brothers had virtually no chance of finding honest work.

Her family had the misfortune of living in a high-rise public-housing project at 7th Street and 15th Avenue, directly across from Newark's Fourth Precinct police headquarters. On a hot day in July of 1967 cab driver John Smith was arrested on a misdemeanor charge. He was cuffed and witnesses claimed he was badly beaten by white arresting officers. Smith's fate was uncertain, but rumors spread quickly through the Central Ward that he had died of a brutal assault.

Authorities failed to report that he'd been smuggled out an emergency exit at police headquarters and admitted to a local hospital.

Angry crowds gathered in the street outside Arlene's building. Firebombs were thrown. Police battled their way into the heart of the mob and hand-to-hand fighting ensued. Arlene was sitting in the kitchen talking with her younger sister when she heard what sounded like gunfire. She and her sister couldn't see anything from the apartment windows, so they went down in the elevator.

By now, the riot had spread. Scores of people moved into the street, coming in from all the surrounding neighborhoods. Arlene and her sister watched from inside the front doors of the project. Two men, fleeing the violence, scrambled into their building's lobby.

"They're crazy! Don't you go get involved, now," one of them warned. "They gone crazy!"

Arlene had no intention of getting involved, but the scene before her would be etched forever in her memory. Before it was all over, nearly a week later, rioters would rampage through the Central Ward, looting, overturning vehicles and attacking authorities. State Police were deployed. They called on the National Guard for assistance when the violence exploded out of the black community and into Newark proper. Twenty-six people died over a bloody six-day period. More than seven hundred were injured and police made at least fifteen hundred arrests.

For Arlene, the Newark riot was the hand of fate. Shortly after the deadly mêlée, she would meet a young boxing champion in a high school auditorium. Jackie Tubbs, New-Jersey hero, addressed a public meeting. He urged black communities everywhere not to despair. Tubbs was convinced that time was on their side, that white America would change its collective attitude and Martin Luther King's dream would ultimately be realized. Non-violence, the young fighter told his audience, was the only course if equal treatment was to be achieved for all races.

Arlene had been impressed. She introduced herself to Jackie Tubbs after his speech. There was a five-year age difference, but she was a headstrong girl who knew what she wanted when she saw it. She was determined to become a part of his life. Tubbs, then twenty-nine, took an immediate liking to the young woman from the projects. They dated briefly and were married within two months of that first meeting. Jackie, Jr. was born in July, 1968 and Arlene's life changed forever.

Security in the Tubbs building on South Munn Avenue was a work in progress. There were elaborate plans to ensure the safety of future tenants but, for the present, the main focus was on renovation. Arlene grew accustomed to chemical smells, sawdust and the jarring sound of power tools. Plumbers, electricians, carpenters and painters moved through the various units at will. No one really checked the individual work crews. Several companies were contracted to do the work and faces changed from day to day.

Jackie had only fond memories of his mother. When she died, his father spent whatever leisure time he had with his best friend, Zachary Johnson. Jackie always called him Uncle Zach. The now seventy-three-year-old became an integral part of his life when his father passed on. Then a teenager, Jackie had been thrust into a dog-eat-dog world. Boxing was his passion. Uncle Zach was his ally and friend. The old man, now grey-haired and stooped from years of manual labor, sat at a desk in the main lobby of the apartment building. Jackie hired him to keep an eye on things in general, to be as helpful as possible to the crews and to make sure that undesirable elements didn't just wander in off the street. He was the only security checkpoint. It was like working in a construction zone, but it was the best job Zachary Johnson ever had.

Razor, Tank and the two Atlantic City bikers sized up the situation quickly. They paid a Texaco dealer a few bucks to let them park their motorcycles at his garage down the block.

"Four white guys on Harleys," Razor said, "kinda stand out in this neighborhood."

Razor wanted to attract as little attention as possible. He and the others stashed their jackets. Hells Angels insignias were ill advised.

Zach looked up at the four men as they entered the building. They weren't carrying lumber or sheetrock or tools. Their clothes weren't covered in paint. Something about them set off alarms.

"What kin I do for you gents?"

Razor stepped up to the desk.

"Not what you *can* do, Pops, what yer *gonna* do."

The blood drained out of Zach's face. Razor leaned over him.

"We're lookin' for Arlene Tubbs. You're gonna take us to 'er."
He grabbed Zach by the arm.

"Now git up and do it. Don't try t' signal anybody on the way. If y'do, I'll slit yer fuckin' throat."

Zachary Johnson believed him. He stood up and obediently led the four men to the elevator.

"Penthouse is locked," he said. "Arlene ain't gonna let'cha in."

"That's why you're gonna knock on the door. We'll stay outta the way until she opens it. Got it?"

Zach swallowed. His spit seemed to have dried up.

"What'cha gonna do?"

"Just gonna talk. Just talk, Pops, 'less you do somethin' stupid."

The elevator doors closed behind them and it began climbing to the twelfth floor.

"I might be old," Zach said, mustering his courage, "but I ain't no fool. You plannin' sumpin' bad."

Razor didn't reply. The elevator doors opened and they found themselves in a wood-paneled alcove just outside the penthouse. There was a crystal chandelier, which Jackie and Arlene had ordered out of a catalogue. The floor was covered in granite tile. Razor waved the three other bikers to one side of the penthouse door. He turned to Zach.

"Knock on it, old man. Make it quick. And no tricks."

Zach hesitated momentarily, realized his situation was hopeless and did as he was told.

Arlene came to the door carrying Jackie Jr. on her hip. The baby had Gerber's Pears running down his chin. Arlene was trying to acknowledge Zachary and wipe off the pears at the same time. Her eyes widened in surprise when Razor shoved Zach aside and stood in front of her.

"Inside," he said. "Close the door."

Tank and the other bikers followed behind. Zach's legs were trembling.

"I'm sorry, Arlene. I didn't know what to do. I couldn't stop them." There were tears in his eyes.

Razor's face was deathly white. He was so tall, thin and pasty, Arlene thought of a milk snake or some earth-dwelling insect that had crawled out from under a rock.

"W-what do you want?"

"Shut yer pie-hole and listen. Listen good, 'cuz I don't like sayin' things twice."

He pointed at Tank and then at a wall-phone, visible off the kitchen.

"Get the phone number. Write it down."

He moved so close to Arlene she could smell his breath.

"You tell the champ we got business with him. You tell 'im about our little visit today and he should wait for a phone call from me tonight."

Arlene felt faint. She held her baby as far away from Razor as possible.

"What for?"

"'Cause if he don't wait for that call, you tell 'im our next visit won't be so nice. Tell 'im there's nuthin' he can do. We'll find you and the kid and you make it clear to the champ, he'll never find either of you again."

His upper lip curled into a cruel smile.

Chapter Thirteen

"Dick Tomlin is lying."

Ty Davis was sure of it. He'd reviewed the events of late August over and over in his head. Now, he openly accused the overnight police reporter. Ty, Jason Moore and Greg Peterson sat in Clyde Bertram's office. It was one more in a series of meetings with the news director.

"What makes you think so?"

Bertram, as usual, was chewing on the butt of a spent cigar.

"We have Maggie Price out of the news room that night for a long enough period to provide access to car keys earlier in the evening. Tomlin swears up and down that nothing untoward happened before he went out on his rounds."

Ty shot a worried expression at Greg.

"Neither of us can prove it, Clyde. We've got Tomlin on tape. He was here for the better part of a half-hour before he went out to the cop shops. Maggie never saw anyone in the newsroom prior to Tomlin's midnight start time. Call it a hunch. Greg and I have the feeling that someone got those keys out of Jason's office before Dick ever left the station on his rounds."

Bertram tried to light the cigar butt. It was too short and too wet. Instead, he pulled another one from his shirt pocket and bit off the end.

"A hunch won't do it, Ty. Anyway, why would Tomlin lie?"

Ty placed a tape recorder on Bertram's desk.

"Just listen, Clyde. Listen to the tone."

There was something halting and uncertain about Tomlin's recorded voice.

"I just don't know," he said. "Maggie claims there were people in the building. I'm tellin' ya, it could have been anybody. I don't know who took the car."

"See what I mean?" Ty asked.

Bertram was scowling.

"To be frank, Ty, no I don't. It's no secret you and Greg here don't get along with Tomlin. If he's involved in some kind of bald-faced lie, what's his motive?"

Jason had been quietly going over his notes.

"Look, Clyde," he said, "we don't particularly like Tomlin, that's true. But look at all the things that happened that night. This we do know. There was a Mafia shindig in the north end. Why didn't Tomlin's police contacts tell him anything about that? *We* didn't even know about it until Réal Gendron filled Ty in a month later. Turns out the woman Greg's accused of beating up is a Mafia lawyer, a powerful one with direct connections to the Positano family. At the very least, if Tomlin's not lying, he's a pretty poor excuse for a police reporter."

Bertram was losing his patience.

"Alright, alright. Let's suppose Tomlin's not telling the truth. I still can't see what his motive would be."

"Well," Moore replied, "we think he's fully aware of who took Mobile 9 off the lot. We think he's covering for somebody. Ty has proof the unit was just across the street from the Mafia meeting at Cabrini Hall. We just can't place the car downtown later on that morning. But we do know a helluva lot more about this Maria Claudio person."

"Like what?"

"An RCMP contact of mine had some pretty interesting things to say. Claudio is not just any old lawyer. She's Salvatore Positano's personal lawyer."

"What's that prove?"

Moore flinched. Bertram was being tough.

"We know, in this room, that Greg wasn't driving Mobile 9 that night. We can't prove it. We just know it. So, if Maria Claudio is as well connected to Positano as my contact says she is, there's no way she was *not* at Cabrini Hall. Whoever Tomlin is covering for, maybe whoever was actually at that Mafia meeting, is powerful enough or scary enough for Tomlin to have handed the keys over without question."

Bertram appeared to be thinking.

"Someone who was in this building on that night."

"Right. And there's something more, Clyde. My contact tells me that Claudio is first-cousin to Massimo Gianfranco, Positano's right arm."

"Here's another tidbit," Ty added. "I've picked up a piece of interesting information. There's this sports doctor, a Dr. Thomas Sinclair. Walt Taylor put me onto 'im. He's Johnny on the Spot at the Sands Family Gym in Ste. Anne de Bellevue. Looks after Billy and his brothers and handles medical stuff for some of the high school kids who take boxing lessons out there."

"I'm listening," Bertram said.

"Seems he overheard a conversation between the infamous Gino Viscuso and Billy Sands' sparring partner, Carmen Acelino. Apparently they were talking about Billy's upcoming fight with the middleweight champion, Jackie Tubbs. It's at the Forum in a couple of weeks. Doctor Sinclair heard them arguing about whether or not to give Positano certain information."

"Information?"

"Yeah, about the possible outcome of that fight. It sounds to me like Viscuso is planning to make book on the match. And if Doctor Sinclair got it right, it appears he's not cutting Positano in. Like he's got his own agenda. Like he's some sort of maverick."

Bertram raised an eyebrow.

"That'll get him dead."

"And," Moore added, "there's something more you should know. The RCMP contact might have provided us with what could turn out to be a major news story. Also, why Viscusco is out there doin' what he's doin' and free to do it. Maria Claudio is paying off some of our Superior Court judges. Positano's money."

"What?"

"Apparently there's a police investigation underway. She gets mob-connected people off. She has Positano's go-ahead to bankroll some of the judges. Cops are trying to pin it all down, as we speak. And that would explain why Gino Viscuso hasn't been sentenced yet for that drug bust in the Townships last August."

Bertram lighted his cigar and took a long drag on it. The smoke curled toward the ceiling.

"Here's what I don't get," he said. "If this lawyer is as important as your contact says she is, Jason, and if whoever actually beat her up was also at Cabrini Hall, why would she tell the cops anything about the beating? Why would she agree to a police lineup, much less finger Greg for the attack? Doesn't make sense. She wouldn't want the attention."

"Because," Moore smiled, "she had no choice. The man who was smoking on his balcony and saw the whole thing is the guy who called the police in the first place. He told them about the CKCF mobile. He told them about the beating. Claudio was stuck. She had to follow through with a credible story, without identifying the attacker. Greg was just a convenient out."

"That's what you think," Bertram said. "But you don't know for sure."

"No, we don't. But we will. Just a matter of time and talking to the right people."

"What's the status of the police investigation?"

Moore looked at Greg.

"No charges so far against Greg. Cops *know* this Claudio. I don't think they're buying her story either."

Paolo Sciascia looked like a bookkeeper. He was balding and short and had the reputation of being a good listener. When he did speak, it was in quiet tones that possessed an unnerving authority. His face was lined and pale. His overall manner appeared benign.

Salvatore Positano knew better. This was the *capoprovincia*, the boss of Sicily's Agrigento Province. Positano knew that the Mafia's regional commission had sent a barracuda into Montreal waters. This was a man whose very soul stemmed from generations of underworld brutality and whose reputation was the product of violence and bloodshed. As *capoprovincia*, he would have to be a calculating and heartless leader who took no prisoners.

Sciascia was accompanied to the Westmount mansion by Pasquale Galante, a Sicilian *caporegime*. They sat in leather chairs opposite Gaetano Lipare and Umberto Madonia, the *capos* from the New York Ragusa family. This was the sit-down that would determine several things: whether Rocco Panepinto would be expelled as *caporegime* in Montreal, whether his soldiers would be dispersed throughout the Positano *borgata*, and whether the Sicilian element should be forced to wait out a probationary period before capitalizing on mob activities in the area. Panepinto was also present. This was the showdown Ragusa's underboss Giovani Lorenzo had wanted. Positano spoke first.

"Welcome to Montreal."

He held up a glass of single malt scotch. The other men followed suit.

"You have all met. You all know why we're here. Rocco has presented his case. He has the right of appeal. The outcome of this mediation will be binding."

Positano turned to the Ragusa family representatives.

"Gaetano Lipare will speak for Frank Ragusa."

Lipare stood up out of his chair. He was a rotund man with a bad complexion. He wore an expensive suit. There was silence in the room as he prepared his argument.

"Panepinto, here, has been in Montreal for less than two years. It's true he was made *capo* by Salvatore. It's true he has pulled his weight. But these truths have flaws. For one, he has been expanding his territory without consulting the *borgata*, buying up real estate, opening dry-cleaning establishments, restaurants and bars. He's brought his crew in from Sicily, again ignoring the *borgata*'s right of approval. And," Lipare paused for effect, "he seems to think he's fucking entitled to share all profits with the other five *capos* in Montreal. This is not right. There should be conditions."

Paolo Sciascia interrupted. "Let me point out that Rocco Panepinto's reputation in Agrigento Province was well established before he ever was sent here." He addressed Positano, purposely ignoring Lipare. "You're lucky to have him. Frank Ragusa should be happy to have him."

Sciascia stood up to emphasize his point and faced the tribunal.

"No one here can complain. Rocco and his crew have, perhaps, expanded their territory but the five other *capos* have reaped the benefits. Legitimate enterprise is the way of the future. Buying real estate, setting up the businesses you referred to has meant additional revenue to everyone in the *borgata*. This is not an issue. Salvatore, you named him *caporegime* because you knew these things to be true."

Positano nodded.

"I did. No one dislikes the color of his money. It's the lack of respect."

"Respect is earned."

"Then goddam well let him earn it. Respect takes time."

The *capoprovincia* grinned.

"You think he should be expelled. Why?"

"Because he's got no fuckin' respect. Not for me. Not for the other *capos*."

Gaetano Lipare resented being cut out of the conversation.

"Me 'n' Umberto got some things to say. As you know, Paolo, it don't matter how much money Panepinto's generating. It's peanuts compared to the bank. He wants an equal cut of everything. Why should he have the fuckin' right? The Positano family, hell, Frank Ragusa himself, have shown over many years that financial gain from the rackets far exceeds what can be expected through legitimate enterprise."

"And," said Sciascia, "when Salvatore named Panepinto *caporegime*, he was fully aware he'd be sharing those profits with him and with his crew. The issue of respect aside. This is no popularity contest. This is more, even, then a clash of personalities. It's Frank Ragusa trying to hold on to control. It's underboss Lorenzo trying to put a cap on Sicilian interests. No more of this. Salvatore Positano made his decision. He gave Panepinto his rank and, like it or not, he and his Sicilian crew have lived up to their end of the bargain. Everyone here is better off financially because of it."

Once again, there was silence in the room. It seemed no one could dispute Sciascia's arguments. By mutual agreement, it was decided that there would be no expulsion. There would be no probationary period and the Sicilian influence would remain in Montreal. Ragusa underboss Giovani Lorenzo would return to New York in defeat.

Chapter Fourteen

It had been a record season for rainfall in the Boston area. Autumn foliage lacked its usual vibrant colors. The saturated ground, instead, produced a muddy complexion on hillsides around Newton Lower Falls to the west. Leaves fell. Raking began. Winter whispered in the night.

Charles Walkley was troubled. He'd spoken twice with his son-in-law in recent days. His daughter, Elizabeth, seemed to have slipped into a deeper depression since the scene at the Billingale Country Club. His wife, Sarah, and he noticed from the very start that Elizabeth was quieter than they remembered. She was an active little girl, growing up on Montreal's West Island. Her energy levels were almost excessive, prompting the Walkleys to consult with her pediatrician about hyperactivity and its potentially negative impact.

Charles was eventually convinced she possessed the kind of outgoing personality that only an intelligent, healthy girl *should* possess. Frenetic energy, he decided, was a byproduct of her need to be popular and to succeed. Elizabeth won a scholarship to McGill University and met TV reporter Ty Davis at a student protest. As far as Charles and Sarah Walkley knew, she and Ty were happily married. Then there was the phone call. She and their grandchildren were on a train to Newton. There was a storm brewing in Camelot.

As a treat, that night he'd taken them all out to dinner at the club. Elizabeth, he and Sarah enjoyed a cocktail, while Catherine had a Shirley Temple complete with a maraschino cherry. Two-year-old Robin wanted apple juice. There was wine with dinner. It wasn't until coffee and dessert that Charles grew concerned. Elizabeth didn't want dessert. She ordered a Drambuie, threw it down like a shot and ordered another. Then her mood changed. She yelled at the children, argued with her mother and ultimately embarrassed her father.

Billingale Country Club was out of his league, beyond his salary-range as a liberal arts professor at Unity College. The college, however, recognized that many faculty members enjoyed golfing. An arrangement was made under which Billingale offered considerably reduced rates. In return, club members were granted free access to adult education programs, library facilities, on-campus concerts and numerous other social activities. Boston's elite considered the college a bastion of intellectualism and good breeding. Charles Walkley simply liked to play golf.

He and Sarah moved to Newton Lower Falls shortly after their first grandchild was born. He gave up teaching at Loyola College in Montreal in 1964 when Unity College underwent extensive staff changes. Several young lecturers failed to meet its standards. The college was looking for seasoned academics and was offering professorships to replace them. Charles heard about an opening in the Liberal Arts faculty, a job that paid fifteen thousand dollars more than he earned in Montreal. It was a gutsy move to make in his fifties, but he liked Boston. Elizabeth had her own family now. Sarah, who was born in Massachusetts, had often spoken of selling their home and moving to the United States.

During the first couple of weeks in Newton, things went from bad to worse for Elizabeth. She drank what she called "elevenses," at precisely eleven o'clock each morning. Usually it was a vodka and tonic. She argued it was a British custom that she enjoyed at home. Charles discussed it with Ty, who warned him about the evening martinis and the blackouts. Charles put a lock on his liquor cabinet, but it didn't act as a deterrent. Elizabeth started clubbing, often driving into Boston and staying out 'til all hours of the night.

"What the hell is wrong with this town?" she'd asked. "Everything shuts down at one o'clock in the morning. Can't buy booze on Sundays. Bunch o' Puritans here."

Charles' second call to Ty Davis was somewhat urgent.

"She borrowed my car keys, without asking. The car came back missing the passenger side headlamp. I'm not sure Sarah and I can do this anymore."

Ty agreed to forward the money for car repairs. He explained, with no shortage of emotion, that Elizabeth had hung up the phone on him on the three occasions he'd been able to reach her at the

Walkleys' home. He wrote to her. She did not reply. It seemed the postpartum depression, of which Charles and Sarah were aware, had evolved into a clinical disorder. The alcohol fed the depression. The depression increased the need to drink. Ty tried to offer Charles whatever encouragement he could.

"As far as I know," he told him, "we had no marital problems prior to Robin's birth. Even the few days after Elizabeth and the baby came home from the hospital, she seemed excited and quite normal."

"What did you do once the depression set in?"

"Everything the ob/gyn suggested. Prescription drugs, counselling. It got worse, not better."

"Did you consult a psychiatrist?"

Ty waited a moment before answering.

"Do you think she's mentally ill?"

"Depression, in and of itself, is a mental illness. The alcohol seems to be symptomatic of a worsening condition. I don't know what to say, Ty. Perhaps Alcoholics Anonymous? I gather you're not keen on psychiatric help."

"No, no I'm not opposed at all. That probably would have been our next step. Then she left. Just left, and I don't know how to get her back." He was on the verge of tears.

Charles cleared his throat.

"I know somebody at the college," he said. "I'll see what I can do from this end. Maybe her mother can get her to open up. I've tried. Since I put a padlock on my liquor cabinet, communication between Elizabeth and me has been nonexistent."

"I'd appreciate anything you can do Charles. Anything. How are Catherine and Robin?"

"The children are fine. They ask when daddy's coming. They think they're on some kind of holiday down here."

"I'm sorry, Charles, I can't get away right now. Things are piling up at work. I'll—"

"First things first, Ty. I'll talk to this friend at Unity. See what he has to say. Sarah will have a go with Elizabeth. Take care of yourself and we'll be in touch."

The line went dead.

Anticipation of the Montreal boxing event reached unprecedented levels toward the end of October. Jackie Tubbs had a loyal following in the city. Billy Sands, however, was the local boy vying for a WBA championship. There was little comparison between the two camps. Billy would have the majority of fans on his side at the Forum.

There were also some rumors that Tubbs had injured his right hand. He'd won international recognition by winning the light-middleweight division title years before. Tubbs wasn't satisfied with that. He changed his weight class and then went on to defeat the middleweight champion. He'd last defended that title only a year ago, with a sixth-round TKO at Madison Square Garden.

Despite the rumors about his hand, Tubbs' promoters said he hadn't lost any of the heart that had put him and kept him on top. Now, those same promoters, managers, trainers and other fighters were gathered at the Montreal Forum for the official weigh-in. More than three thousand people showed up, underlining the significance of the event in the Montreal boxing world.

Billy Sands was a showman. He drew catcalls and screaming from his fans, many of whom were wide-eyed teenaged girls. Sands was as popular with women as he was with men. When he stripped to his underwear, he threw his T-shirt into the crowd. That brought another round of wolf-whistles. He stood some eighty feet from Tubbs. Sands shook a fist at the champ and pointed to the floor, indicating that Tubbs was going to go down.

Tubbs responded by planting a fist under his own chin, suggesting the power of his knockout punch. He was nearly a head taller than Billy and his build was almost lanky. Sands was meatier and his musculature was more sharply defined, a characteristic that can play against a fighter. Muscle-bound might appear formidable, but it's stamina that counts in the ring.

"The time has come," Sands declared to the crowd, "for Jackie Tubbs to step up and show what he's got."

The fans cheered. For his part, Tubbs merely eyeballed his challenger and said nothing. The entire weigh-in lasted only twenty minutes. Newspaper articles the next day would speculate on the possibility that Jackie Tubbs was not the champion he'd once been; that the younger Billy Sands looked in better trim, that this would be a fight for the record books.

There was more. Tubbs, according to the articles, might have suffered a blunt injury to his hand a year ago and the injury might not have healed properly. A photograph in the *Montreal Star* showed Tubbs looking down at the floor as Billy held him in a fierce gaze. The photo seemed to suggest that Tubbs had even lost the eyeballing contest.

Chapter Fifteen

The coffee tasted bitter. Greg Peterson sat in his mother's kitchen pondering the injustice of his suspension from CKCF TV. He sipped the coffee and stared blankly at the walls. Two months without a paycheck were weighing on both his pride and his bank account.

Greg was grateful for the moral support from Jason Moore and Ty Davis. He knew that Clyde Bertram was also on his side, but bills had to be paid. His mother's retirement money went only so far and trying to squeeze some dollars out of the bureaucracy in Quebec City was demoralizing. Greg spoke a decent French. It meant nothing to the francophone civil service. Peterson was an English name. His file was nobody's priority.

He thought of his photography. Hundreds of black and whites were in his portfolio, along with as many full-color shots. Greg was sure they were saleable, but marketing the material was something else again. He had no idea where to begin.

Suzie was always upbeat. She felt his talent knew no bounds. "Sort the stuff out," she suggested. "Separate landscapes from portraits. Think themes. Choose personal favorites and start to put those into a selective portfolio. You're so good, Greg. You don't have enough faith in your own ability."

Greg's favorites were no mystery to him. They were all shots of Suzie Waldon. Suzie by candlelight. Suzie asleep. Suzie, Suzie, Suzie. His chest ached for her. He wondered how he could ever offer her the kind of future she deserved.

Anger began mixing with sadness. He knew that Jason and Ty were making progress in their investigation of Maria Claudio. It rankled him however, to have his fate determined by everyone else. Hal Nichols, the operations chief at the TV station, didn't seem the slightest bit interested in the possibility of his reinstatement. The technicians' union, of which he was a dues-paying member, had hung him out to dry. Ty Davis proposed paying Greg at least a portion of his salary out of the strike fund. The union executive considered and then rejected the idea. Criminal matters, they said, were outside the parameters of union business.

"Fuck 'em all," Greg told the empty room. He'd had a vivid dream the previous night of free-spirited days before his job in the Photo Department. He and three friends, backpacking in Nepal one summer. The magic mushrooms they carried into the high country around Kathmandu. The "brothers times four," as they called themselves, climbed along centuries-old trails into the Himalayan foothills, each mile of their journey carrying them deeper into an alien world. In those carefree days of the early '60's, the entire region was known as a kind of hippie mecca.

They passed incredible views, making camp beside whitewater rapids, pausing on mountain cliffs to peer downward into the Newar Kingdoms of the Kathmandu Valley. Greg's camera was always with him. He captured fairy-tale images of huge palaces with intricate facades, farmlands, livestock, and women carrying water jugs into the lush fields. There were temples decorated with dream-like impressions of birds, insects and religious symbols.

One memory in particular stood out from that experience, which now seemed so long ago. His anger subsided as he rewound his dream and played it back in his head. He and his friends had rented a houseboat, using it as a staging place for new adventures. On one occasion they packed their tent, heavy clothes and enough food for at least a three-day expedition. From Kathmandu, they took a train into the southern foothills.

"Pick a mountain," he'd said, pointing at a horizon that swept from eye-level into the very clouds. That adventure took them on wooded trails across impossible bridges, over stunning mountain passes and ultimately into snow country.

The four pitched their tent above the tree line. Greg estimated they'd wound their way along the footpaths and up the side of a major peak. They were above the twelve-thousand-foot level. The mountain beyond melted into the clouds, its highest face disappearing altogether from view. They set up camp against a cliff side under an overhang and, thus, out of the wind. When darkness fell, the "brothers times four" sat inside the tent passing a cup of hot tea laced with the powdered mushrooms. Gradually, the psilocybin wrapped itself around their collective imagination. To this day, Greg wasn't sure whether what happened next was actually real or a hallucination.

They heard a noise. All four heard the same peculiar sounds outside the tent, blending with but definitely not part of the wind's shrill notes. This was more like voices. High pitched. Unearthly. If it was some type of auditory hallucination, the remarkable thing was that it became a shared phenomenon.

No one wanted to venture outside. Greg was closest to the front of the tent, so he was elected. He remembered unzipping and lifting the flap and crawling halfway out. An evening storm had cut jewel-like facets in the snow just beyond the cliff side overhang. That, however, was not what startled him.

Sitting in a semi-circle in the orange glow of their fire were six white apes. Greg's mouth hung open in amazement. He didn't think to grab his camera. He didn't think to summon the others. He merely backed into the tent on all fours and zipped-up the flap. When his friends asked him what he'd seen, Greg told them he didn't want to talk about it. Now, as he sat alone sipping coffee on Querbes Avenue, his situation seemed almost as bizarre and unreal as that Himalayan adventure.

Montreal Police Detective-Sergeant Pierre Maillot silently cursed his smoking habit. At the same time, with another busy day ahead of him, he opened a new pack of Mark Ten cigarettes, pulled one out and lit it. He could set aside concerns about a heavy caseload for the three or four minutes it took to draw the smoke into his lungs. He didn't get the chance. His phone was ringing.

"*Oui, âllo?*"

Maillot frequently overlooked protocol, ignoring his Captain's orders to always identify department and rank when answering the phone.

"Is this Detective Maillot?"

The voice was gruff. "*Oui, monsieur.*"

"This is Clyde Bertram. I'm the director of news at CKCF Television."

"*Oui, monsieur.*"
"I'd like to know what's going on with a matter involving one of my employees."
Maillot butted his cigarette. He wasn't enjoying it anyway.
"You're referring to Greg Peterson?"
"Right. Why hasn't he been charged?"
Maillot didn't like Bertram's tone.
"I'm not at liberty to discuss an ongoing investigation, *monsieur.*"
Bertram decided to change his approach.
"Detective, I apologize if I sound impatient. Let me give you some information about Greg if I may."
"As you wish."
"Greg is a good kid, in my opinion. What you might not know, Detective Maillot, is that my superiors here at CKCF have a rigid policy about stuff like this. Greg has been suspended without pay for better than two months. Until your case is resolved, one way or another, the kid is screwed."
Maillot wasn't aware of the fact that he'd begun smoking another cigarette. He scowled at it and blew out smoke.
"*C'est dommage.* It's too bad," he said. "But this is a homicide investigation, *Monsieur* Bertram. These things, they take time."
"Homicide! What do you mean, homicide?"
Maillot hesitated.
"As I said. This is an ongoing investigation. I'm not at liberty to—"
"Yeah. I know. But homicide? That makes no sense, detective. Greg was a suspect in an assault, not a murder."
Maillot realized he'd have to divulge some details if he was ever going to get off the phone.
"*Monsieur* Bertram, I can trust this will be confidential?"
"Absolutely."
"My personal feeling is that Greg's not involved. But we 'ave to look at every possibility. For now, he is not charged."
Bertram took a deep breath.
"Charged with what, though? So far as I know, there's nothing but an alleged attack on this lawyer, Maria Claudio."
"*C'est vrai.*"
"Then what does this have to do with homicide?"

"In fact, two homicides, *monsieur*."

"What?"

Maillot jammed the second cigarette into an ashtray on his desk.

"Two women. Same m.o. Same victim profile."

"I see. How do you know that?"

"Both women were grabbed off a downtown street. The incidents were after dark. Same general area where Maria Claudio was attacked."

"And these other women were murdered?"

"Raped and strangled with an article of their own clothing."

Bertram's journalistic instincts kicked in. He started taking notes.

"Look. Detective. I give you my word. None of this is on the record. What do these two murders have to do with Greg Peterson, or for that matter with Maria Claudio?"

"Similarities, *monsieur*. *C'est tout.* Downtown. Late at night. Maybe she just got lucky."

"Okay, okay, but Claudio wasn't murdered."

"*Mais non.* But look at it from a police point of view, *Monsieur* Bertram. If someone wanted to have as little trouble as possible engaging a potential victim in conversation, do you not agree that a marked news vehicle would be useful? Less threatening? We can't rule it out, you see."

Bertram decided it would be unproductive to question Maillot any further.

He understood the implications all too well. He admonished himself for not asking follow-up questions, then decided to delegate that responsibility. There was little likelihood Greg Peterson was involved in the attack on Maria Claudio, much less the sex slayings of two other women. Bertram had no intention of violating the trust between himself and Maillot. On the other hand he wondered why more attention hadn't been paid to the murders. Jason Moore was sitting in his office. Bertram would hand off the problem to him. The assignment desk was heaped with teletype copy, file folders and the remains of a ham on rye sandwich.

"Got a situation," Bertram said.

Moore appeared frustrated.

"Join the club."

Bertram told him about his conversation with the Detective-Sergeant.

"Jeez, Clyde, that explains a lot."

"But not everything. Not by a long shot. Make some phone calls will ya? Get back to me soonest."

"I'll get on it. I can think of two or three things right off the top."

Bertram smiled. He was planning a little visit with the CKCF president. Victor Gordon was going to get an earful about the Peterson suspension and, by extension, he thought, ops chief Nichols would get his balls squeezed by Gordon.

"Thanks, Jason." He stepped out of the glassed-in office and headed for executive row.

Moore was aware of the two murders. They were the forty-eighth and forty-ninth of the year in Montreal. He had not been aware that the police believed a serial killer might be on the loose. He checked his files. Moore didn't want to waste time on Detective-Sergeant Maillot. He had his own contacts in the homicide division.

Lieutenant Peter Loughlin was thinking about lunch when his phone rang. He headed up the public relations department at Gosford Street headquarters. His career, he realized with perennial resentment, had reached its pinnacle. Loughlin was of Irish descent. Francophone colleagues who'd joined the force years after him had bypassed him when promotions were handed out. He thought of breaking for lunch and ignoring the damn phone, ruled it out and answered it on the fourth ring.

" 'Lo there, Peter," Jason said. "Long time no talk."

"Hello, Jason. How're they hangin'?"

Moore grinned. He'd known the Lieutenant for years and got some of his best tips from him over beers at the McGill Tavern.

"Peter, you abreast of the Maria Claudio case?"

"The Mafia lawyer?"

"The same."

"Yeah, I know about it. Got herself beat up? One o' yer guys fingered for it?"

"That's the story. Her story, that is."

Loughlin chuckled.

"You not buyin' it?"

"No way. And I'm pretty sure Pierre Maillot isn't either."

"We talkin' as friends or as P.R. chief and reporter?"

Moore thought about Bertram's pledge to keep things off the record.

"To be honest, a little of both. I've got some questions that could help my colleague. I've got some that could easily become a news story."

"Fair enough. You tell me when we're helping your friend and when we start talking headlines."

"I'll make it absolutely clear."

"Well, fire away."

"Okay. As regards Greg Peterson. He's the cameraman who's out of a job unless this thing about Claudio is officially dropped."

"Uh-huh."

"If homicide believes the attack on Claudio was somehow related to two recent sex killings, why hasn't Greg been asked to account for his whereabouts on the nights *they* occurred?"

"I gather, Jason, this is the part of our conversation where we're only helping your friend."

"Right."

"Frankly, then, I'll tell you off the record that we're following other leads on the homicides. We're treating the Claudio matter as an isolated incident."

Moore clicked his tongue.

"So, it's not likely Greg will be charged with anything?"

"That's current thinking. Maillot got it into his head that the killer might be posing as a newsman, driving around town in a marked car. I don't think even he believes it. Besides, this Claudio is about as shady as they come."

"You got that right."

"Jason, it's safe to say the marked car theory is a non-starter. Claudio has quite a history, so we're looking twice at her allegations against Peterson."

"But it's still an open file?"

"Has to be. She picked him out of the lineup. It's just not a priority for now."

"Got it. Now here's where I'm changing gears, Peter. My boss has told Maillot that all of their conversation was confidential. I don't want to compromise that, so I'm simply talking to you to clear up some things about the murders."

"Shoot. But I'm not guaranteeing anything."

"Understood. Okay. Getting back to the marked car business. If there were no witnesses to the abductions of those two other women, how do you know *any* car was involved?"

"Because the bodies turned up miles away. One in a wooded area of Laval. The other in the Morgan Arboretum in Ste. Anne de Bellevue. They had to be driven and dropped."

"Then how do you know they were actually grabbed in downtown Montreal?"

Loughlin was beginning to sound cautious.

"We're getting close to the fire here, Jason. I can't fuck up the investigation."

"Alright. Here's my promise and you know I'm good for it. Anything you tell me now remains strictly between us. I'm really only trying to get Greg off the hook."

"I believe you. But if this stuff ever goes public, it could jeopardize everything. The killer isn't aware of what we know or don't know about his movements."

"Lips are sealed. You have my word as a friend."

"Okay. Both victims were picked up near the same bar on Crescent Street. We know this because victim number one was drinking with a girlfriend. She promised the girlfriend a ride home and went to get her car out of a nearby parking lot. That's the last time she was seen. Just five nights later, victim number two was in the same bar. She lived a couple streets west. Bartender says she was a regular, was drinking alone and left the club around midnight. She never made it home."

"So you know that both women were abducted in the same area."

"We never would have known if the second victim's address hadn't popped up. The boys did some door to door. Checked the clubs because of the late hour involved and got lucky. The killer probably thinks we're way off the trail because of where he ditched the bodies."

"How'd you get on to the girlfriend of the first victim?"

"She called us. Heard about the second murder."

Moore recognized the pattern.

"So you're thinking serial killer?"

"Looks like the same guy in both cases."

"Were you ever gonna tell the media?"

"Like I said, Jason, we're following several leads. We wanna nail the bastard. We don't wanna tip him off."

Moore had to agree. "Thanks, Peter. We never had this conversation."

Chapter Sixteen

Clyde Bertram's bulk filled the doorway. He leaned his shoulder against the wall and fixed his eyes on Amy Sebastien's legs. Victor Gordon's secretary had her back to him and was sorting through a filing cabinet. She was a recent acquisition at CKCF. Bertram had to hand it to Gordon. He knew how to pick them and his choices had very little to do with secretarial ability.

"Hi, Toots," Bertram said.

Amy wheeled around. Three buttons of her blouse were undone revealing an ample bust line, another qualification for the job.

"Mr. Bertram. How nice to see you."

"Is the boss in?" Bertram inquired, puffing on the requisite cigar. She winked at him.

"For you, he's always in. Give me a minute."

Amy walked through the door at the rear of her office and disappeared into the executive suite beyond. Bertram noted she swung her hips suggestively in crossing the room. He didn't like Gordon but admired his taste in women. Moments later, Amy returned to her desk.

"He's waiting for you."

"Thanks, kid." She showed her dimples in a broad smile as he walked past her.

The president's office was more like a luxury hotel suite. The huge desk occupied the better part of one wall. There were three built-in television monitors, positioned for easy viewing from Gordon's desk. Upholstered chairs were placed in front.

At another end of the room were a leather couch and two matching chairs, circling a glass-topped coffee table. Two large lamps spilled soft light into that section, designed to relax potential clients.

A third wall featured a gigantic aquarium. Tropical fish floated through an ethereal scene of miniature castles, mountains and rainbow colors. Bertram figured just one of the fish would fetch the price of a good steak dinner.

"How's tricks?" he asked Gordon, whose five foot six frame seemed all but overwhelmed by his surroundings.

"What's up, Clyde?"

"Got a beef, Vic. I've nursed it for two months. Haven't brought it up until now."

Not to be outdone, Gordon opened a humidor on his desk and withdrew a Cuban Monte Cristo cigar. It was an intentional, albeit indirect, comment on Bertram's preference for the cheaper House of Lords brand.

"That's why I'm here, Clyde. What's the problem?"

"Greg Peterson's the problem. More specifically, the decision to fuck the kid up the ass with this suspension."

Gordon felt a headache coming on. Clyde Bertram had the unsettling ability to instantly put him ill at ease.

"Nobody's trying to do any such thing," he protested.

Bertram sat down in one of the chairs facing the big desk.

"You know me, Vic. I've put my job on the line on several occasions in the past, because of something I believe in. I know about policy. Well, fuck your goddam policy. Greg Peterson doesn't deserve this shit."

"Chrissake, Clyde, he beat up a woman. Company property was involved. Even if the news car *wasn't* involved, this is a police matter and until it's not, Peterson is out."

Bertram proceeded to tell him what he'd learned from Detective Maillot.

"This is a murder investigation, Vic. Cops haven't filed charges in the Claudio beating because it has nothing to do with their big picture. You're not gonna sit there and tell me you think Greg Peterson is some kind of serial killer."

Gordon leaned back in his chair.

"You hired him, Clyde. You tell me. I don't know this guy or what he might be capable of."

"Aw, for goddsakes, Vic. Give the kid a break."

"Can't do it. Alright, I'll give you this. You know more about his character. Maybe the police are satisfied he had nothing to do with the murders, but the fact remains that Maria Claudio was attacked. A CKCF car was involved. The victim pointed at Peterson."

"He didn't do it."

"And you know this, how?"

"Because there was another news mobile on the road that night. It was seen at a Mafia gathering in the north end, not two hours before Claudio was pushed around. Mobile 9 wasn't on any authorized assignment."

If Victor Gordon felt a headache coming on before, it was now a full-blown migraine. He reached into a drawer for some aspirin and swallowed two with a gulp of lukewarm coffee.

"This Mobile 9. It was the car involved in the downtown incident?"

"Can't prove it. Not yet. But Maria Claudio is part of the Salvatore Positano crime family. Whoever was behind the wheel was at that Mafia party. You think Claudio *wasn't* there?"

Gordon was at a momentary loss for words. After what seemed an awkward interlude, he leaned his elbows on his desk.

"Doesn't alter the facts, Clyde. This is still an open police file. You can't say for sure that Peterson did not beat up Claudio."

He took a deep breath, as though regretting his decision. "The suspension stands."

Gino Viscuso had ringside seats. A buxom blonde, a stripper with top billing at the Club Coquettes, sat on his left. The Montreal Forum was nearly filled to capacity for the middleweight championship fight. It was comparable to the type of excitement generated by a Stanley Cup playoff. Viscuso's jaw was working on a wad of gum. He had reassurances from Razor that the champ would carry Billy Sands through all fifteen rounds and ultimately lose on points. Viscusco had tens of thousands of dollars riding on the outcome. Jackie Tubbs promised to throw the fight after a good show, but Viscuso wouldn't feel comfortable until it was all over.

Sands appeared first. He danced his way through a gauntlet of reporters and fans, waving into the white light of dozens of flashbulbs. Photographers were having a field day. The crowd cheered. Billy shadowboxed an imaginary opponent, displaying the confidence he was famous for. His black silk robe was open down the front, revealing a washboard stomach and impressive pectoral cuts. The name "Billy Sands" was monogrammed on the back in orange lettering, followed in smaller lettering by "Sands Family Gym." He climbed through the ropes and into the ring. The Forum resounded with thunderous applause.

The reverse was true for the champ. Jackie Tubbs wore a white robe. The hood was up. His sash was tightly tied. Tubbs emerged from the dressing rooms, walked through the crowd and was greeted by a chorus of boos. This was Montreal. Tubbs felt East Orange, New Jersey was a million miles away and the safety of Arlene and Jackie Jr. was in his hands. He stepped through the ropes into the ring and, according to ritual, made a perfunctory dance around his corner. The fans responded with more boos, interrupted by the master of ceremonies.

"Good evening, ladies and gentlemen. Welcome to the Montreal Forum." Cheers erupted. "This evening's main event. Fifteen rounds for the World Boxing Association middleweight championship. The challenger, wearing the black trunks, weighing 163 pounds. From the City of Montreal. Bill-e-e Sa-ands-s-s."

There was a huge reaction from the crowd. Many rose to their feet.

"Wearing the white trunks," the MC continued, "weighing 160 pounds. From East Orange, New Jersey. The undefeated middleweight champion of the world, Jack-e-e-e Tubbs-s-s."

Scattered cheers. Mainly jeers from the fans. Tubbs and Sands, now without their robes, were sent to the center of the ring for the referee's instructions, then to their respective corners. Billy sat down. Carmen Acelino leaned over him.

"Feel him out. Don't be in no hurry. He's got the reach. Don't let 'im stick ya. Bob and weave. Feel 'im out."

Billy adjusted his mouthpiece and took a deep breath as the bell rang for round one. Tubbs charged out of his corner. The ringside announcer, broadcasting on a New York-based radio network, began shouting into his microphone.

"There's the bell. And the champ comes out of his corner like a man with a mission. This is the first time these two fighters have met in the ring and it looks like Tubbs wants to make it the last time. A series of jabs by Tubbs. Sands appears caught off guard. A left by

Tubbs. Another and another. He's not giving Sands any opportunity to get used to his style. Sands replies with a jab and a cross. Both misses. Tubbs slips away and comes back with a combination. Sands is being out-boxed, here. No question about it."

The bell ended round one. Carmen Acelino noticed some blood coming from Sands' left nostril.

"Don't let 'im catch ya. Circle to the left. Stay away from 'im."

Round two began. Sands opened it up a bit, circling left as Acelino advised and, at the same time, trying to keep Tubbs in the center of the ring. The announcer sized-up the action.

"Sands appears to be in great shape. He took a battering in the first round and seems none the worse for wear. Tubbs still using the jab but not connecting as often. So far we haven't seen him throw his right, the knockout power this middleweight champion has exhibited so many times in the past. There's a clean, solid blow from Sands. Tubbs not fazed. Sands, forcing the champ to circle around him in the center of the ring. Staying away from the ropes. A combination from Tubbs. Sands runs away. One would have to say, a conservative round so far. There's a left to the champ's head. Sands misses with his right. Tubbs backing off. And there's the bell.

Tubbs' corner man was concerned.

"What're you waiting for? This guy's a bum. You're the champ. Act like one."

The third round got underway with a flurry of punches from both fighters.

"This is more like it," the announcer told his radio audience. "This is starting to look like a fight. Tubbs, with a combination. Probing Sands' defenses. Another left. There's the cross. A left again. One two. One two. Sands, bobbing and weaving. Tubbs gets him in the corner, jabbing at Sands. Wait a minute. Sands comes back with a hard blow to the mid-section of Tubbs. An uppercut rocks the champ back on his feet. Sands is out of the corner. There's a left. A right. Tubbs, backing away from the smaller man. And the bell. An exciting round three here at the Montreal Forum. I'm no judge, but I'm scoring that one for the challenger."

"Move! Move!" Tubbs was getting an earful from the corner man. "Dismantle the sonofabitch."

The crowd began chanting "Bill-e-e-e, Bill-e-e-e," as the bell ended rounds four and five. The ringside announcer questioned whether Tubbs was displaying championship qualities.

"Where's the sting? Tubbs doesn't seem to be on his game. He's actually fighting defensively. This is not the Jackie Tubbs we're accustomed to. Sands appears both physically and mentally strong. Some punishing combinations from the challenger. Very little back from the champ."

Round nine began with more of the same.

"Tubbs, throwing his left. Jab. Jab. He's chasing Sands. There's a solid left to Sands' head. A cross from Tubbs. Sands is stunned. But look! Look at Tubbs' face! He appears to be in serious pain. That right cross has hurt him, maybe more than it hurt Sands. Well, we heard about this. Tubbs has apparently been nursing his right hand, after suffering what his promoters called a blunt injury last year. Sands doesn't seem to have noticed. He gets inside that two-inch reach advantage. One to the body. Another punishing uppercut to the jaw of the champion."

The bell rang. Acelino pounced excitedly on Sands.

"Yer doin' good. Stay inside. Stay inside. Jab. He ain't got no knockout punch. Get 'im!"

He got him as often as possible in rounds ten through twelve. Tubbs kept up the pressure, chasing him with a series of powerful jabs.

"A fight that is going the distance," the announcer declared. "Very close on points. Tubbs, connecting repeatedly with his left. Sands, counter-punching effectively. This is too close to call. And the champ, noticeably in pain every time he throws that right. As we head into the final rounds, Tubbs has literally become a one-handed fighter."

"You're free to do some damage," Acelino told Sands. "He's fuckin' crippled."

Sands came out swinging in rounds thirteen and fourteen. It was still very close on points.

"Tubbs is running back," the announcer shouted. "Here's a series of hard blows to the body from Sands as he gets inside Tubbs' reach. Round fifteen, folks, and who'd a' thunk it? Sands is not only on his feet. He appears to be in command of this fight. The champ is trying to stay alive. There's another uppercut from Sands. The crowd is going crazy!"

"Bill-e-e. Bill-e-e."

"And another combination from Sands. The champ is in the corner. Tubbs, using that jab, trying to fight his way off the ropes. There's a left to the temple of Tubbs. He's in trouble. Another left. He dodges it. He's trying to get out of the corner. Jabbing. Jabbing at Sands. A solid right cross from Tubbs. He's hurt! The champ is wincing. That right hand of his is giving him some serious pain. Here comes Sands!"

"Bill-e-e. Bill-e-e."

"A left. A right. Tubbs is in trouble. Can he last the round? Sands now hitting the champ, seemingly at will. One to the head. One to the body. Another combination from Sands. Tubbs is taking it. A jab to the face of Sands. The referee separates them. Another jab from Tubbs as round fifteen comes to an end. What a finale. What a tremendous fight this has been!"

Both fighters raised their arms in a victory dance. There was pandemonium among the fans.

When Sands approached Tubbs to congratulate him on a good match, something unusual happened. Tubbs turned his back on him and retired to center-ring to hear what the master of ceremonies had to say.

"Ladies and gentlemen." The crowd gradually settled down. "Judge number one scores the fight 117 to 111 for Billy Sands."

Cheers resounded through the Forum.

"Judge number two scores it 115 to 113 for the challenger, Billy Sands."

This time the noise level dropped only slightly.

"Judge number three," the MC continued, "115 to 113 for Jackie Tubbs."

The cheers lapsed into nearly unanimous audience disapproval.

"We have a split decision. And an upset for the ages. Ladies and gentlemen." He held Billy's arm in the air. "The winner and new, WBA middleweight champion of the world, Bill-e-e-e Sands-s-s!"

The fans went wild. In row three, Gino Viscuso and his stripper companion stood up and began working their way toward the aisle. Viscuso was grinning from ear to ear.

Chapter Seventeen

"I'm sorry, Ty. So terribly sorry."

Elizabeth Davis stood in her nightdress by the telephone in her father's study. Ty was taking a shower when he heard the phone ring. He scrambled over the edge of the tub, stumbled and hit his hip on the bathroom sink. He picked up on the fourth ring.

"Elizabeth?"

"Dad and Mother have gone to bed."

"What time is it, anyway?" Ty was dripping all over the hardwood floor in his hallway. He'd left his watch in the bedroom.

"A little after ten-thirty."

"I was in the shower. What's going on, Liz?"

"Maybe what's going on is that I love you. Catherine and Robin too. We all miss you."

Ty found he couldn't reply.

"Ty, are you still there?"

"Yes. Yes I'm here."

"Did you hear what I said?"

"I did. I love *you*, Liz. I never stopped. Everything seems meaningless without you and the kids. I swear. It's so depressing around here. All I do is work and sleep. I can't eat. I keep hearing the kids upstairs and think it's Robin or Catherine. You don't answer my letters. You're distant when we talk on the phone."

"I know. I know, Ty. I'm sorry. I haven't been myself for a long, long time."

Ty ignored the fact he was soaking wet and sat down on the cushioned chair by the telephone stand.

"It doesn't matter," he said. "Nothing matters if we aren't together."

"A little more time, Ty. I'm seeing one of my father's colleagues over at Unity College. We meet twice a week. I've learned a lot about myself, about what's been happening."

"Like what?"

"Like what postpartum depression can do to a person. Chemical and hormonal changes in the body. Stuff like that."

"Who is this guy?"

"He's a psychologist. A doctor. A professor at Unity."

"And what's he saying?"

"That I'm recovering, but it's a slow process."

"Can't you come home and see somebody here?"

Elizabeth momentarily went silent.

"Liz?"

"I want to be home, Ty. More than anything I want that. Professor Hall referred me to a local doctor who changed my medication. The anti-depressant I was taking wasn't effective."

"This new one is working?"

"That's just it. I've been on it for only a little while. He says it takes several weeks to really kick in."

"But you sound fine."

"I'm making good progress. That's not the result of the pills though. It's because of these sessions with Professor Hall. He's honestly helping me to understand why I've been drinking. Why I've been so—" she began to sob, "so very unhappy."

"It's alright, Liz. Everything's going to work out."

"God, I hope so."

"It will. I'm here. I'm going to be here when you're ready to come back."

"I do love you, Ty. I wasn't even sure of that, before I left."

"Tell you what, Liz. I'll call you every damn day. We can talk about your meetings with the professor. Anything you want to talk about."

"Okay."

"I actually think I'm going to get some sleep tonight."

"I'm glad."

"Kiss the kids."

"I will. G'bye."

"Bye, Liz."

Montreal newspapers devoted widespread attention to the Sands-Tubbs fight. One headline read "Middleweight Mismatch." Another declared "Tubbs Tanks," and the story questioned why reports of the champion's injured hand hadn't surfaced earlier. "Jackie Tubbs," it pointed out, "easily defended his title a year ago against up and comer Lyle Osgood at Madison Square Garden. A TKO in the sixth round dispelled earlier speculation that Tubbs had begun to feel his age. The middleweight champ, interviewed after the match, was quoted as saying he was in great shape and looking forward to a real challenge to the title. He referred to Osgood as a cocky kid, not prepared to step into the ring with a veteran like himself." The story made no mention of an injury. Tubbs' promoters had brought that up only recently.

A French language paper went even further, suggesting that for reasons unknown Tubbs seemed to have held himself back intentionally. Only one newspaper carried the headline "Sensational Sands." There was a photograph of Billy Sands with his arms in the air, holding the championship belt above his head. There was a brief reference to Billy's brothers and the Sands Family Gym. The writer conceded that it had been a split decision and a rematch was most likely.

Jason Moore was frustrated. He felt he was on the fringes of a significant story. The problem was that he'd obtained most of the information through confidential sources. He couldn't develop it on the air without compromising those sources and identifying powerful people who might take CKCF to court. What could he prove? How would it all help Greg Peterson? Moore was connecting the dots. He started by putting another call through to the RCMP. Corporal Normand Francoeur wasn't overly pleased to hear from him.

"You promised me this would go no further," he reminded Moore.

"And I've kept my promise. It's just that there are several angles to this thing. Maria Claudio seems to be at the center of most of it."

"She gets around."

"No doubt. Look, I'm not planning to turn this into a Flash News report, at least not for the time being. If it ever comes to that, you have my word that your name will never come up."

"I'd be out of a job, Jason."

"I know and I appreciate any help you can give me."

"I'll try."

Moore wasn't sure where to begin. He told Francoeur about the alleged attack on Maria Claudio and the subsequent police lineup. He mentioned Greg Peterson's suspension.

"We know Peterson is innocent of the assault charge, but that's been complicated by a Montreal murder investigation."

"How so?"

"The primary on the murder case, a Detective-Sergeant Pierre Maillot, had some theory that the killer could have used a marked news mobile."

"And?"

"And it seems to be a dead end. Meantime, Greg's outta luck because Maillot's theory hasn't entirely been discounted and the Claudio case is on their back burner."

"Well, how can I help?"

Moore got a steno-pad and pen out of his desk drawer.

"I'm not sure. Can you tell me anything more about these judges who may be on the take?"

"What's that got to do with Peterson?"

"It's more about Maria Claudio. If I can throw dirt at her, talk about bribery and so on, it might cast doubt on anything she's telling the cops about Greg."

Francoeur thought it over.

"That's a stretch."

"Maybe it is. I gotta start somewhere."

"Okay. First thing is, we've got jurisdictional issues. If judges are peddling their influence in Quebec, the Provincial Police want to know about it. We've got our own interests at the federal level, because organized crime extends beyond provincial boundaries."

"I understand."

"So, here's what we know. Claudio has represented a number of clients who didn't seem to stand a chance of beating the charges against them."

"But they did."

"They did. Since then, we've had the undercover boys following her into court. Y'know. Watch the proceedings?"

"Yeah?"

"Every time it seems there's solid evidence against them, some of her people are given a clean bill. Not guilty, by reason of some technicality the judge digs up."

"What if it's a jury trial?"

Francoeur sighed.

"All the mob has to do is get to one juror."

"And they beat the rap?"

"Case is thrown out, or if it's too serious a charge and the judge gets nervous, they might be found guilty. The judge just keeps finding reasons to delay sentencing and the bastards are out on the street."

"Can you positively establish that Claudio is paying off some of the judges or that there's jury tampering or intimidation?"

"Not yet. On two occasions we've spotted her having lunch with a particular judge."

"If nothing else, wouldn't that be some sort of conflict of interest?"

"But not without precedent. Lawyers with ambition often associate with other court officials. Maybe they covet an eventual appointment to the bench. Maybe they just wanna get laid. Who knows? Anyway, there's nothing illegal about lunching with a magistrate."

Moore scribbled something on his pad.

"Unless that magistrate is about to rule on one of Claudio's clients."

"That's it. Look, Jason. We're keeping a tail on her. We've even got a court clerk who's been doing a little spying for us, on this one judge. You know. Who gets to meet with him in chambers, that sort of stuff. But we still don't have the goods on Claudio."

"Thanks, Normand. Can I check in with you from time to time?"

"It's your dime."

Moore smiled. Montreal Police Lieutenant Peter Loughlin was next on his list. He waited a few minutes, sipping slowly on a cup of vending-machine coffee that tasted more like lukewarm water and powdered milk. The news department had tried to set up its own coffee corner. Nobody but Maggie Price ever washed the pot or cleaned up the spilled sugar and discarded paper cups. Clyde Bertram finally closed down the entire operation. Good coffee in the building was at a premium. He dialed the number for police public relations.

"Loughlin here."

Moore put the cup down on his desk. The aftertaste from the foul liquid was disgusting.

"You guys have decent coffee down there in cop land?"

"Rather have a Molson."

"Sounds good. How y'doin', Peter?"

"Same shit. Different day."

Moore sat back in his chair. He watched Ty Davis enter the newsroom and sit down at his typewriter.

"Got a couple follow-ups to our last conversation."

"Oh yeah?"

"Nothing really. Mostly impatience with this whole business about Greg Peterson. What is it with Detective Maillot anyway? Why's he putting off either charging Greg with something or tossing the case?"

Loughlin hesitated, then said "Because he can."

"Seriously, Peter. Greg's a friend of mine. I'm one-hundred percent positive he had nothing to do with Maria Claudio."

"That may be, Jason. Maillot's got his own way of thinking."

"And what exactly *is* he thinking?"

"Maillot's a bit of a Quebec nationalist. *Maîtres chez nous* and all that. He's no fan of the press, particularly of the English media. Doesn't like to have his authority questioned.

"So you believe he's just being an asshole?"

"You said that. I didn't. But here's the way I see it. Maillot gets the idea his serial killer might be a news reporter. His theory is shot down by the brass. Now, he's no closer to solving the murders and he's pissed off."

"That would explain why Greg's never been interrogated about the two victims or what he was doing on the nights they were killed."

"Exactly. So what's he got? He's got a Mafia lawyer pointing the finger at a *maudit anglais* TV guy. He isn't fond of the Italians. He's absolutely certain he dislikes Anglos and he despises the English media."

"Nice," Moore replied.

Loughlin let out a breath.

"I don't see any alternative, Jason. This thing is going to have to play out in its own time."

Chapter Eighteen

The wind was out of the east on the first day of November 1969, drawing with it the noxious odors of Montreal's east-end oil refineries, launching transparent waves of stench as far west as Ville St. Laurent. Shortly after his phone call to Peter Loughlin, Jason picked something up on the police radio that piqued his curiosity. A body was found on BP Canada property. Ty Davis was already en route.

BP's downstream refining operations went hand in hand with its upstream oil and gas exploration in Canada's Arctic Islands region. The Montreal-based holding company distributed its refined product to consumers through a vast network of nearly two thousand gas stations in Quebec and Ontario. In an era of growing government interest in oil industry affairs, BP made sure security was tight and the Montreal refinery was fully prepared for sometimes frequent visits from bureaucratic officials. No one, least of all security chief Ron Irvin, was sure how the BMW came to be parked in the shadows of the holding tanks.

"Everything coming in and going out overnight is checked and cleared," he told the television camera.

Ty held the microphone midway between himself and Irvin in an effort to keep their voices at the same level. Two Quebec Provincial Police cruisers flanked the BMW parked in the background. The auto manufacturer's first fuel-injected vehicle was capable of doing 130 miles an hour. It hadn't been fast enough for the car's lone occupant.

"So how do you explain an unauthorized vehicle on company property?" Ty asked.

Irvin frowned.

"I don't. Not until I've had the chance to debrief my graveyard crew. Obviously one of them opened the gates."

"When do the overnight guys go home?"

"Eight o'clock. I got in shortly after nine. The BMW was discovered by one of the dayside guards when he made his rounds at eight-fifteen."

"You called the QPP?"

"I did."

"And what happened next?"

"They jimmied the trunk and found the body."

Ty thanked the security chief. He'd ask the cameraman to shoot some silent footage of the car, wait for the morgue truck to arrive and do an on-camera standup. In the meantime, he decided to ask the cops to pop the trunk.

"Any objections if we take a few shots?"

They didn't have any. Ty wished, in retrospect, that they had.

"Small space," one of the officers said as he raised the trunk cover. "Big body."

Ty nearly lost his breakfast when he saw what was inside. The torso was big-bellied and generally huge—impossible to stuff into the BMW in one piece. The legs had been severed and lay neatly beside the torso on a blood-covered tarpaulin. Frozen in horror were the dead eyes of Mafia *capo* Massimo Gianfranco.

Victor Gordon seldom paid a visit to the newsroom. When he did, it was usually late afternoon after Maggie Price came in. Gordon believed he possessed the ability to charm all women. Maggie was a challenge. She criticized his cigar smoking and objected strenuously when he hung over her workstation. Today, however, Gordon pushed through the newsroom door at 10:28 a.m. He was on a mission.

"Clyde around?" he asked.

Keith Campbell was rushing toward the radio studios with his 10:30 report.

"Down the hall. Had to take a leak."

Gordon nodded and walked into Bertram's office. The news-director joined him a few minutes later.

"Social call, Vic?"

Gordon recognized the animosity in Bertram's voice.

"A little of that, Clyde. Always good to see you."

"Sure it is."

Gordon parked himself in one of the three chairs grouped around Bertram's desk.

"Wanna discuss one of the stories I've been hearing from Campbell on morning radio."

"Oh yeah?"

Bertram braced himself for an argument.

"What story is that?"

"The one about Billy Sands. The fight the other night at the Forum."

"That's sports. Why not take it up with Walt Taylor?"

"Already have."

"Well, what about the fight?"

"Walt's agreed to stay away from speculation that the champ, Jackie Tubbs, might not have been in it to win."

Bertram raised an eyebrow.

"Walt might have agreed to keep it out of the sportscast, Vic, but it's the sort of story that warrants attention. To put it in context, the papers are talking about mob interference. That makes it a news story in my book."

"It's just speculation, Clyde. Since when have we been in the business of reporting gossip?"

"It's all over town, Vic. If Tubbs threw the fight, question is why?"

Gordon wasn't backing off.

"Again," he said, "nothing but speculation."

"And if we don't talk about it, all the other media will, Vic. What the hell's your interest in this?"

"No particular interest. Just something on the radio that caught my attention."

He stood up to leave. Bertram hadn't agreed to drop the story and Gordon appeared far from pleased.

It was a dream come true for two reasons. Suzie had a week off and decided to spend it with Greg, and they had discovered the commercial space, together, in Old Montreal. It was large enough to accommodate a dark room and photo studio. There was even a separate area where he could set up an office, establish contacts by phone and book clients.

They stood at the large windows looking out on St. Paul Street. The view of Montreal's oldest street seemed to exist in a timeless space all its own. Greg put his arm around her waist, warmed by the pleasure of her company.

"I hate asking for money," he said.

Suzie squeezed his arm.

"You're not asking. I'm offering."

"Yeah, but five hundred a month? There's the first and last month deposit. We're talking big bucks, Suzie."

"Let me worry about that. Besides, you'll pay me back."

"How?"

"Well, think of it this way. When you're a rich and famous photographer and working at CKCF Television is just a hobby."

Greg turned her around and kissed her on the forehead.

"You're too much, Suzie Waldon. How do you know I'll even get my job back?"

"Because you're an excellent cameraman. Because you and Ty and Jason are going to prove that you had nothing to do with that woman being attacked. Because I love you. That's how."

"Look at this place!" he suddenly exclaimed, doing a three hundred sixty degree turn. "It's perfect."

The ceilings were at least fifteen feet high, ideal for studio lighting. The floor was finished in wide plank pine. One wall was the original antique red brick. Below the windows, four hot-water radiators kept the winter chill out.

"I just can't believe it, Suzie. This is. This is far-r-r out!"

Word spread quickly through the media about the death of Montreal's second most powerful crime boss. Newspaper reporter Réal Gendron was first off the mark with an analysis of Mafia politics. He pointed out that Massimo Gianfranco was widely seen as the eventual heir to the Positano empire. Gianfranco was fifteen years younger and the *borgata's* most influential *caporegime*.

Gendron's headline story provided a brief history of the rapidly evolving underworld hierarchy. It referred to a possible changing of the guard, from the Calabrian wing's focus on traditional racketeering to the Sicilian emphasis on legitimate enterprise. It raised the possibility of an imminent war between the two factions.

There was mention of the influence on Salvatore Positano's operations, by New York's Frank (The Shark) Ragusa. It speculated that even Ragusa's "boss of bosses" reputation was being eroded by an FBI investigation of several murders in the late 'fifties. A whistleblower named Alphonse Scarpa was being kept in witness protection. He was providing the Feds with valuable information on the Ragusa family. "By extension," the article said, "there'll be renewed efforts by U.S. drug enforcement agents to stem cross-border traffic in heroin and cocaine." The story concluded that the loss of Gianfranco, the FBI's targeting of Frank Ragusa, and the emerging power of Sicilian *capo* Rocco Panepinto were putting unprecedented pressure on Montreal's most colorful hoodlum.

Chapter Nineteen

News Department shifts overlapped at CKCF Television. The flow from one shift to the next was seamless. Information on the location of reporters, story deadlines, the status of film processing and upcoming events was passed from one lineup editor to the next. Production meetings were scheduled to coincide with personnel who were winding up their day and those who came in to replace them. All shifts were of nine hours' duration, including a union negotiated half-hour for lunch and two fifteen-minute coffee breaks to be taken at the discretion of reporter-camera teams and at the convenience of the assignment desk. Lunch was supposed to be taken on or before the fifth hour. Assignment could override that provision of the labor contract if a news conference or unfolding story warranted a work-through.

It was virtually impossible to organize meetings that involved all newsroom personnel without the issue of overtime being raised. Valid reasons for extra hours included developing stories and management briefings. To refuse the overtime was to show a lack of enthusiasm for the job. The meeting Jason called November 7 did not fit into the category of valid reasons.

"It's only Dick Tomlin," he told the news director.

Clyde Bertram was chewing on one of his cigar butts.

"What about Ty and Maggie?"

"If we try to bring Tomlin in, let's say around nine, he'll hit you with three hours. Maggie's already in. Ty and I have agreed to waive overtime, so it's only Tomlin who won't appreciate the call."

Bertram discarded the cigar butt in one of several filthy ashtrays on his desk.

"What purpose would it serve?"

"Maybe none. But we think there are giant holes in Tomlin's account of events that night. Maggie has offered up some interesting points and we hardly ever have the opportunity to get everybody in the same room at the same time. Greg'll be here too."

"It means a twelve-hour shift for Tomlin."

"Yeah well, fuck 'im, Clyde. We've got to get to the bottom of this thing."

"The sooner the better," Bertram agreed.

Jason returned to his office, secure in the knowledge that Bertram was as anxious as he was to clear Greg's name and get on with business. The day ahead was grueling. He assigned Ty to a follow-up on the Gianfranco killing. The French papers were already miles ahead of him on the story. There were at least two must-cover items in the rolodex file and the ten-to-seven reporter wouldn't be able to deal with both of them. The overnight police-run included a possible arson, a shooting in the east end and two more in a series of penny-ante holdups in the Pointe St. Charles district.

When his shift was over at four, Jason walked over to The Hole and tried to relax with a beer. He watched the six o'clock show on a TV set located over the bar and made small talk with Nick, the bar-keep. Ty joined him at seven. They nursed their beers, discussed the possibility of a blood feud in the Montreal mob and walked over to the station at eight forty-five. Maggie Price was hard at work.

"Should have the show lined up in time for the meeting," she informed them. "But I'll have to bow out no later than ten."

Anchorman Art Bradley demanded her full attention after he reported in. He liked to think of himself as a contributing editor. All he ever did was read over Maggie's script and, as she put it, bitch and complain. Art often labored over simple word changes, argued with the lineup editor, questioned the need to run certain stories and frequently threw temper tantrums. Art was a star. He wanted every-body to treat him like one.

"Clyde says to use his office," Moore said. Greg, Maggie and Ty followed him in. Moore sat behind Bertram's desk.

"Guess we just wait 'til Tomlin gets here."

He glanced at his watch. The overnight police reporter finally arrived, ten minutes late. He wasn't happy.

"Christ. Is this shit ever going to end?"

Greg battled an urge to take a swing at him. Instead, he retrieved a fourth chair from the newsroom, brought it into Bertram's office and gestured at Tomlin to sit down.

"At least you're getting a steady paycheque," he said. "Try being unemployed for a couple of months."

Moore held up his hands.

"Look. We've got about forty-five minutes. Maggie's gotta get back to her show. Bradley's coming in at ten. So, can we get on with it?"

Everybody nodded. Tomlin crossed his arms over his chest, defiant.

"I'm booking for three hours."

"Already approved," Moore replied. "Okay. We've gone over a lot of this before, but that was weeks ago and quite a few things have happened since. I think the issue of the missing keys is still extremely important."

Tomlin sighed. Moore ignored him.

"Maggie, Dick is suggesting they could have gone missing before he came in at midnight. What time did you leave the station, that night?"

"Just after midnight. In fact, I saw Dick, briefly, as he was arriving."

"You had a regular show? I mean, eleven-thirty to twelve? No network delays for a movie or sports event?"

"Nope. I headed home at about twelve-ten."

"Right. Well what do you think about Tomlin's idea that the keys disappeared on your watch?"

Maggie shrugged.

"Could have happened, I guess. As I've said, I had to go to the bathroom a couple of times. The nighttime reporter was on assignment. And one other time, about nine, I went down to the studio to look for a fountain pen. The early lineup editor had left it on the anchor desk."

Ty had been looking over his notes.

"Is that when you noticed the lights were on in Victor Gordon's office?"

"That's right. I heard voices in Vic's boardroom. Not all male voices, so it could have been a sales meeting or something like that."

"Conceivably then, someone from that meeting could have gone up to the newsroom, while you were in the studio."

"Sure."

Greg was quiet, until now. He'd been watching Dick Tomlin's reactions to Maggie's account.

"Maggie, you're on three to midnight every day aren't you?"

She smiled. "They let me out for good behavior every now and again."

Greg chuckled.

"Glad to hear it. But here's the question. Based on your experience, Monday through Friday, isn't it a little unusual for Vic Gordon to be holding sales meetings at nine o'clock at night?"

"It is. I remember thinking it was strange. Especially when I heard the female. To the best of my knowledge, we don't have any females in the sales department."

Moore leaned forward, placing his elbows on Bertram's desk.

"No we don't. Maybe ol' Vic was havin' a party. He uses that boat of his, y'know. I mean, it's possible this was a social occasion in the boardroom, not a business meeting at all."

"And," said Maggie, "I don't think it was over, three hours later."

"Why do you say that?"

"Because when I left the building, I spotted Gordon's Chrysler Imperial."

"Where?"

"Not inside the executive garage as usual. It was parked beside his yacht, behind the station."

Dick Tomlin suddenly shifted his weight in his chair.

"What's that prove? He was probably on the boat. Everybody knows what goes on. Gordon likes to get a little on the side. So what?"

Moore was adamant.

"Here's what. So far we know about a Mafia meeting at Cabrini Hall. We know that news Mobile 9 was at that meeting. Ty, did you ever find out what time the woman who was walking her dogs that night actually saw the mobile?"

Ty shook his head.

"No. But she could have been walking the dogs before she went to bed or something."

"As late as midnight or after?"

"Anything's possible. I'm sorry. I didn't think to ask. A lot of dog owners like to walk their animals before they turn in, though. Otherwise, they're likely to piss the rug."

"Alright, let's assume Maggie's right and the party in Vic Gordon's office carried on for some time after she heard the voices at nine. Let's also assume that the dog owner spotted Mobile 9, say, sometime around twelve-thirty. That would allow someone from the Gordon party to steal the keys and get over to Cabrini Hall at least an hour before Maria Claudio was attacked downtown. The guy who just happened to be smoking on his balcony at one-thirty that morning said a CKCF car was involved. However, he couldn't say whether or not it was actually Mobile 9. Dick, you say the keys were likely taken during Maggie's shift. I'm beginning to have my doubts."

"Fuckin' A! Why?"

"Because," said Moore, "it now looks like the nine o'clock boardroom meeting continued for some time. Gordon's car was parked beside his boat at midnight or at ten minutes after midnight when Maggie left. You were already in. Whatever was going on, you haven't mentioned any of it in the past."

"I've told you what I know."

"And it seems you know very little. You're a goddam reporter. And for a reporter, you're not very observant."

"Whaddya mean?"

"Well, for one, you apparently didn't know anything about this meeting in Vic Gordon's office. You never mentioned seeing the boss's Chrysler parked beside his boat. Hell, that's right at the corner of the building. You couldn't have missed it on your way in. You then did not notice that a set of keys was missing from my office, even though it's your business to check on those keys. You didn't know about the Mafia meeting at Cabrini Hall, where Mobile 9 was seen, even though there was an RCMP operation right across the street. And you didn't know about the attack on Maria Claudio at one-thirty that morning, despite the fact the information was on the fucking police radio. I told you about that, when I called you after four, to tell you about the police lineup."

Tomlin was beginning to perspire. Beads of sweat dotted his forehead.

"Gimme a break will ya? To begin with, when I sign in at midnight I go straight upstairs. I don't make a habit of walking past the executive offices. And, no, I didn't notice Gordon's Chrysler by his boat. Even if I had, I prob'ly wouldn't have thought twice about it."

Maggie interrupted. "I didn't mention it before because it didn't seem relevant I guess. But if Vic was doin' the nasty on his boat that late in the day, then the nine o'clock meeting in his office takes on new significance."

Ty was nodding enthusiastically.

"I'll say. It means there were three occasions for someone from that meeting to filch the keys while you were out of the newsroom, Maggie. You say you were in the bathroom twice before nine. You were in the studio, looking for the fountain pen, at just about nine."

"Yes, but I've gotta point out," Maggie replied. "I was in the ladies' very briefly. Couple minutes at most. I doubt anyone could have got into the newsroom, located the keys in Jason's office and made off with them in that short a time. Besides, if they had, I would have heard them. The bathroom is right at the top of the stairs. I'd have heard something in the corridor."

"That's true," Moore interjected. "The men's can is right next door. Even during the day, when things are busy around the place, you can hear phones ringing, people walking, people talking."

"When you're sitting on the throne," Greg said grinning in agreement, "makes you up-tight about farting too loud."

Everybody laughed, except Tomlin.

"So, we're back to where we started. The keys could have been taken anytime that evening."

Moore scowled at him.

"Not so. I think we've moved the issue along tonight. Maggie's right. I don't believe they could have been stolen while she was in the john. Too little time. And Maggie would have heard something. That leaves only the nine o'clock visit to the studio."

"That's probably when it happened." Tomlin added.

"Or," Moore pointed at him, "you're not telling us the whole story. You were here until nearly twelve-thirty. Maybe you handed the keys over to someone. Fact is, Dick, you're the only one who actually knew they were hanging on a pegboard in my office."

"Why would I do that?"

Moore glanced at Ty and Greg.

"I don't know, Dick. Why would you?

Chapter Twenty

A storm was brewing. Its potential for violence couldn't be measured in meteorological terms. It was entirely emotional. Salvatore Positano was in a rage. He paced back and forth across the Persian rug in his library, waving his arms and intermittently shaking his fist at *caporegime* Tony Soccio.

"If I told you once, I told you a hundred times, Tony. The cops knew exactly where to go and some fucker in your crew must o' told 'em. Ragusa's up my ass. He's under indictment for a bunch o' murders. Christ, we haven't had the balls or the brains to move shit over the border since August."

"Like I said, Sal, we got a rat."

"You said that more'n two months ago. It's your goddam crew. The fuck you doin' about it?"

Soccio's face drained of color.

"It ain't easy. I got fourteen soldiers."

"And one of 'em is talkin' to the cops."

"I'm on it, Sal."

"You are, are you? Well, what a fucking relief. You're on it. I got pressure from New York to move product. I got a dead *capo*, a Sicilian sonofabitch tryin' to muscle in and you're fucking on it."

Soccio swallowed hard.

"Here's what, Sal. One o' my guys has been flashin' money around. Big bankroll. Twenties, hundreds. He bought a new set o' wheels last week."

"Who? Gimme a name."

"Gino. Gino Viscuso."

"So, he bought a car. So what?"

"It's come to my attention he might be into other shit."

"Like what?"

"Maybe stuff on the side. Comes t' me from the Hells. They got their own problems. One of 'em, he's done a lot fer me in the past. He says Viscuso and a coupla' bikers might a' fixed the Billy Sands fight."

"Fixed it how?"

"Word is Jackie Tubbs, he's the champ who went down?"

"Yeah, yeah. I read all about it. What about 'im?"

"Okay, but my contact is regional boss in the Hells and he tells me it's true. Viscuso was workin' with Sands' trainer. He says a couple mavericks put the squeeze on Tubbs. Threatened his wife and kid."

"So Tubbs threw the fight?"

" 'Zactly."

"Any money come our way?"

"That's it, Sal. No. No it didn't."

"What's this got ta do with last August?"

"Nuthin'. But if Viscuso went solo on the fight, maybe he's the rat we been lookin' for over what happened in the Townships."

"What's he gain? Why would he tell the cops about the drugs? No connection I can see."

"He's not doin' no time, is he? Sal, think about it. He was the only direct link to us when those raids took place. Rest of 'em were jus' sittin' on the shit, waiting t' truck it to Ragusa's boys."

Positano stopped pacing and sat down, facing Soccio.

"Maria got him off. That's why he's not doin' time. Maria Claudio got him off."

"That's not what I hear, Sal. Maria tried to get him off, yes. The fuckin' judge wasn't buyin'. She came close to bein' charged herself."

Positano appeared skeptical.

"I talked to Maria this week. After Gianfranco was hit. She never told me none o' this. If she didn't get him off, why's he out on the street?"

"Good question. I'm guessing here, Sal, but suppose he wanted to go on his own, long before the RCMP raids. Maybe he got hungry. Maybe he didn't wanna be dependent on the *borgata* no more. So he decides to make a deal. He tips off the cops. He gets himself arrested, sure. But he never gets sentenced. Nobody's the wiser. We all figure Maria paid off the judge and nobody thinks twice about it."

Positano thought it over.

"What would Viscuso get out of it?"

"Immunity. He gets to be big man with the Feds. He don't serve no time for the Townships bust. He's free to operate on his own."

"Fuck. We'll be havin' a little talk with Gino Viscuso."

"Like I say, Sal. I'm on it."

Montreal is not, and never was, a football town. Hockey reigns supreme throughout the Province of Quebec. November 1969, however, was different. Ty Davis, among many of his CKCF colleagues, was anticipating mid-month finals in the western and eastern conferences of the Canadian Football League. Sports bars across the city had their TVs tuned to all developments, amid reports Montreal would play host to the fifty-seventh Grey Cup, the CFL's championship game. It would be quarterback Russ Jackson's last regular game before retirement, presuming the Ottawa Rough Riders could defeat the Toronto Argonauts in the finals. It would mark the first time the city hosted the Grey Cup in nearly forty years.

Ty was thinking football stats' as he pulled up to the gates of the BP refinery. He had another meeting scheduled with security chief Ron Irvin. Irvin was reluctant at first, claiming he'd taken harsh criticism from BP's executive branch for allowing Flash News to film Massimo Gianfranco's mutilated body. Ty reminded him that permission to open the BMW's trunk was granted by the Quebec Provincial Police, not him. He also told Irvin this would not be a television interview. Just a friendly chat.

The stocky security chief was waiting at the gates. He wore a business suit, obviously tailored to accent an athletic build. Natural shoulders. No pads. Irvin waved at a uniformed employee to open the gates. Ty drove Mobile 14 past the guard shack and parked it beside a red brick administration building that housed Irvin's office, among others. He glanced at the nearby holding tanks. The BMW was long gone. There was no evidence of the recent violence. Irvin held the front door open and pointed Ty down a corridor to another door, marked "security."

"So what's this *friendly chat* all about?" he asked, emphasizing the two words Ty had used in their telephone conversation.

"First of all, let me ask what you've learned about the Gianfranco hit."

"You're saying it was a hit?"

"A mob hit, yes. An assassination."

"Well you know more about it than I do."

Ty realized Irvin was being difficult, intentionally. He decided to try to embarrass him.

"You do know who he was, don't you?"

Irvin sat down at a desk that looked like a fugitive from an elementary school classroom. It was ink-stained and out of date.

"I read the newspapers," he replied, not seeming in the least embarrassed.

"Then you know this was the second most powerful gangster in Montreal."

"So I understand."

Ty wasn't getting anywhere.

"It begs the question, Mr. Irvin. Why were the gates opened to the BMW in the middle of the night, in the first place?"

"That's what the police wanted to know. I'll tell you what I told them."

"Okay."

"I told them I hadn't the foggiest idea."

Ty reached into his pocket for his cigarettes. He'd noticed an ashtray on Irvin's desk.

"Mind if I smoke?"

"Go ahead."

He lighted up, offering one to Irvin who declined.

"You told me you'd be talking to the guards who'd gone off duty that morning."

"And I did."

"So, what did they say?"

Irvin suddenly appeared uneasy.

"There were four men on the graveyard shift. I talked to three of 'em. They were in the western and northern quadrants of the refinery at about the time the car must have come in."

"What about the fourth guy?"

"Gone."

"What do you mean, gone?"

"Cops're looking for him."

"You mean he disappeared?"

"That's what I mean."

Ty was losing patience.

"What's the background?"

"I hire through the regular security services. This one was sent over by Pinkerton's."

"He was new?"

"Two weeks. Yeah, he was new. When these guards are assigned to BP, it's my job to show 'em the ropes. They get the grand tour. They do regular rounds. Fill out a report at the end of their shift."

"What's his name?"

"Cristina. Natale Cristina. Italian."

The information rocked Ty back in his chair.

"And I'll bet his report never mentioned the BMW."

"Not a word."

Newton Lower Falls, Massachusetts, was tucked away in the northwestern corner of the City of Newton, one of thirteen villages in Newton Proper. Its distinguishing characteristic was the Charles River, along which one of the first paper mills in the United States was built. The Charles dropped eighteen feet over a distance of less than a quarter mile at Lower Falls. It flowed over three dams in that short stretch and when a dam was opened, calm upstream waters were suddenly and dramatically transformed. A powerful undertow swept invisibly beneath the surface, as the Charles began rolling more rapidly toward lower ground. Swimming and boating weren't recommended directly above the dams. Fish ladders were located along what locals referred to as The Drop.

Elizabeth Davis wasn't planning to swim. She found the river peaceful, even on this chilly, early November day. She sat on the banks, munching on a cheese sandwich. Her mother, Sarah Walkley, was watching Catherine and Robin while she had her final session at Unity College with Doctor Wayne Hall. She had bought the sandwich and a large coffee in the college cafeteria.

Seagulls wheeled into the wind above one of the dams. Elizabeth passively watched two men, who were doing something near the fish ladder, as she recalled her conversation with the professor.

"You should be aware," he said, "that you're not alone. Up to eighty percent of new mothers experience mild depression within a year of giving birth."

Elizabeth's mild depression had escalated. Hall agreed that some of her more recent symptoms were worrisome. However he remained upbeat.

"Some women experience actual psychosis. The so-called baby-blues, unfortunately, can produce this extreme but related disorder. You're definitely not there, Liz, but I believe you advanced past mere emotional letdown. You exacerbated the problem by drinking far too much alcohol."

Elizabeth swallowed a mouthful of coffee.

"What are the symptoms I should be watching for?"

"You've already displayed signs of a mood disorder called PPD. That's full-blown postpartum depression, Liz. Usually happens before a baby's first birthday. Your Robin is two. So this has been festering for some time."

"Feels like forever."

"It tends to feel just like that. PPD is on a par with clinical depression. Despondency, a sense of inadequacy as a mother and wife, impaired concentration and memory."

"What's even worse, Doctor Hall, is that I used to get such pleasure from the children. I've felt terribly guilty, because I lost interest in everything. Nothing's fun. Nothing's enjoyable."

Hall had smiled at her.

"The good news, Elizabeth, is that we're treating it and you're getting well. A little more time. Talk to your husband. Discuss going back to Montreal. The medication that's been prescribed for you should provide even more help. Fact is, you're talking about it and that's half the battle. You have to recognize that this is not some sort of failure on your part. You've been suffering from a fairly common illness and you're getting better every day."

The Charles River seemed far more placid than she was, as it continued its journey toward The Drop.

Elizabeth drank the last bit of coffee, stuffed the paper cup into her overcoat and began walking toward the Walkley's Grove Street residence. She felt cautiously optimistic for the first time in months.

Chapter Twenty-one

Francine Landry stood in front of the mirror and gazed disapprovingly at her reflection. She was thirty-four years old, single, and still trying to find meaning in life. She frequently went clubbing after a day's work at Fairchild Insurance, usually heading uptown from the company's McGill Street offices and stopping for supper at one of the many restaurants along Ste. Catherine Street. Tonight, she headed east.

Francine turned sideways, examining her breasts in the bathroom mirror. The blouse she'd worn to work did nothing to enhance them. She thought her pleated grey skirt made her look fat and there were fatigue lines under her eyes.

"Oh well," she told her reflection. "Onward and upward."

The words of self-encouragement had little effect on her mood.

Francine tucked the blouse into her skirt, took one last look at her waistline and went back to the bar. She ordinarily set herself a two-drink limit. On this occasion, because of the man she'd met earlier, she threw caution to the winds. They eventually migrated from barstools to a quiet table-for-two. She was already halfway through her third Manhattan.

"I've never been here before," she said, as if the revelation had profound significance. "It's quite nice."

He took a sip of his rum and coke.

"It's okay."

"Yes, well I didn't mean it's the best bar in town."

Francine felt she was always apologizing for something. Talking for the sake of talking.

"It's nice, though."

La Violette Bar and Restaurant was, in fact, a hole in the wall on

Rue St. Denis south of Dorchester Boulevard. The motif was early who gives a shit. The food was fast. The drinks were watered down.

"Whaddya say we split?" the man said. It was more of a statement than a question.

He'd been reasonably communicative during their brief time together, but Francine had the uncomfortable feeling that his eyes were somehow not in unison with his mouth. They weren't unattractive. Dark, with heavy lashes, but they lacked expression. If eyes are the windows to the soul, she thought, these windows had the blinds down. More disturbing than that possibility was her gnawing feeling that the soul itself wasn't normal.

"I, uh. I don't think so," she replied. "You go ahead if you want to. I'll just—"

He grinned.

"I'm way over on Atwater Avenue. It's a weeknight. Another day at the mines tomorrow. Y'know, this place isn't as nice as you say it is and the neighborhood can be downright dangerous for a woman as young and pretty as you are. Let me drop you somewhere."

"Young and pretty? Well, thank you sir."

She managed to smile back at him.

"I don't know."

"Oh, c'mon. I'm a nice guy. Just tired, is all. Figure it's time to pack it in, know what I mean? My car's down the block. It's no trouble at all."

Francine reluctantly began to think there was some sparkle in his eyes, after all.

"Alright. I'm on your way anyway. St. Marc Street."

He stood up, still smiling, and walked over to the bar to pay the bill. It was a quarter-to-one, Wednesday morning, November 8th. The office manager at Fairchild Insurance reported Francine Landry missing on Friday, the 10th.

"If the Mounties can't make a case against Maria Claudio, what chance do we have?"

Jason Moore was sitting in his glassed-in alcove with Ty Davis.

"Let's face it, Ty, we've made a hell of a lot of progress. If you look at where we were when she identified Greg as her attacker, we knew essentially nothing. Now we know Claudio is a Mafia insider.

We know she's first cousin to the late Massimo Gianfranco. And, according to Francoeur, she's probably involved in a conspiracy to influence the outcome of certain court cases."

"Can't prove it."

"Neither can the RCMP. That's not the point. If we can blacken her name, without being sued for defamation, maybe that bastard Maillot will realize he can't trust anything she says."

Ty glanced at his watch. It was just after eleven.

"Want me to put something together?"

"I think so. Get the librarian to pull stock footage. Let's look at the possible components of a six o'clock report."

"Well, we can start with the raids in August. Viscuso's connection to Claudio and the Positano crime family."

"She defended him in court. That's a non-libelous fact. He's walkin' the street a free man. That's also a fact. Really, we can't get into the whole thing about the judges."

Moore nodded in agreement.

"I promised Francoeur we wouldn't. I'll call him later today, to fill him in on what we're planning for the early show."

"There's no reason we can't use the Gianfranco hit. And it would be entirely legit' for us to identify Claudio as a close relative. We obviously can't go with her position as legal advisor to Positano because that also came to you from Francoeur and we could be challenged on it."

"Not to mention, Francoeur would have my nuts."

Ty chuckled.

"You know the problem, though? Our dutiful Detective-Sergeant Pierre Maillot hates the English media."

"So?"

"So, I doubt he ever watches Flash News, unless he's pissed off at something."

"We'll send him the film. His curiosity won't allow him to ignore it. And, we can include a cover letter that fills him in on some of the speculation about Claudio. Things that aren't proven and can't be used yet on the News."

Moore's face lit up.

"Another thing, Ty."

"What?"

"Maybe you can incorporate some of the analysis Réal Gendron used in his column. You know, about the possibility the Gianfranco killing was just the beginning of a power struggle in the Mafia."

"Good idea. I can talk about it when we're using the footage from the BP refinery. Could you talk to Clyde?"

"About what?"

"Get his permission to show some of the blood and guts shots, when the QPP opened the trunk and we got to see what really happened to Gianfranco."

"He won't like it."

"Yeah, but what's the point of whitewashing everything? This is what gangsters do to each other."

"You know Clyde's argument. We're a family newscast."

"Yeah, but if we want to make an impression on Maillot about Claudio's first cousin, about the kind of world she's a part of, we need to show something more than just a body being loaded into a meat wagon."

"I'll see what he says."

"Tell him about Maillot. Tell him why we want him to get the point that Claudio wouldn't think twice about lying. We can run a disclaimer as a lead-in to the story. Warn viewers that some of the stuff they're about to see is graphic, blah, blah, blah."

Moore clapped his hands together.

"Pull the shots. I'll talk to Clyde."

Greg was taking inventory. He surveyed the large room where he hoped to set up a profitable photo studio. Acquiring the space was one thing. Suzie had handed him the necessary thousand dollars for first and last month's rent. He'd sealed the deal with the landlord, but it would be awhile before the place could become a viable, commercial enterprise. He realized equipping the studio would cost thousands more. Greg was making a list of what he had and what he would need to get started. It was a discouraging task.

Suzie told him she had nearly ten thousand dollars in her savings account. She returned to Ottawa, after telling him he would have full access.

"Sure," he replied, "but there are good and there are bad business investments."

Suzie smiled reassuringly.

"I'm investing in us. How can that be bad?"

Sunlight streamed through the windows, cutting a swath between low-rise buildings on St. Paul Street. The weather wasn't behaving like mid-November. Christmas decorations already filled display windows in downtown department stores and the outside temperature was approaching the high sixties.

Greg sat on the wide-plank floor. His equipment list started with cameras and related accessories he already owned. Several categories included cameras, lenses, tripods, backdrops, props and lighting.

He owned a high-end Canon that came on the market in the middle of the decade and featured an externally coupled exposure meter, an interchangeable pentaprism viewfinder and an automated aperture control system. When Suzie asked him what all that gobbledygook meant he'd said only that it produced one fuck of a good photo. Greg had nine of the sixteen lenses available for the Canon.

He also owned a Super-8 cinecamera that he intended to use for weddings. Combined with high quality stills, the moving pictures would likely be popular with brides- and grooms-to-be. He planned, however, to emphasize portraits, preferring the controlled studio environment.

There was the tripod he'd used on the Himalayan trip. It had a three-way pan tilthead that enabled him to stabilize the camera with a maximum of maneuverability. Greg recalled the shots he'd managed to take near Kathmandu of an elderly man whose craggy features reflected decades of exposure to sun and high altitude. On that occasion he'd been using his smaller Canon Color Demi. He made a point of listing the more compact, lightweight, lens-shutter camera. It would come in handy in fashion shoots, where the model had to strike numerous poses in rapid succession.

Backdrops and props would be a problem. He possessed neither. Greg decided to ask for advice from the photo department at CKCF. He was aware of a variety of backdrops in commercial use. Some were made of canvas. Others were muslin and entirely wrinkle free and washable. There were even hand-painted backgrounds that could be purchased, giving the three-dimensional impression that a subject was in the midst of some exotic setting. Props ranged from wigs and hairpieces to period costumes. All necessary. All very costly.

Greg's knowledge of lighting was more extensive. He had some of the necessary equipment, but there was always the danger of too much light. He'd need filters to diffuse it, and he'd need lighting stands, ceiling clamps and fixtures. He was a strong believer in the dramatic use of shadow, especially in black and white.

His mission in the St. Paul Street building was not exclusively aimed at making lists. Greg brought a scrub-brush, wash-pail, broom, dust cloths, various cleaning rags and detergents. He'd parked his mother's Ford Fairlane just off the Rue de la Commune on the waterfront. By the time twilight descended on Old Montreal, he was very tired and very hungry. He reminded himself to start costing a few of the items he'd need immediately. A conflicting mixture of excitement and apprehension accompanied him to the car.

"*C'est lui*! That's him!" Detective Sergeant Pierre Maillot told his partner.

Alain Rainville started the engine of the unmarked Montreal police cruiser. He kept the headlights off. The two men watched Greg Peterson get into the Ford, back into a sidestreet and head west along de la Commune.

"*Il va vers l'ouest*," Rainville said.

Maillot made a palms-down gesture with his left hand.

"*Ne le laisse pas te voir. Il se dirige vers la rue McGill.*"

Rainville had no intention of being spotted. Fairchild Insurance was just around the corner on McGill Street. It was the last place Francine Landry was seen alive, by anyone who knew her. Rainville never turned on the cruiser's headlights, as the Ford headed north. Greg was thinking about Suzie. He had no idea he was being followed into the downtown core.

Chapter Twenty-two

It couldn't be called Grey Cup fever. CKCF sports director Walt Taylor was looking for a way to describe the excitement that was building in Montreal as CFL fans prepared for the league's eastern and western conference finals. The word fever had become a sportscaster's cliché and generally was a reference to hockey's Stanley Cup.

Taylor shared an office with Mark Carter who handled the station's late show. Carter had just arrived for the beginning of his three-to-midnight shift. Taylor was puffing on his pipe, laboring over his six o'clock script and looking perplexed.

"How would you phrase the lead-up to the CFL finals?" he asked.

Carter sat down at his own typewriter. The two men respected each other's writing talents.

"Tell you the line I was planning to use for the eleven-thirty 'cast. You're gonna steal it from me aren't ya, you bastard."

He was grinning.

"I just don't want to go with Grey Cup fever."

"Don't blame you. It's lazy writing."

"Fact is," Taylor added, "football's not very popular in the Francophone community."

"True, but our audience demographic is mostly west of St. Lawrence Boulevard. 99.9 percent English."

"Okay. So what would you go with?"

"Well, I'm gonna ask Moore to assign a camera to some of the bars around town this evening. Have you noticed the growing number of cowboy hats and western boots on the streets these days?"

"Now that you mention it."

"If I can get the film, I'm planning to lead into the story by asking a question."

"I'm all ears."

"You're a goddam plagiarist is what you are."

Taylor tapped his pipe on the edge of his ashtray.

"Not if I use the line first. Don't forget, I'm on the air before you are."

"Bastard. Okay, how about this? Have you noticed, lately, that the city is taking on a distinctly western flavor?"

"Not bad."

"No good, though, unless I can get Moore to free up a camera. He usually has other priorities. I'm sure, though, we'd find some cowboys in the bars tonight."

"I'll speak to Moore. It's a good idea."

Moore was chewing on a wad of gum when Taylor walked into his office.

"Trying to quit smoking," he said. "Every time I get the urge, I pop in a stick of gum."

Taylor shrugged. He had little sympathy for cigarette smokers.

"Must be you get the urge often. That's one huge mouthful."

"Yeah, well it seems to help. What's on your mind, Walt?"

"Need a camera."

"Don't we all."

"Mark's planning a piece for the late show. Wants some shots of westerners in town. You know, the cowboys are already comin' in for Grey Cup."

"Shouldn't be a problem. The late guy comes in two, two-thirty. I've nothing for 'im. At least, nothing urgent."

"Good. Ask him to see Mark Carter, will ya?"

"Will do."

Taylor turned to leave, then seemed to have a last minute thought.

"By the way, what's happening with Greg Peterson? He may be the best cameraman on staff. Really knows how to put things together and we miss him."

"Ditto," Moore agreed. "He's doin' okay. Still on suspension 'til the whole thing is cleared up."

"Fuck of a thing. I know you and Ty talked with Carter and the night crew and so on, but I wondered if Carter mentioned the Green Room party."

"Green Room party?"

"The night Peterson was supposedly involved in that downtown incident. What was it, August 27th?"

"That's right. No, Mark never said anything about a Green Room party."

Taylor sat down next to the assignment desk.

"Mark and I were talking about Peterson the other day. He said you'd asked him about one of the news cars being out on the road that night, and whether he might have any information."

"Right. He didn't know about the car being taken."

"Apparently, though, you also asked him about a meeting in Vic Gordon's office?"

"He did know about that. Said he'd seen some people go into Vic's boardroom about seven-thirty."

"I guess Mark didn't make a connection between the meeting and whatever was going on later that evening."

"Obviously not. What'd he tell you?"

"Well, we were just chewing the fat about Peterson. Wondered how the police case was proceeding. Mark said you and Ty were investigating on your own. That's how we got on to discussing August 27th. Anyway, Mark says he spoke with the news anchor, or vice versa. Art Bradley was bragging that he'd had a drink in the Green Room."

"Really? Who with?"

"Mark assumed they were clients and they'd been part of the earlier meeting in Gordon's office. I imagine that's why he didn't think it was important to tell you and Ty about it. You already knew about the meeting."

"So the bar was open in the Green Room. Bradley doesn't report in until ten, so he must have had the drink after ten o'clock."

"Not unusual for Bradley," Taylor smiled. "He's the only guy I've ever met who can have a three-martini supper and go on the air without a problem."

"But did he get invited, or just crash the party?"

"You know Art. If Vic Gordon was around, he'd have had his nose up his ass in a second. He wouldn't need an invitation. He's big man on campus. He'd just walk in and expect everybody to be duly impressed."

"Did he actually say Vic Gordon was in the Green Room?"

"Carter didn't mention it. I imagine he would have been there, though. It's not likely Vic would leave clients by themselves."

Moore made a mental note to telephone Art Bradley. The timeline surrounding the events of August 27th was becoming ever more sharply defined.

The six o'clock news was on as Maria Claudio prepared her dinner. It had been the kind of day most lawyers would find tedious. A lot of paperwork. Billing old clients. Chasing new ones. Claudio ran her own law office, preferring an independent-contractor status to employment in one of the major firms. She enjoyed a six-figure income, drove a Mercedes and lived in a large greystone on Peel Street north of Sherbrooke. At thirty-seven, Maria was slim, attractive, self-assured and on course to bigger things.

Dinner, on this mild November evening, would consist of a green salad followed by a linguini and shrimp dish and key-lime pie for dessert. She sipped on a tall-stemmed glass of white wine as she worked. Cooking was more a pleasure than a chore.

A thirteen-inch television was built into a wall of cabinets on one side of the kitchen, allowing her to watch the screen while moving freely about the room. It was tuned to CKCF. Anchorman Art Bradley completed a report on a counterfeiting ring that had been broken up in Pointe Aux Trembles. He turned, for dramatic effect, to face a different camera.

"You might recall a multi-million dollar drug bust by the RCMP last August in the Eastern Townships."

Bradley's tone and facial expression were serious. He believed in combining good journalism with no small degree of acting.

"Eight men and four women were rounded up in a series of five police raids."

At this point, he began voicing over film shot by Greg Peterson at the August news conference.

"Three-million dollars of cocaine was seized, along with an undisclosed amount of cash and a variety of weapons. Of those arrested, seven men and one woman were charged and later sentenced for intent to traffic drugs into the United States. Three women faced lesser charges of simple possession. Ty Davis has some of the more recent developments."

Davis appeared on screen, standing in front of the Old Courthouse on Rue Notre Dame.

"Only one individual, arrested that day, is still walking the streets a free man."

A courtroom artist's drawing was shown, full screen.

"Of all those charged and found guilty, no sentencing date has ever been set for Gino Viscuso. A Flash News investigation of this man shows two past arrests on drug-related charges. Viscuso served two years of a ten-year sentence for importing heroin from Marseilles. He was acquitted in the second case."

Here, Ty introduced French newspaper crime reporter Réal Gendron.

"At that time, *La Voix* newspaper reporter Réal Gendron, in published reports, linked the Marseilles connection to Montreal businessman, Salvatore Positano."

Gendron began speaking to the camera.

"Let's be honest, eh? *Monsieur* Positano is much more than a businessman. He is reputed crime boss in Montreal, *n'est-ce pas*? Might's well, as you say, call a spade a spade."

The picture faded to a shot of the Club Coquettes near Knowlton. Gendron continued. "Gino Viscuso was arrested at Club Coquettes in *les Cantons de l'Est*."

Ty threw in a question. "What's his connection to the strip club?"

"Part owner. When the RCMP pick 'im up, they found most of the drugs inside."

More shots of the Townships appeared. Ty asked another question.

"Your newspaper linked the earlier heroin case to Salvatore Positano. What about Viscuso? How does he fit in?"

Gendron smiled. "He work for Positano."

By this time, Maria Claudio was glued to the television. Her appetite for linguini and shrimp had all but disappeared.

The Davis report was far from finished.

"*La Voix* crime reporter Réal Gendron. Thanks, Réal."

"*Plaisir.*"

Davis appeared again on close-up.

"Flash News has learned that in all three of Viscuso's appearances here at the courthouse, he was represented by a lawyer named Maria Claudio."

Maria dropped her wine glass on the kitchen floor. The report continued.

"We don't have a photograph of Claudio, however, we do know that she is related to this man."

A picture of Massimo Gianfranco came on screen.

"Massimo Gianfranco, sometimes referred to as the second most powerful gangster in Montreal, was found murdered a few days ago."

The BMW appeared on screen. Bertram had given his permission to use a few seconds of Gianfranco's remains.

"His mutilated body turned up in the trunk of this BMW at an oil-refinery in the east end, triggering speculation the killing could mark the beginning of a factional war within the Mafia. Maria Claudio is first cousin to the late Massimo Gianfranco. And, for reasons as yet unexplained, her client, Gino Viscuso, has never been sentenced in connection with what the RCMP have described as the biggest cocaine bust in Quebec history. Ty Davis reporting for Flash News."

As the report came to an end, Maria Claudio was already on the telephone. She was dialing the unlisted number for Salvatore Positano.

Chapter Twenty-three

Greg Peterson searched his memory. He sat, staring at his hands, in a chair beside the desk of Montreal Police Detective-Sergeant Pierre Maillot.

November 7th you say?" He looked into Maillot's eyes.

"That's correct."

"That would have been what day of the week? Do you have a calendar?"

Maillot stared back at Greg.

"Tuesday. It was a Tuesday."

"Well, let me think."

"Take your time, *Monsieur* Peterson. If you need to make a call, you can use my phone."

Greg was at a loss.

"A lot has happened in eight days." He ran his fingers through his hair, nervously.

"We know what you were doing two days ago," Maillot said.

"You do?"

"You were driving a Ford Fairlane on de la Commune. At precisely eighteen minutes past seven on Sunday night you turned right, off de la Commune, onto McGill Street."

"Jesus! You were following me?"

"*C'est vrai.*"

"Why?"

"Because, *monsieur*, we are investigating a possible murder."

"A murder! Whose murder?"

"A young woman, last seen on McGill Street at her place of business on Tuesday, November 7th."

Greg tried to absorb the information.

"But, why were you following me? I have nothing to do with a murder. Good God!"

"That's what we're trying to establish, *monsieur*."

Greg thought he might be sick.

"Look. Maybe using your phone *would* be a good idea."

Maillot pushed the telephone to the edge of his desk. Greg dialed the private line to CKCF News. It rang three times before Keith Campbell answered.

"Keith. It's Greg Peterson."

"Yes Greg. How're you doin'?"

"Not well at the moment, Keith. Is Jason Moore around?"

Campbell glanced over at Moore's office.

"Behind the glass, as usual," he replied.

"Ask him to pick up, will ya?"

Moore came on the line. "Well, Greg," he began, "what's goin' on?"

"I'm at police headquarters."

"What for?"

"With Detective-Sergeant Pierre Maillot. Remember him?"

"Certainly do. What's he want?"

"He's questioning me about a murder. Listen, Jason, I can't remember now. When did we have that late evening meeting with Ty, Maggie, and Tomlin?"

"Exactly a week ago."

Greg swallowed, but there was no spit in his mouth.

"Thank Christ," he said.

Moore wanted to know more. "Whose murder are we talking about Greg?"

"Not sure. Some woman, who disappeared last Tuesday."

"Missing or dead?"

Greg held the telephone receiver away from his ear and addressed the detective.

"The assignment editor at CKCF Television wants to know who the victim was."

Maillot scowled. "We have no body yet."

"I'm confused, then. You said you were investigating a murder."

"No, *monsieur*. I said a possible murder."

Greg went back to his phone call. "Jason, there's no body. So it's officially a missing persons case."

"And what do they want with you?"

"For some reason they were following me on Sunday when I came down to clean up my photo studio. Rather, when I left."

Moore was silent for a moment.

"Okay, Greg. Now, don't shit yourself when I tell you this. The cops have been investigating two other killings. Both women. Both last seen in the downtown area. Their bodies were found in Laval and in Ste. Anne de Bellevue. We didn't tell you about it, because you had enough to worry about."

"Tell me what?"

"That Maillot tried to sell his superiors on the idea that the attack on Maria Claudio was somehow related."

"You mean, they suspected me?"

"I think Maillot's theory was shot down."

Greg suddenly felt angry.

"Well, fuck this. First I'm accused of beating up someone. Now they think I'm a serial killer?"

Moore tried to sound reassuring.

"I think they're grasping at straws. Just tell Maillot where you were last Tuesday and that should be the end of that."

Greg lowered his voice. Maillot was shuffling papers on his desk and didn't appear to be listening.

"Jason, please, don't keep me in the dark about stuff like this. Next time you hear I'm suspected of something, tell me. Tell me right away."

"10-4. Read you loud and clear."

Greg hung up the phone and spoke to the detective-sergeant.

"To begin with," he said, "on Sunday I was at my own place of business on St. Paul Street. That's why you saw me on de la Commune. That's where I parked my car."

"What place of business is that, *monsieur*? I thought you worked for Flash News."

"I do. At least I did, until that woman was attacked and she pointed at me. In the meantime, I've started a photo studio in Old Montreal. I was there, cleaning it and doing inventory most of the day, Sunday."

Maillot raised an eyebrow.

"That doesn't explain what you were doing on Tuesday, the seventh."

"I was in a meeting at CKCF Television."

"This can be verified?"

"Yes. By several people."

"And what time was this meeting?"

"It didn't start until nine in the evening. Before that, I was at home. My mother can vouch for that fact."

"How long did the meeting last?"

"About an hour. I hung around the television station for a bit after it broke up. Then, the man I just spoke with and I went for a drink."

"How long were you in the bar?"

Greg thought back.

"I didn't get home until after midnight."

Maillot was rapidly taking notes.

"And after that?"

"Goddam it, I went to bed."

"Your mother was at home?"

"Yes she was. She was asleep, though. I don't think she even heard me come in."

Maillot displayed a sarcastic smile.

"Your story sounds familiar, *monsieur*. Your mother was home, but she cannot provide you with an alibi."

"An alibi for what? You don't even know if this was a murder."

"*Merci, monsieur* Peterson."

"Fuck this. How many people can come up with an alibi for the hours they sleep at night?"

Maillot was unresponsive. It seemed Greg Peterson was being summarily dismissed.

Chapter Twenty-Four

At four-thirty in the afternoon the Monkland Tavern was filled with a mixture of daytime drinkers and men back early from work and hoping to down a couple of cold ones before heading home to their wives. Ty Davis didn't fit into either category. He parked his car on Old Orchard Avenue near the tavern. His shift was due to end at seven p.m., but he was tired and made a deal with Jason Moore.

The assignment editor told him Montreal Police Lieutenant Peter Loughlin had some new information on the Gianfranco killing. Loughlin lived in the Snowdon district, five minutes from the tavern. Ty was just around the corner on Oxford Avenue. He agreed to meet Loughlin, get the information and knock off an hour or two early.

He found a corner table facing the street. Ty wondered why Moore hadn't simply obtained the information on the telephone. Loughlin, after all, was his drinking buddy. The tavern was dimly lit, reflecting the gloomy Tuesday afternoon. Wet snow fell on passing traffic. Rivulets of water ran down the window next to his table.

"Hello, Ty."

Peter Loughlin waved at him from just inside the front door. He grinned and walked over to the table. Ty thought his ruddy complexion, rust-colored hair and slightly twisted nose made him look like an Irish prize-fighter.

"'Lo Pete. How's the P.R. game?"

Loughlin sat down and flagged a waiter.

"Ask me again after my first boilermaker. Life always seems rosier when viewed through the bottom of a shot glass."

"That bad, eh?"

"Nah. I'm just a little down."

Ty swallowed a mouthful of Labatt 50.

"Y'know, I used to come here all the time."

"The Monkland?"

"Yeah. We lived over on Girouard. When I wasn't skipping school and sitting in the Monkland Theatre for a matinee, I'd come over here to kill time."

Loughlin laughed.

"A regular high school lush, eh?"

"I looked older than I was. Never got asked for an I.D. I used to get a kick out of watching people here. There was always some guy who obviously had a buzz on and was worried about catching shit from his wife."

"Yeah?"

"He'd always head over to the men's room, usually about this time. When he'd go into the can he'd look disheveled and pissed. You know. Tie pulled down. Shirt untucked?"

"Uh-huh."

"He'd be in there for about five minutes. Then, when he came out his hair'd be combed. His tie would be pulled up and his shirt carefully tucked in."

"Ready to go home and face the music."

"Well, he thought so. But even if he straightened up his shoulders, he still wasn't walking a straight line."

Loughlin shook his head. A waiter wearing a white shirt, black pants and an apron was standing next to their table.

"A draft and a shot of Irish," Loughlin said.

"I'll go for another Labatt," Ty chimed in.

The waiter wrote it down. Outside, a bus made a slushy noise as it passed by in the street.

"Shitty day," Loughlin gestured at the window.

"So what're we doin' here?" Ty asked. "Jason told me you had some news on the Gianfranco hit?"

"Some news and a photograph. Moore figured I could hand it directly to you rather than courier it all the way into the north-end. That way, he thought, you could trim a couple hours off your shift like you wanted and I had a valid reason to leave my office early. We both win."

"What a guy," Ty replied.

Loughlin shrugged.

"Anyway, saw your piece on the tube Monday night. Some ugly mess they made in the trunk of that BMW."

"We don't usually show stuff like that on the six o'clock news. It's sort of an unwritten rule."

"Well, it got me to thinking. I made a call to a P.R. friend of mine over at the QPP."

"Oh yeah?"

"Wondered what their investigation turned up. How that BMW got on to refinery property in the first place."

Ty recalled his conversation with Ron Irvin. The BP security-chief had told the Quebec Provincial Police he hadn't the foggiest idea.

"And?" he asked.

"They've pinned it down to a guard by the name of Natale Cristina."

"Right. BP told me about him."

"Moore said you had the name. The provincial boys, however, did a little more digging."

"Okay."

"Cristina worked for Pinkerton's, as you're aware. He's also a *made man* in the crew of Rocco Panepinto."

"The Sicilian *capo*."

"Right. Here's Cristina's photograph. Got it from Pinkerton's."

Loughlin put a sealed envelope on the table. Ty picked it up.

"Well that clinches it. Gianfranco was definitely killed by the Sicilian faction of the local Mafia. Salvatore Positano has a major problem on his hands."

Loughlin nodded in agreement.

"Question is, who gets whacked next?"

On Thursday, November 16th it was still not clear which teams would be finalists in the Grey Cup game. Ottawa or Toronto could be playing either Saskatchewan or Calgary. Montreal was prepared for any scenario. The Autostade lay in waiting. CFL fans watched the finals in anticipation of the big game. On the 15th, the Saskatchewan Roughriders defeated the Calgary Stampeders 17-11. Game two in the western conference was scheduled for the 19th. In the first of two between the Toronto Argonauts and the Ottawa Rough Riders,

Ottawa was trounced 22-14. Game two was slated for November 22nd, to wrap up the eastern conference finals.

Jason sat in his cubicle listening to the police radio. Sometimes he felt almost guilty for his general lack of interest in professional sports. He never engaged in water cooler discussions about one athlete or team versus another. It just seemed, in the normal run of things, to be insignificant.

The department was quiet, in comparison to recent days. Clyde Bertram was in Halifax attending a meeting of the RTNDA, the News Directors' Association. Keith Campbell had been leading his hourly radio reports with international news. Nothing was happening locally.

Two days had passed since Loughlin came up with the photograph of Natale Cristina. So far, there had been no reprisal attacks for the Gianfranco killing. It seemed the mob's Calabrian faction was biding its time before moving on the Sicilians. Jason was trying to figure a way to help the story along when Ty walked into his office.

"How about them Roughriders?" he asked, showing his teeth in a broad grin.

"Who gives a shit?"

Ty knew he'd provoke that very response. He decided to push the assignment editor's buttons.

"That depends on which Roughriders we're talking about, the Ottawa or the Saskatchewan variety."

Moore leaned back in his chair.

"They're all the fucking same. Bunch o' hairy Neanderthals, knocking each other down for money."

"You're just envious."

"Why, because I'd rather be concerned about something that actually matters?"

Ty chuckled.

"Alright, have it your way."

Moore realized he was being teased, but he couldn't help the way he felt. He'd had the same conversation a million times, mostly with guys who believed there was something fundamentally wrong with him for not caring. He was aware Davis was just good-naturedly pulling his leg.

"So what's on tap this morning?" Ty asked.

"Absolutely nothing. I've got the early reporter covering some fundraiser at the Children's Hospital. One o' the guys is on the mountain shooting the first signs of winter. Snow on the ground. People skating at Beaver Lake. That sort o' crap. You got any ideas?"

Ty placed a copy of *La Voix* on Moore's desk.

"Interesting column from my good pal Réal Gendron. Seems the Positano clan is comin' up dry in its efforts to move drugs over the border. The cops haven't had a serious bust since August. According to Gendron, Salvatore's on the warpath trying to deal with the Gianfranco thing and what appears to be trouble in his ranks."

"Trouble?"

"Yeah. Of course, Réal's got contacts we don't have. Some kind of an inside track. It's speculation for the most part, but according to this morning's piece, someone in Positano's operation is spilling the beans to the police."

"About what?"

"Gendron claims the RCMP were tipped off in advance about the Eastern Townships raids last summer."

"Someone connected to Positano."

"Exactly."

"Uh-hmm. Okay, maybe it's time to take another scenic trip down the Ten. God knows we've made good use of the original film footage. Shoot some new stuff. Maybe revisit that strip club."

"Should we credit *La Voix*?"

"Story's under copyright. Yeah, mention the paper, but try to find our own angle."

Ty stood up, throwing a military salute at Moore.

"I'm as good as gone, chief."

"Yeah, yeah. Get out of my office."

"It looks like a Rockwell painting."

Suzie walked hand in hand with Greg Peterson along St. Paul Street. Huge flakes of fluffy, white snow floated down on Old Montreal. There was virtually no wind. There was a damp chill in the air, but it was still mild enough to be pleasant. Suzie was excited.

"Isn't it wonderful?"

Greg acknowledged her enthusiasm by putting an arm around her as they walked toward the studio. He hadn't told her about the murders and his own mood was far from exuberant.

"How long can you stay?"

Suzie clasped his hand tightly, swinging both their arms as they approached the building.

"Just today and the weekend. I might sleep overnight Sunday and head back early Monday morning."

"That'd be great. Well, here we are."

He pulled a set of keys out of a pocket in his winter jacket.

"I think you'll like what I've done with the place so far."

She watched him unlock the door and followed him inside. A staircase at street level led to the second-floor studio.

"Can't wait to see it," she replied.

Greg's spirits were gradually lifting. Suzie's innocent pleasure at being with him and her genuine enthusiasm for the new business were proving contagious. They emerged from the stairwell into a corridor. Her eyes widened when she spotted the inscription on the door leading into the photograph studio. It read "Suzie-Q Agency."

"Too much," she smiled. "But it should be in your name. Not mine."

"You're paying for it."

"And you'll pay me back."

Greg used a second key to open the door. Suzie stepped through into the darkened room. Steel-grey skies over the city weren't providing much natural light. He reached around to his left and found the switch. The huge space was suddenly bathed in a golden hue, reflecting off the polished, wide-plank floor.

"It's beautiful!" Suzie exclaimed. "And it smells so clean."

By now, he was equally excited.

"I've become a regular domestic. Ma gave me scrub-buckets and the like. So, I was here all day Sunday, workin' my little hoofies to the quick."

Suzie pointed in the direction of the bricked-over south wall.

"And what is that?"

Greg was grinning.

"That, my darlin', is a day-bed. Couch by day. Bed by night, or whenever you want it to be a bed. Bought it Wednesday and had it delivered."

"You planning to get it on with some of the models?"

He rested his chin in one hand, appearing to consider the idea.

"Hadn't thought about it, but now that you mention—"

Suzie was suddenly all over him, kissing his mouth, moving her lips down his neck, pressing her body against his.

"Y'know," he said, "it's even too early in the morning to call this a nooner."

She pushed his long hair back over his shoulders, playfully sticking her tongue into his ear. Then she whispered.

"We'll call it a christening. The Suzie-Q Agency is officially named and open for business."

Greg kissed her back, holding her tightly against him.

"If I decide to change the name, can we do this again?"

They gradually moved toward the bed. Beyond the four huge windows a blanket of November snow was beginning to accumulate on St. Paul Street.

Chapter Twenty-five

The game was five-card stud. The players were friendly, but not friends. The first hand was dealt at ten-thirty Friday night, in a backroom of the Club Coquettes in Knowlton. It was not a rich game. No mortgages on the table. Neither was it penny-ante. There were hundreds of dollars in the pot. Tension filled the room like acrid smoke.

It was now ten-thirty Saturday morning. The four men had played, with only occasional breaks, all night long. *Caporegime* Tony Soccio was dealing. Four cards were face down around the table. All but the last card had already been dealt.

Gino Viscuso and the Hells Angel, Razor, grudgingly folded, after surviving three betting rounds. Viscuso's nerves were on edge. The *capo* rarely visited the strip club unless something other than a card game was on his mind.

Soccio had an ace of diamonds showing and was betting as though he had another ace in the hole. Tank was still smiling confidently. His exposed cards showed a benign 7, 9 and 10 off-suit, but something about his smile didn't sit right with Soccio. He wondered if he could be missing something.

The *capo* rubbed his eyes, stretched his arms over his head and took another careful look at Tank's face cards. He figured even if he had the 8 in the hole, a straight was still a long shot on the river. Soccio was determined to kill the hand there and then. He bet big. Everything he had.

Perhaps it was the dusty shaft of sunlight, filtering through the room's only window. Maybe it was the empty vodka bottle on the table, serving as a reminder of the many hours that had passed, but Tank decided to call. He pushed a wad of cash into the center of the table and his smile didn't falter.

"Hit me," he said.

Soccio stared at his opponent and dealt the final card.

"Whaddya got? Tank asked.

Soccio turned over his card. "Pair of aces."

"Not good enough."

Tank's last card was a six. He slapped a straight on the table and began dragging well over a thousand dollars toward his chair.

"What the fuck." Soccio said. "The fuck were you doing? You had nuthin' in that hand. That was one sonofabitch of a gamble."

"I felt lucky," Tank replied.

Ty Davis agreed to meet a cameraman at the Club Coquettes. It was snowing lightly, with intermittent breaks of sunshine, as he steered Mobile 14 into the parking lot behind the wood-frame building. He couldn't get his mind off Maria Claudio.

Her name kept coming up in connection with nearly every major development since the August drug raids. She provided legal counsel to Montreal's number one gangster. She was a blood relative to the victim of the Mafia's highest-profile mob hit in decades. RCMP Detective-Lieutenant Normand Francoeur had tied her in with possible corruption in the judiciary. She was directly responsible for Greg Peterson's suspension from CKCF Television and she was the reason the Club Coquettes' part owner and Mafia underling, Gino Viscuso, was not behind bars.

There was no sign of the camera car. Ty lighted a Belvedere and took a long drag on the cigarette. If Réal Gendron's column was accurate, the multi-million dollar cocaine bust was thanks to a stool pigeon in the Positano organization. He wondered how long it would take for the crime family to figure out who had broken the cardinal rule of *omerta*, the Mafia's code of silence.

Ty decided to wait in the parking lot for the cameraman. He butted his cigarette and rolled down the driver's side window. It had temporarily stopped snowing and a bolt of sunshine sliced down through thinning clouds. It was precisely ten forty-seven in the morning.

Tony Soccio watched as Tank cleared the card table of cash. The biker stuffed bills into the pockets of his jean jacket, gradually becoming aware of the *capo's* cold scrutiny.

"So, you felt lucky," Soccio remarked.

Tank lost the cocky attitude he'd displayed at winning the poker hand.

"Yeah. Lucky."

Viscuso and Razor were still sitting in their chairs, relieved that the marathon game was finally over.

"We ought t' get some breakfast in here," Razor said.

Viscuso shook his head.

"No food for me. Coffee though. I could use a fuckin' gallon."

Soccio stood up and walked around behind Viscuso.

"Maybe luck wasn't the only thing at work here." He placed his hands on Viscuso's shoulders and fixed his eyes on Tank. "Maybe you wouldn't o' called that hand if you didn't give a fuck whether you lost."

Tank glanced at Razor then back at Soccio.

"Whaddya mean?"

"Maybe you guys got so much money it don't matter whether you win or lose."

Viscuso started to get up. Soccio applied downward pressure on his shoulders.

"Maybe the odds played in your favor when Jackie Tubbs threw that fight at the Forum."

Viscuso suddenly realized why the *caporegime* had made his surprise visit to the strip-club the night before. He shifted uneasily in his chair and tried to stand up again.

"Stay put," Soccio said in a tone of voice that sent shivers up his spine. "I ain't finished."

A door opened and two men stepped into the room. One was bald headed and built like a wrestler. The other was at least six and a half feet tall. Both were holding revolvers.

"Now," Soccio continued, "let's talk."

Razor knew that the next few moments could be his last. His survival might depend on a simple choice of words. The straight razor he kept strapped to his ankle was no match for a bullet.

"We was followin' orders, is all."

Soccio bared his teeth. He did not remove his hands from Viscuso's shoulders.

"Salvatore Positano don't know about no orders. Whose fuckin' orders you talkin' about?"

Razor felt no loyalty to anyone but himself. He leaned his head back, pointing his chin at Gino Viscuso.

"His," he replied.

Tank didn't move. His eyes danced wildly back and forth between Tony Soccio and the gunmen.

"That's right," he said. "Gino tol' us."

Soccio relaxed the pressure on Viscuso's shoulders. He stayed behind him and slipped one of his hands into the side pocket of his suit coat.

"You givin' orders these days, Gino?"

Viscuso tried to turn in his chair.

"Don't fuckin' look at me. Just answer the question."

"Okay, okay. So we leaned a little on Tubbs."

Soccio's grin bore a distinct resemblance to a hungry wolf.

"And you got fat bettin' on Billy Sands. How much you make?"

"Forty, fifty large."

"Forty, fifty large eh? The fuckin' car you bought 's worth more'n that. And where's my cut? Where's Sal's?" He glared at Razor and Tank. "How much he pay you?"

Razor saw no point in lying.

"Five thousand each. Plus expenses."

"Expenses?"

"You know. For the trip. Gas and such."

"Pretty generous for a guy who made only forty thousand himself. You holdin' out, Gino?"

Viscuso said nothing. Soccio patted his shoulder, keeping the other hand in his jacket pocket.

"Another piece o' business now. Sal's concerned. We lost big on that coke bust last summer. Anything you wanna tell me about that, Gino?"

By now, Viscuso was squirming in his chair.

"Like what? Tony, honest I—"

"Shut the fuck up. Like why the cops knew where to look for the shit. Like everyone arrested is doin' time 'cept you."

"I got convicted."

"No time though. How you fuckin' explain that?"

"I had a good lawyer."

Soccio was waiting for just that answer.

"Maria had no pull with that judge, Gino. You got no sentence for another reason you fuckin' sonofabitch."

"I don't know what you mean."

"Yeah you do."

Soccio withdrew his hand from his suit coat pocket.

"Maybe this'll help jog yer memory."

He raised his arm and brought his fist down hard. Gino Viscusco rolled off the chair and began thrashing around on the floor. An ice pick protruded from the top of his head.

The area to the south of Club Coquettes was heavily wooded. It wasn't an old growth. The young trees and underbrush were thick and even impenetrable in parts. Ty Davis and the cameraman were shooting film of the building's exterior, when two men emerged from a side entrance. One was a giant. Ty estimated he was close to seven feet tall. The second man was bald and heavy set. They were carrying something between them.

"Looks like a rug," Ty said.

He and the cameraman were concealed behind cars in the parking lot at the rear of the strip club.

"Wonder why they're dragging a rug into the woods. Get a shot of 'em. Stay behind the cars. Don't let 'em see you. Something's not right about this."

The cameraman aimed his Bell and Howell silent camera at the two men as they disappeared into the woods. He was still shooting film when they reemerged. They were still carrying the rug, but it was no longer rolled up and it no longer seemed heavy. The giant had it slung over one shoulder. The two men reentered the building by the side entrance.

"Something's up," Ty said. "Let's just sit here for a few more minutes. We've got all the shots we want of the Club Coquettes. Let's just see what happens next."

What happened next was a repeat of what had occurred minutes before. Another trip into the woods. Another rolled up heavy rug. Another return to the building.

"Jesus!" Ty exclaimed. "I think we're lookin' at bodies. What else could it be?"

Once again, the two men appeared at the side door, carrying the rug between them. And, as before, it was obviously heavy.

"We'd better get the fuck out of here," the cameraman said. "That's three trips into the woods. If you're right and we're spotted, I don't want to be number four."

"You're absolutely right. We'll wait 'til they come back, then get the two mobile units outta here. There's a motel about a mile up the highway. I'll meet you there. We'll let Jason know what we've seen and then get in touch with the cops."

The giant and his bulky companion reappeared. This time, they'd left the rug behind. Ty and the cameraman retreated to their cars, engaged barely above a whisper in a frantic conversation.

"Ground slopes downhill to the highway," Ty said. "We'd better not start the engines 'til we're at the bottom. If we've just witnessed murder, the last thing we want to do is attract attention."

Jason Moore hadn't heard a 10-5 emergency call on the mobile radio since a natural gas explosion tore through a burning building in Verdun two years before. At that time, Greg Peterson had been filming the fire and literally screamed into the microphone. This call from Ty Davis was breathless and frightened.

"10-5," he repeated the code. "Mobile 14 is 10-30."

Moore responded immediately.

"What's happening, Mobile 14?"

"Can't talk on the radio. Call you on the phone. We're en route to a motel in Knowlton."

"But, what's the emergency?"

"Don't want to explain on the air."

"10-4. I'll wait for the call."

Ty and the cameraman pulled into the Redfern Motel just before noon. There was a pay phone in the lobby. Ty dropped a couple of coins into the slot, waited for a dial tone and dialed the direct line to news. Moore picked up.

"Ty?"

"Yeah. It's Ty. Christ, Jason, I think we've just seen a triple murder! Or at least, the aftermath of one."

"Where?"

"At the Club Coquettes. We were shooting outside at the rear of the building. There's a narrow stretch of pavement running down the south side. They keep a dumpster there. It's on the club's property, not accessible or visible from the highway."

He proceeded to describe the events of the morning. Jason listened attentively before replying.

"Stay where you are," he said. "I'll contact a guy I know in the Cowansville QPP detachment. He'll dispatch people. Shouldn't take long. I'll monitor the police-band and let you know when the cops are in the vicinity of the strip club. Then you and the cameraman can appear to have been on some nearby news assignment and simply showed up to film what happens. Did anybody see the CKCF cars?"

Ty explained how they'd kept the engines off and coasted to the highway's edge.

"Couple of customers came into the parking lot earlier. Looked like they were just heading into the club for a beer, though. I don't think there was any connection with the two men and the rug."

"Good. Stay put. I'll be in touch."

Chapter Twenty-six

A narrow footpath led south from the Club Coquettes through a tangle of prickly underbrush and young maples. It sloped downward to a small pond, the oily surface of which rippled silently around the remains of an old air-conditioner. It was warmer now under a climbing sun, but wet snow and melting ice still clung to the path.

Half-a-dozen Provincial Police officers had no trouble locating a section of ground that appeared to have been disturbed. It was about twenty yards into the underbrush. Ty imagined it would have been buried in snow during the winter, concealed under new growth in the spring and hidden from sight by early summer.

Approximately an hour had passed since Moore's phone call to the QPP. It was sufficient time for the information to go out on the police radio and for *La Voix* reporter Réal Gendron to respond. He stood next to Ty as the shoveling began.

"Thought you might be here," he said. "You think our good frien' Gino Viscuso is involved?"

Ty shrugged.

"You're the one who told me he was part owner of the Club Coquettes."

"*Mais oui.* What were you doing out here on a Saturday morning?"

"Just updating. Shooting some new footage. We're chasing your story, actually."

Gendron nodded.

"As you English say, two plus two equals four. Someone informed the RCMP before this place was raided in August. Drug traffic over the *frontière*, the border, has been crippled. The mob is losing millions."

Ty raised an eyebrow.

"So you think this, whatever this actually is, might be some sort of retribution?"

"*C'est possible.* They find anybody inside?"

"Just a woman behind the bar. Couple of strippers. They said they knew nothing about any of this and there were no arrests."

Suddenly, one of the police officers shouted. His shovel had uncovered a white substance, some three feet beneath the soil. Ty and Gendron moved in to get a closer look. The CKCF cameraman was busy at the edge of the pit.

"Quicklime!" Gendron exclaimed. "*Lechada!*"

"What's that?" Ty asked.

"A corrosive. It's an old Mafia method. Dissolves the bodies, eh?"

A milky white liquid oozed to the surface of what now appeared to be a prepared burial ground. Ty backed away.

"Where do you get this stuff from? What exactly is it?"

"*Très facile.* It's easy. Anyone can buy caustic lime. Building suppliers sell it all the time for many reasons. Mostly construction. The mob adds some acid to the calcium oxide and it goes to work on the evidence."

"How long does it take for bodies to, uh, melt?"

Gendron pointed at the police officers.

"We're about to find out."

An arm stuck out of the white soup. Shovels and grappling hooks were used, over the next couple of hours to retrieve three bodies from the pit. All were in accelerated states of decomposition. One of the faces was literally peeling back from a deep scar that ran across the forehead and right eyebrow. Ty had never had a photograph, but recalled the artist's courtroom drawing. He had no trouble identifying the rapidly dissolving face of Mafia soldier, Gino Viscuso.

The six o'clock Flash News report covered all the Knowlton events in detail. Ty's stand-up introduction to the story was done at graveside. New film footage was used to show where the various drug raids had taken place in August. Another interview was conducted with Réal Gendron, who proceeded to speculate on the significance of the triple murder. He talked about Frank Ragusa in New York, the Positano *borgata* in Montreal and the fact that the recent mob hit on

Massimo Gianfranco, indicating a blood feud between the Mafia's Calabrian and Sicilian factions, appeared to have little to do with this morning's developments.

"This," he declared, pointing to the quicklime pit, "was located soon after three bodies were buried, which will allow forensic experts to positively identify the remains. We know, however, that one of the bodies was that of Gino Viscusco, a crew member of the reputed gangster, Tony Soccio."

Ty interjected.

"Réal, if this was not part of a factional war in the Montreal mob, what was it?"

"As I said in my column in *La Voix* this morning, the drug raids of last summer were probably the result of a police informer. It's my guess that informer was one of the three people killed today."

"And what of the other two?"

"*Alors*, two Harley-Davidson motorcycles are parked behind the building, eh? Both bodies are wearing Hells Angels insignias. We'll have to wait for the official results before they can be named, but they were probably working with Viscuso."

Ty thanked Gendron and turned to the camera.

"Three bodies. Three more mysteries. Was this, in fact, linked to the recent murder of Mafia *capo* Massimo Gianfranco, or was it, as you've just heard, a settling of accounts? Did someone violate the mob's unwritten code of silence...*omerta*? And did that someone pay with his life? Ty Davis, at Club Coquettes in Knowlton, for Flash News."

Montreal Police Detective-Sergeant Pierre Maillot was fuming. He received the package containing sixteen millimeter film from CKCF Television. There was no projector available at police headquarters and his superiors had ordered him to accept the TV station's invitation to screen it there. He resented having to speak English to the young woman who greeted him at the door. He resented being called in on a weekend.

"This way," she said.

He followed her from a security guard-post off the main parking lot.

"Newsroom is up a couple of flights. We're all set up for you in film-editing."

"*Merci, mademoiselle.*"

Maillot realized his investigation of two murders and the missing Francine Landry was going nowhere. A cover letter, signed by news director Clyde Bertram, was cutting to say the least.

"*It is clear,*" it declared, "*that CKCF employee Greg Peterson is being held hostage to your current murder investigation, and that you have not been able to demonstrate Peterson was in any way involved. You are unable, as well, to link him to the recent disappearance of another woman. Our own inquiries indicate he was mistakenly identified by one Maria Claudio, in connection with an assault on her August 27th of this year. We firmly believe Peterson is innocent of that attack and that Claudio picked him out of your lineup in order to conceal the true identity of her assailant.*"

The letter went on to mention possible bribery or intimidation of judges, Claudio's alleged connection to the Positano crime family and her relationship to the slain Massimo Gianfranco. It underlined the fact that, because of the potentially defamatory nature of the letter, it was for police eyes only.

Clyde Bertram welcomed Maillot to the newsroom.

"Our film editing section is just behind that wall," he pointed at a door leading off the assignment office. "I gather, Detective, that you seldom watch English television?"

Maillot didn't like the question.

"*Mais non, Monsieur Bertram.* We 'ave our own media in Québec. Often, we 'ave different opinions."

"The collective we, is it?" Bertram scowled. "You versus us?"

"*De temps en temps.* Sometimes it comes down to that, *monsieur.*"

"Well, I hope you'll find our little film to be helpful."

The two men were joined by assignment editor Jason Moore.

"Detective-Sergeant Maillot," Moore was smiling. "I've spoken to you a number of times on the phone." He extended his hand. Maillot shook it.

"*Oui. Plaisir.*"

They stepped into a darkened room where two film-editors were hard at work on the late news. It was just after seven-thirty in the evening. One of the editors was introduced by Bertram.

"Detective, this is Mike Greer. Mike, Detective-Sergeant Maillot."

Greer nodded and shook hands with the police officer.

"Got the stuff on projector. Take a seat."

As Maillot watched the first part of the Ty Davis report of Monday the 13th, his facial expression remained unchanged until the artist's drawing of Gino Viscuso appeared on screen. Moore noticed a flicker of recognition in the policeman's eyes. There was no reaction to the information about Salvatore Positano, but Moore noted a definite response to Davis's standup on the steps of the Old Courthouse.

"Of all those charged and found guilty," Davis was saying, "no sentencing date has ever been set for Gino Viscuso."

After the screening Maillot confirmed that he knew Maria Claudio was first cousin to Massimo Gianfranco. He knew about the August drug raids, but was unaware that Viscuso had been represented by Claudio. Moore didn't plan to leave it at that.

"You've been informed," he asked, "about the murders this morning in Knowlton?"

Maillot nodded affirmatively.

"Then you know that Claudio's client, Viscuso, was one of the victims. This woman, Detective-Sergeant. She has a lot to hide. Do you really think she is telling the truth about Greg Peterson?"

Chapter Twenty-seven

"Three down. One to go."

Walt Taylor winked at Ty as they passed each other in the corridor outside the sports department. Ty appeared tired. It was the first full weekend he'd worked in nearly two months. He gave a thumbs-up to the sports director.

"You still an Argos fan?"

"If the Als aren't playing. Yeah, I like Toronto."

"I'm not sure," Ty replied smiling, "but as a Montrealer that might border on sacrilegious."

Taylor shrugged.

"My money's still on Toronto. They beat the crap out of Ottawa on the 16th. I don't think the Rough Riders have the balls."

"Wanna put your money where your mouth is?"

"Sure. Fifty bucks on Toronto winning."

"What about today's game? The western conference."

"Saskatchewan all the way."

"Okay. Let's make it an even hundred. I'll bet fifty on Calgary today and fifty on Ottawa on the twenty-second."

The two men shook on it. Taylor disappeared into the sports department. Ty crossed the hall and pushed through the door into news. Jason Moore was on a day off, but Clyde Bertram was catching up on paperwork and was busy filling his office with cigar smoke.

"Mornin' boss." Ty stood just outside Bertram's door. His eyes began watering from the odiferous clouds wafting into the newsroom.

" 'Lo Ty. Nice job yesterday. Moore told you to find our own angle on the Gendron piece. You sure as fuck did."

"Pretty scary stuff. For awhile there, it was fucking dangerous."

Bertram pursed his lips.

"You handled it like a pro'. One hell of a story."

"Thanks. Any follow-ups today?"

"Could be. What about all this speculation that Viscuso fixed the Sands fight?"

"I've been thinking about that. The two Hells Angels who were killed yesterday. Either they were just in the wrong place at the wrong time or they were involved with Viscuso in something that pissed off the mob."

"Could be they had some role in the drug seizures."

Ty shook his head.

"I don't think so. If Gendron's right, Viscuso acted solo. If he was a police informer he wouldn't have told anyone, much less a couple of thugs like that."

Bertram chewed thoughtfully on his cigar.

"What then?"

"Somebody had to get to Jackie Tubbs. No one's ever proven he threw the fight, but if he *did* there had to be a damn good reason."

"Threats?"

"He's got a wife and kid."

"You believe Viscusco hired those two guys?"

"The Mafia uses the Hells all the time for just that sort of strong-arm stuff. Contract killings. You name it."

"Right. Well, look into it. You self-assigning today?"

"Yep. Moore's off."

"Try to come up with something for the six o'clock. Not much in the day-file."

Ty turned to leave.

"Famous last words," he said.

Carmen Acelino seldom slept at the Sands Family Gym. Last night, he'd pulled out the hide-a-bed couch in his office and watched the late news on an old Admiral TV set next to his desk. Billy Sands had been in the gym earlier in the day when the six o'clock Flash News report carried a story about the triple murder in Knowlton. Billy was oblivious. He believed he was the middleweight champ, fair and square. No one told him about threats against Arlene Tubbs and Jackie Jr. No one told him the greatest moment of his boxing career was nothing but a sham.

Acelino threw cold water on his face and looked at himself in a cracked mirror above the sink in a corner of the office. He hadn't profited from the fight, despite his knowledge of Viscuso's plans. Billy was his boy. He'd never have bet against him. Billy might have had a legitimate chance against Tubbs at some point in the future. He was strong and fast and had the heart of a champion.

"Too soon," he told the mirror. "He wasn't ready yet."

Acelino knew about Tubbs' phony hand injury. He knew that if the champ had actually thrown his right more often, Billy wouldn't have made it even through the early rounds. Tubbs was a seasoned pro. Billy had been out-boxed from the get-go.

Acelino shut off the bathroom light and walked out into the gym. The boxing-ring stood empty. He didn't expect any of the regulars to train on a Sunday and Billy had said he wouldn't be in until early in the business week.

He felt the weight of his years and a deep sense of guilt as he picked up his duffle bag and headed out to his battered old Chevy Biscayne station wagon. Acelino was thinking about Gino Viscuso's assertion that "what Positano don't know won't hurt him," as he turned the key in the ignition and the Chevrolet exploded in a blinding fireball.

Snow came down like a theater curtain by mid-morning Sunday. Ty shivered in a north wind that drove the storm out of the Laurentian Mountains on a head-on course with the Island of Montreal. He chastised himself for not listening to the weather forecast before leaving home. He was wearing only a flannel shirt and jeans. Now, standing in an open lot outside the Sands Family Gym in Ste. Anne de Bellevue, he began to wonder if there were some other way to earn a living; somewhere warm, somewhere free of the violence and bloodshed he'd witnessed this weekend.

"Not much left of that Chevy," he said to a fireman who was rolling up a length of hose. The explosion had tossed the station wagon's engine and the driver's side door several yards across the parking lot. The remainder of the vehicle was charred black. Its roof yawned open in a jagged pattern of twisted metal.

"Not much left of the body inside," the fireman remarked.

Ty leaned in for a closer look. Part of an arm had been blown into the wagon's rear storage space. The victim's legs had literally been vaporized. His torso was seat-belted in place.

"Any idea who we're lookin' at here?" Ty asked.

"Not my business. Ask the police officer-in-charge. Over there." He pointed to a uniformed Provincial Police corporal.

By now, media people were swarming the place. TV reporters were setting up cameras. Radio personnel were clutching tape-recorders and the print people were busily writing shorthand into their notebooks. The officer-in-charge was about to preside over an impromptu press conference at the entrance to the Sands' Gym. Ty walked toward the CKCF camera position and was greeted by the same individual he'd spent the previous day with in Knowlton. The cameraman was using a shoulder-mount, in order to stay portable.

"Hate to make this a habit," he said offhandedly.

"10-4 on that."

Ty watched a four-wheel drive jeep pull into the parking area. The words *La Voix* were written across both doors.

"Here comes Gendron. Right on cue."

Gendron joined the other reporters as the press conference was getting underway, grinning at Ty as he squeezed into the growing crowd. It reminded Ty of a Parliament Hill scrum, when journalists surround a federal politician in hopes of getting a useable sound clip. Ty waved at the cameraman to roll film.

"*Monsieur*," he shouted in the face of newspaper reporters who liked to monopolize the first few minutes of any press conference, "can you confirm this was a bomb?"

The officer glanced over at him. It appeared he wasn't used to questions in English.

"*Absolument*," he replied. "*Les morceaux ont été trouvés sous l'auto.*"

"In English, *s'il vous plaît*," Ty asserted.

"*Oui*. It was a bomb."

"Do you know anything yet about the victim?"

"You 'ave to check with the coroner's office."

"What about the license plate? Who's the vehicle registered to?"

"Again, *monsieur*, *'sais pas*. I don't know."

"Okay. Thanks."

Ty told the cameraman to switch off.

Réal Gendron emerged from the crush of reporters as one of the French journalists was saying something about the F.L.Q.

"This has nothing to do with the separatists."

"I know that."

"You want an I.D. on the victim?"

"I think I know that too."

"Billy Sands' corner man, *n'est ce pas*?"

"The same. Carmen Acelino. It's all tied in with yesterday. Viscuso, the Hells, Acelino, Billy Sands and Jackie Tubbs."

"Don't forget the RCMP drug raids."

"Separate issues. But yeah. Viscuso was a dead man the minute he started singing to the Feds."

Gendron agreed.

"*Mais oui.* And when he fix the fight, these guys get caught in the web."

"Now they're dead," Ty said.

"Same message, my frien', don't you think?"

"What's that? What message?"

The *La Voix* reporter grinned knowingly. "Don't fuck with Positano."

Chapter Twenty-Eight

Film-editor Mike Greer was in Clyde Bertram's office. Ordinarily, he'd have taken up the matter with Jason Moore, who was enjoying a Sunday off duty.

"You've seen the footage from the Club Coquettes?" he asked.

Bertram was shuffling papers on his desk.

"Guys did one hell of a good job."

Greer was holding a circular tin container. He held it up in front of the news director.

"I think you'll be sending this to the RCMP."

Bertram sat back in his chair.

"What's that?"

"The outs on the Knowlton job. The shots that weren't used on the air."

Close-ups of the two men who had carried the rug into the woods next to the strip club fit into a journalistic grey area. It was obvious the men had a direct connection to the murders of Gino Viscuso and the bikers, but they hadn't been found or charged. Ty Davis and Jason Moore had decided not to use their faces on the air.

"Good thinking," Bertram said. "Maillot didn't seem too happy with our backgrounder on Maria Claudio and company, but I'm sure the Feds'll be glad to take a look at a couple of murder suspects. Leave it with me. I'll make some calls to the Mounties and the QPP."

Greer nodded and left the office. Bertram lighted a House of Lords corona and decided to step across the hall to sports. Ty Davis was just coming up the corridor. His long hair, shirt and jeans were soaked through.

"Here comes winter," he said, as Bertram passed by.

"Snowing, is it?"

"And this time it's staying on the ground. Well, boss, we've got our lead story for the day."

"Been listening on the police radio. Figure it's this Acelino character?"

"Gotta be. Remember, we had him tied in with Viscuso on several fronts. Viscuso frequently visited the Sands Family Gym. We know that. And when I spoke recently with the sports doctor who works at the gym—"

"Thomas Sinclair. Yeah, I remember. A point of caution, though. It's strictly word of mouth from Sinclair that Viscuso and Acelino were somehow in cahoots on the Billy Sands fight."

Ty nodded in agreement.

"I wouldn't bring it up in my report. Fact is, I don't think we can even identify Acelino as the victim of today's bombing until the cops get the coroner's report."

"So how do you want to frame it?"

"Let me screen the stuff with Greer. I'll come up with an approach and run it by you later this afternoon."

"Do that."

Bertram tucked his cigar into the corner of his mouth and walked into the sports department. He liked Ty Davis. He didn't like his haircut, or the fact that his star reporter would be wearing jeans and a sports shirt on CKCF's flagship newscast. He planned to remind him about the station's dress code.

Mark Carter was covering the weekend shift for sports. Walt Taylor seldom assigned himself to a Saturday or Sunday. He'd come in earlier, merely to do some paperwork. Carter was pawing through the sports pages of the *Montreal Star* when Bertram stepped into his office.

"Hey there, Clyde," he said, smiling. "You work here on weekends or just slumming?"

Bertram blew out a mouthful of cigar smoke.

"Playing catch-up with my budget is all. Mark, a couple things I wanted to ask you about."

"Fire away."

"Apparently, Walt told Jason Moore about a Green Room party way back last August. August the 27th, to be precise. You know anything about that?"

"I'm the one who told Walt about it. That's the night Greg Peterson got nailed for beating up some woman."

"That's why I'm interested. One of the news cars was commandeered. It showed up later at a Mafia party in the northeast end of town. All this happened before the beating incident."

Carter made a clucking noise with his tongue.

"Greg's one of the best. Hate to see this all comin' down on him."

Bertram shrugged.

"Vic Gordon's policy," he said.

"Anyway. Yeah. I heard about the Green Room from Art Bradley. He checked in about nine forty-five that night. Apparently had a drink with some people."

"In the Green Room."

"That's what he said."

"Was Gordon around?"

"At first."

"What do you mean, at first?"

"Well, Bradley says he was there when he had the drink, around ten. Then he took off."

"And didn't come back?"

"He didn't specifically say. But Bradley would have had to head back to the newsroom to get ready for the late show. No idea about Vic, whether he left or came back to the party."

Bertram paused before speaking again. He was thinking about Gordon's Chrysler being spotted on the parking lot just after midnight.

"Any ideas on the nature of this Green Room thing?"

"No. At least, Bradley didn't know. He hadn't seen any of those people before, but he assumed they were clients."

"Right. Another thing, Mark. What did Gordon tell you and Walt about the Billy Sands fight? I know you guys agreed not to play up speculation about Jackie Tubbs losing on purpose."

"Why do you ask?"

Bertram scowled, appearing somewhat impatient.

"I'm not being critical of that decision, Mark. I'm asking for good reason."

Carter had witnessed the news director's temper in the past. On the one hand, he wanted to uphold Walt Taylor's autonomous approach to sports. On the other, he had no intention of risking Bertram's wrath.

"Vic simply pointed out that it was just speculation. Said we weren't in the gossip business."

"Uh-huh. He said the same thing to me. I told him to fuck off."

Carter swallowed hard. He couldn't imagine telling Victor Gordon to fuck off.

"News *went* with it, then?"

"We did. Now we've got several people dead, and it's all connected."

"Jesus," Carter said. "What's Vic got to do with it?"

Bertram withdrew the cigar from his mouth and stared at the sportscaster.

"No idea. But I intend to find out."

Elizabeth Davis had always felt claustrophobic when traveling through mountainous country. Today was different. Saying goodbye to her parents had been difficult, but as the train wound its way north through Vermont's Green Mountains, it was almost as if her spirits were in sync with the high terrain. She had her act together. Doctor Hall, of Unity College in Boston, advised her father that her postpartum depression was under control. She had stopped drinking. Day by day she derived an increasing sense of pleasure from Catherine and Robin.

"Mommy, look at that!"

Four year-old Catherine pointed out the train window. There, standing very near the train tracks, was a bull moose, complete with massive antlers. Two year-old Robin, who'd been sitting on the aisle to Elizabeth's right, climbed over his mother's lap to get a look. The moose was quickly left behind.

"What was it?" he asked.

"See if we can guess," Elizabeth replied. "Do you think it was a bear?"

"No-o-o, silly." Catherine giggled.

"It was a cow," Robin decided.

Catherine muffled her laughter with her hand.

"Wasn't." she said.

Elizabeth realized this was the simple process she'd been missing for much too long, that of enjoying her children.

"Maybe it was a deer," she suggested.

Catherine thought it over.

"A very big deer."

"I think it had a headache," Robin added.

"Why do you think that?"

" 'Cause. 'Cause it had bumps all over."

Elizabeth couldn't stop herself from laughing out loud.

"Those are called antlers. What we saw back there was a moose."

"A mouse?" Catherine appeared astonished. "It couldn't have been a mouse."

"No, dear. A moose. It's sort of like a deer but much bigger. That was a moose and it didn't have a headache, Robin. It had antlers on its head."

Robin crawled off his mother's lap and said "Oh." He seemed entirely satisfied with the explanation. Catherine stared out the window.

"I didn't think it was a mouse," she said.

The train was crossing the Lamoille River. White water churned across rocks far below. As they moved north toward the U.S.-Canada border, the weather gradually closed in. It was snowing quite hard.

"Do you think Daddy will be glad to see us?" Elizabeth asked her children. Robin was beaming all over.

"It's a soo-prize," he replied.

"A surprise. That's right, it is, Robin. We didn't tell him we were coming."

"Did we get him a present?" Catherine asked.

Elizabeth hugged her daughter.

"You and Robin are all the present he'll need."

Chapter Twenty-Nine

Clyde Bertram made a decision. At three-thirty in the afternoon of Sunday, November 19th he called Ty Davis into his office. He'd already made two phone calls to network officials in Toronto. Bertram's motor was running at full throttle. He was almost purring. "I've reformatted the six o'clock show," he announced. "Talked with programming. The usual claptrap that runs six-thirty to seven is pre-empted. We'll go with a half-hour special. I want you to co-host it with Art Bradley."

Ty felt the cold thrill of an adrenalin rush. He'd always harbored aspirations of becoming a news anchor. He figured there might be an opportunity, at some point, in the next few years, but it had never occurred to him Bertram thought he was ready now.

"Co-host?" he asked, haltingly.

"With Bradley," Bertram grinned. "Here's what's happening. The network has agreed to offer the half-hour to the affiliates. It may not be picked up by all of them, but Toronto will run with it. Probably Ottawa and Vancouver. There's a lot of interest in Mafia and the Hells Angels out west. Don't look so damn terrified, Ty."

Ty realized he'd actually begun to tremble. There were times when he'd been on the air live with Bradley for a debriefing on one story or another. Then, it was just a matter of one or two lines to a live camera and directly into an edited report.

"It's just a little scary, Clyde."

Bertram was still grinning widely. He believed in throwing his people into the deep end to see if they could swim. It was a time-proven method of finding those who could function well under pressure.

"You'll be fine," he said. "Maggie's coming in to assist weekend lineup. Bradley will anchor the news from six to six-thirty. We'll lead with the car bomb, of course, and we'll plug the six-thirty special at the end of your report from Ste. Anne's. Maggie will script the entire special, so you've nothing to worry about on that score. Greer's pulling stock footage going back to the August drug raids. We'll touch on the drug seizures, the Gianfranco thing, the Sands fight, the Knowlton killings and today's bombing. It's been your story from the beginning, Ty. Take ownership. You've built some credibility and it's time to expand on it."

Ty had begun to sweat profusely.

"If you say so, Clyde."

"I say so."

"Okay. What do you want from me?"

"Three things. Finish up your piece on the bombing. Do a sign-off from the parking lot here at the station and use it to promote the upcoming special. Then get your ass home. Shower and come back in a suit and tie."

"What, you don't like my soaking wet plaid shirt?"

"You look like something the cat dragged in. Go home. Clean up. Back here by five."

It was Ty's turn to smile.

"I kinda' thought this could be the new look for television anchors."

Bertram scowled.

"And you know what?"

"What?"

"You'd be dead wrong."

"Just joking boss. I'll do you proud."

"I'm counting on it."

Ty's wet clothes clung to his back and shoulders as he scraped off the windshield of Mobile 14. Winter was making its mark on Montreal. Mixed emotions accompanied him into the N.D.G. district. Trees along Oxford Avenue hung heavy with snow and an icy wind blew out of the north.

On the one hand, Ty realized his career was undergoing profound change for the better. Dreams of anchoring Flash News no longer seemed impossible. On the other hand, he thought, what good were dreams? What benefit was there in working hard if there was no one to share the rewards?

Ty parked the car in the lane next to his home. A blast of Arctic air lifted a white cloud along the sidewalk, momentarily obscuring his view of houses across the street. What began as a light snowfall earlier in the day was now a blizzard. At least two inches had already accumulated on the ground, and the storm showed no signs of abating.

He climbed his front stairs, fishing in a jeans pocket for housekeys and hunching his shoulders against the wind, when the door opened seemingly on its own. Suddenly, Ty felt his daughter's arms hugging him around the legs. An inside doorway leading into the hallway was open. There stood Elizabeth, holding two-year-old Robin on her hip. She was smiling, but a tear ran down one cheek and her lips were trembling.

"Ty," she said. "Ty, we're home."

"Daddy, daddy!" Catherine exclaimed, as he picked her up and squeezed her so hard she could barely get the words out.

"Oh my God," he said. "What? Why didn't you tell me?"

"Soo-prize," Robin shouted.

"Soo-prize," said Elizabeth. She stepped across the threshold into a warm embrace. She held Robin. Ty held Catherine. All four rocked back and forth, as one.

It could be described only as organized chaos. A network special was not run of the mill for Flash News. As predicted by Clyde Bertram, Toronto, Ottawa and Vancouver decided to pick up the live broadcast out of Montreal. Edmonton and Halifax were also planning to use it. Ty walked into the eye of a storm. Maggie Price was hammering the keys of her typewriter.

"Ty, when Gianfranco's body was found at the refinery, what's the story on how he was killed? Or, do we know?"

He was somewhat taken aback by the question. He made a sweeping motion with his hand.

"Jesus, Mag, this is insanity."

"I know. Believe me, I know. What can you tell me, though? We're ninety minutes from air-time."

"We know squat about how or when. What we do know is that

one of the guards at the BP refinery opened the gates for the BMW. Gianfranco's body was in the trunk."

"What do we know about the guard?"

"Natale Cristina. He was hired by the BP security chief, Ron Irvin, out of Pinkerton's. It came out later that Cristina's part of the Sicilian wing of the mob. Works for Rocco Panepinto, the *capo*."

Maggie kept typing while she talked.

"Okay. I've got shots of the BMW. Bertram's agreed to show some of the gory stuff, after the cops let you film Gianfranco's body. Was there any follow-up on this Cristina?"

"Just that he's in the wind. The provincial boys are still lookin' for 'im."

"So we can say he's wanted in connection with the Gianfranco killing?"

"That's safe," Ty agreed.

"What about Salvatore Positano?"

"What about him?"

"I mean, what's the significance of the hit on Gianfranco. How's it affect Positano?"

"Big time. Frank Ragusa, the big boss in New York, heads up the Calabrian faction of the Mafia. When his underboss came to Montreal—his name is Giovanni Lorenzo, G for short—when G came to Montreal, Ragusa wanted to put the Sicilians on a five-year probation before they could cash in on Positano's Montreal operations. Ragusa got shot down and the Sicilians are here to stay. Panepinto's been putting the squeeze on Positano ever since. The Gianfranco thing is a major part of it. He was Positano's number two in Montreal."

"Good. Good." Maggie's typewriter was almost on fire. "That gives me a solid bridge into this whole business of Gino Viscuso, the Sands fight and what happened down in Knowlton. I take it Viscuso's death is related to the fight?"

Ty hovered over Maggie's work-station.

"It's all related," he said. "But I don't think Positano would have ordered a hit on Viscuso for going maverick. I mean it's serious shit that the Sands-Tubbs match might have been fixed. But I don't think they'd have killed him because of that. And we can't say, for certain, that Tubbs actually threw the fight. We can talk about the speculation.

* * *

All the papers had it. We had it. No, I'm pretty sure Viscuso was whacked because of last summer's drug raids."

Maggie nodded. "I remember. This crime reporter from *La Voix*, Réal Gendron, had a lot to say about that."

"So did we, Mag. But we've framed it all in the form of a question. In my report I simply asked whether Viscuso paid with his life because he'd broken the Mafia's most sacred rule. *Omerta.* The code of silence. If Viscuso tipped off the police, if he was directly responsible for Positano losing millions of dollars in those drug seizures, the mob would have had to set an example."

"So, that's why he wound up in that lime-pit in Knowlton."

Ty shook his head.

"But don't say that. We can't know for sure. Just write it the way I originally reported it. Like a question. Gendron's guessing like everybody else. We just don't know."

"And all of this is connected to the Gianfranco murder? How?"

"Really, it's not. Just with respect to the pressure Positano's been exposed to, in general. He's got a possible war with the Sicilians. He's lost big on cross-border drug traffic. Ragusa's facing murder charges south of the border. It's a shit-storm."

"Where do these Hells Angels fit in? The two guys who were killed, along with Viscuso?"

"Looks like they might have been working with Viscuso on the Sands-Tubbs fight. Probably threatened Tubbs' family."

"Can we say that?"

"Again, it's a question. None of this is anything more than a question."

Maggie appeared frustrated. "Well, Christ. What can we say for sure?"

Ty smiled.

"Mag, we might never know any of the answers. All we can say for sure is who's dead. We can only speculate on why."

"Same thing for this Carmen Acelino?"

"All part of the Sands-Tubbs connection. If the Hells Angels leaned on Tubbs to throw the fight, all we really know about Acelino is that he was Billy Sands' trainer and corner man. Did he know about the fight being fixed? Who the fuck can say? All we can report is that his car blew up today and he's history."

"Alright. Say, by the way, what's happening with Liz and the kids?"

Ty felt his legs go numb. He'd forgotten confiding in Maggie about his marital problems.

"They're home, Mag. Came in by train today. Liz is doin' great. I think everything's going to be okay."

"Oh, Ty, that's wonderful. And you're stuck here."

"Liz understands. This special *is* special. She's behind me a hundred percent."

"Will she be watching?"

"All of it," he replied. "And, Mag, finally, I'll be going home to my family."

"Quite a day for you. This'll be a piece of cake. You have more information in your head about all of this than we can possibly report in a half-hour format. You deserve this, Ty. You've earned it, whether Art Bradley likes it or not. Thanks for your help."

"Is Bradley upset?"

"Pissed off. Doesn't like working a Sunday. Doesn't like sharing the spotlight."

Maggie grinned. "Fuck him," she said.

Chapter Thirty

The letter was received and read almost simultaneously in two separate locations. Greg Peterson's mother put it on her breakfast table, along with the rest of the mail, at nine forty-five Monday morning. Greg read it while eating toast and strawberry jam, thirty minutes later. Clyde Bertram's mail was delivered to the CKCF newsroom at ten. Bertram spotted the City of Montreal letterhead and read it promptly.

It was addressed to Mister Greg Peterson, c.c. Mister Clyde Bertram and Detective-Sergeant Pierre Maillot. It was brief and to the point. It stated that the body of thirty-four year old Francine Landry had been found and positively identified. A suspect was in custody in connection with her murder and those of two other women. The letter went on to say that formal charges were being brought and that Mister Greg Peterson was no longer a suspect in the case. It was signed by the head of the Montreal Police Homicide Division, Detective-Captain Bernard Levasseur.

Marg Peterson was sure Greg had suffered some horrible accident. His shrieks could be heard all the way down Querbes Avenue to Jean Talon.

"Ma!" he shouted. "Ma, it's over! They know I had nothing to do with the murders! They found that Landry woman, or at least her body. They *have* a suspect, Ma! They *have* a suspect!"

Marg threw her arms around him. Greg led her in a spasmodic dance around the kitchen.

At CKCF Television, Clyde Bertram's reaction to the letter was considerably more sober. He read it aloud to Jason Moore and quickly came to a conclusion.

"Doesn't get him off the hook with the Claudio thing. Maillot's been dragged through the dirt over this by his superiors. It'll just make him more determined to nail Greg on the assault charge."

Moore shook his head in disagreement.

"Could be. But this is great news just the same. Don't you think Maillot will have to back off a little?"

"Not his style. He doesn't like Anglos. He doesn't like the English media. Did you notice his ranking officer, this Detective-Captain wrote this in English? That'll piss Maillot off even more. No, I don't think he'll back off. Not unless we can come up with solid evidence that Greg was home in bed when Claudio got slapped around, or that she is a goddam liar."

"Both things are true, Clyde."

Bertram shoved the letter into a desk drawer.

"You and I know that. Maillot's made a fool of himself, so far. Now, it's up to us to find proof."

Ty Davis was riding the crest. No one he spoke to thought he'd come off second best, co-anchoring with Art Bradley. His biggest cheerleader was Elizabeth.

"If you were nervous," she said, "it certainly didn't show. Anyway, I always thought Art Bradley was a self-important, pompous old poop."

His arrival home the night before had felt like rejuvenation. Nothing seemed more innocent and peaceful than the sleeping faces of his children. Ty stood outside their bedrooms remembering the emptiness he felt during their absence. He wondered how he'd kept going, how he'd had any motivation at all. The memory was like a physical ache.

Elizabeth greeted him at the top of the stairs, after he parked the car in the basement garage. They held each other for a few moments and the warmth of her body next to his brought tears to his eyes.

"Never leave me again," he said.

She rested her head in the crook of his neck and whispered—"Never."

Supper included all his favorites. As he cleared dishes from the table, Ty realized that nothing was more important to him than loving and being loved. His job, which had been the focus of his life while Liz and the kids were in Boston, ranked only as a means to an end.

Its importance paled in comparison to the sense of worth and purpose he derived from his family. Without them, he was nothing. Without them, he had been a hollow shell.

"Let's take our coffee into the living room."

Elizabeth was pouring hot water into the kitchen sink and stacking plates and glasses in to soak.

"We could even build a fire in the fireplace if you'll bring some logs up from the garage. We haven't done that in a while."

Ty looked at his wife. She had dressed in a light green angora sweater that accented her breasts and a brown suede mini-skirt that showed off her long legs.

"Good idea. And a fire kind of sets the mood for something else we haven't done in a while."

Her eyes twinkled mischievously as they walked, hand in hand, into the living room. A late November snowstorm obscured the view across Oxford Avenue. Patterns of soft light from a nearby street lamp filtered through frosted windows and played on the walls. They forgot their coffee in the kitchen. They didn't build a fire in the fireplace. They were too busy losing themselves in each other.

Monday morning congratulations followed Ty all the way from the CKCF entrance to the news department. He felt exhilarated. Everything was coming together. Liz and the kids were home. His career was taking off and, sitting in Jason Moore's office, he learned about the letter.

"Greg's off the suspect list."

"Meaning what?"

"Cops're convinced they've got their serial killer. Clyde still thinks Maillot will push the Claudio business."

"So, essentially, we're back to where we started."

Moore wrinkled his forehead.

"Not entirely. The RCMP has Claudio under close scrutiny. Francoeur says it's just a matter of time before they pin something on her. If she's been bribing judges, Maillot's gonna have to realize her credibility is out the window."

"I suppose."

"Meantime," Moore continued, "why don't you call your partner in crime, Réal Gendron."

"And ask him what?"

"You said he was with the RCMP August 27th, across the street from Cabrini Hall?"

"That's right."

"Ask him about the guest list."

"Guest list?"

"Find out what he knows about who was actually there, besides Salvatore Positano and the other Mafia big-wigs. Didn't you say Gendron was taking photographs?"

Ty nodded.

"The cops were. I imagine Gendron snapped a few of his own for *La Voix*."

"Exactly. See if he'd look over his files for anything that might help us place Claudio there."

"Hell of an idea. Why didn't we think of it before?"

"We've been going off in a thousand directions. We *should* have thought of it. I think the most important piece of business right now is to find any way we can to discredit her. Maillot knows about the mob connections. Apparently, he was unaware she'd represented Gino Viscuso after the August drug raids. Now that Viscuso's been murdered, it underlines her involvement with undesirable elements. So, we just keep doing what we're doing. Eventually Maillot is gonna have to ask himself some serious questions about her charges against Greg. And if he doesn't, his superiors will."

"I'll check with Gendron."

Ty stood up to leave. As he walked into the newsroom and sat down at his typewriter, he reminded himself to go to the bank. The Calgary Stampeders had lost 36 to 13 in game two of the CFL's western finals, to the Saskatchewan Roughriders. He owed Walt Taylor fifty bucks.

Victor Gordon was a worrier, a trait never revealed to anyone else. He sat in his office, feeling the weight of another Monday morning and staring at his fish tank. A Clarion angel fish swam slowly by his field of vision. It was one of his favorites. He'd paid a fortune for it on a recent holiday in Acapulco. The angel's black eyes seemed fixed on his own, prompting him to wonder whether it might possess some ancient memory of its Mexican origins. Gordon's thoughts were abruptly interrupted by Clyde Bertram. His secretary, Amy Sebastien, stood behind him, shifting nervously from one foot to the other.

"Sorry, Mr. Gordon. He said it was urgent."

"That's, uh. That's okay, Amy. Come on in, Clyde." He showed his teeth in a broad smile.

" 'Lo, Vic."

"So, what's urgent?"

Bertram chuckled.

"Just said that so I could walk in unannounced. Thought I might catch you jerking off or something."

Gordon pretended to be amused.

"Very funny."

"Actually, it's the latest on Greg Peterson. I thought you'd want to know he's been cleared of the murders."

"Cleared?"

"They have a suspect behind bars. Three counts of pre-meditated."

"That's good. What about the Maria Claudio case?"

"Same shit. But, Vic, we're going to make sure that one goes away too."

"How? She says he did it."

Bertram raised an eyebrow.

"She's lying."

"So you say."

"We can't prove it yet. Trust me. We will."

"Monday, November 20th. This is Flash News. I'm Art Bradley."

The CKCF anchor's booming voice resonated throughout Studio Two. It was a three-camera operation at six o'clock, with an in-studio crew that included three cameramen, a floor-manager who counted Bradley into film segments and provided numerous other verbal and hand signals, a lighting man and two stage-hands. The newscast director, script-assistant, audio-man, switcher and others occupied a control room about fifty feet down the corridor from the studio. Steven Collyer, the director, was barking orders to the switcher.

"Take camera two."

Bradley simultaneously heard the script-assistant's voice in his earpiece and turned to the appropriate camera.

"Camera two. Floor in ten, nine, eight...."

The floor-manager matched the count with finger signals.

"Tonight's headlines," Bradley continued. "The latest on Montreal's serial strangler. And an update on Mafia mayhem in the Eastern Townships."

"Take camera three," Collyer shouted.

Bradley turned. His facial expression had changed from one of high-energy excitement needed for the headlines, to one of fatherly concern. His voice rumbled on at a lower volume, as the script-assistant chimed in.

"Film in fifteen, fourteen, thirteen...."

Bradley led into the story.

"Montrealers are breathing easier tonight. Police have arrested and charged a forty-two year old man *they* believe is responsible for three recent murders in the city. Ty Davis has been following the story. Here's his report."

Ty began voicing over stock footage of Ste. Catherine Street. The shots, taken from a moving news mobile, showed the bright lights of nightclubs, bars and restaurants.

"Montreal after hours. As night falls, city streets take on a new character. Offices and stores close. Clubs and restaurants open in the downtown core to a different set of clientele ... men and women finished with the business day ... looking for recreation."

A full-frame photograph appeared on screen.

"Was this man looking for something more? This photograph, supplied to Flash News by Montreal Police homicide investigators, is that of forty-two year old William Bentley. He is now charged with three counts of murder. Bentley was arrested over the weekend outside the Crescent Street bar where two of the murder victims were last seen alive."

The TV picture changed. An area of deep woods appeared.

"The body of twenty-eight-year-old Linda Martin was found at the Morgan Arboretum in Ste. Anne de Bellevue. An autopsy report showed she had been sexually assaulted and strangled. Just five days later ... another body. The remains of thirty-one year old Thérèse Fortin were discovered by hikers, along a wooded trail in Laval. She too had been raped and strangled."

Ty appeared on screen. He was walking past office buildings on McGill Street.

"Then, just twelve days ago, thirty-four-year-old Françine Landry finished her work day at Fairchild Insurance Company, here on McGill Street. It's not clear where she went that evening. Police are investigating the possibility Landry might have headed for the same Crescent Street bar where Martin and Fortin were last seen. Francine Landry was officially reported missing on Friday, November 10th. Her body was found on the banks of the St. Lawrence River, off the eastern tip of Montreal Island ... yet another victim of the strangler. Montreal Police, meantime, have offered no explanation as to why very little information was disseminated to the media about the murders. Women's groups, in particular, argue that a general alert should have gone out to the public as soon as police knew a serial killer was on the loose. Ty Davis reporting for Flash News."

Chapter Thirty-One

RCMP Corporal Normand Francoeur was bubbling over with excitement. He was on the phone with Jason Moore early on Thursday morning.

"We got 'em!" He could barely contain himself. "Tell your boss he made me a hero around here."

Moore wasn't sure what Francoeur was referring to.

"How so?"

"The film, Jason. The film you guys shot down in Knowlton."

"Right, of course. But you said you got *them*?"

"Two heavyweights in the Positano organization. Their faces were up close and personal. Your cameraman zoomed right in."

Moore reminded himself to show the film-outs on the Knowlton murders to Greg Peterson. He felt sure the tall man, who helped carry the rug into the woods behind the Club Coquettes, was the same thug who assaulted Greg on Querbes Avenue.

"How'd you get to be a hero?"

Francoeur laughed.

"Bertram called me. Sent the film directly to me, so I got the jump on the homicide case. The Provincial Police had to step aside when it became apparent this involved a long-standing federal investigation. And it's pretty rare that a lowly public relations officer like me gets to collar the bad guys."

"Good for you. So what happens now?"

"Well, we've got three bodies. Looks like Positano's boys were doing a little house cleaning. These arrests might prove to be significant. Who knows what we can learn from these two characters?"

Moore smiled. "Probably nothing," he said.

"What makes you say that?"

"If they acted on Positano's orders, which they probably did, you can bet they'll take that little secret all the way to prison. If they didn't, they'd be dead meat before the end of week one on the cellblock."

"You're right. Anyway, it's good to get the bastards off the street."

"No doubt. By the way, I think one of them beat up Greg Peterson. Maybe both of 'em."

"Oh yeah?"

"The big one almost certainly. Greg described him in detail. Six and a half feet tall at least."

"Not too many guys that big," Francoeur agreed. "Likely Positano used this one for enforcement."

"A regular Sherman Tank in human form."

"Soon to be out of commission. Thank Bertram for me, will ya?"

"Consider it done."

The restaurant was nothing fancy. The menu was one step up from greasy spoon. Salisbury steak that had looked like a good choice to Ty Davis turned out to be glorified hamburger floating in brown gravy and surrounded by mixed vegetables that included lima beans. Ty couldn't stand lima beans. He pushed the food around on his plate with his fork and waited for Réal Gendron to arrive. The *La Voix* reporter had said he had something of interest to show him.

Ty was summoning up the courage to sample the mystery meat when Gendron strolled in. He was carrying a manila envelope and wearing a shithouse grin.

"*Allo* my frien'." He flopped down in the booth and stared at Ty's lunch. "Should have 'ad the rib steak," he said. "Not so bad."

Ty smiled back. "It's not often I can say I'm terrified of my food."

"*Alors*. We'll 'ave coffee." He placed the manila envelope on the table. "I look through all my photos from August. The RCMP 'ave more, but this one, *c'est important*."

Ty picked up the envelope and slid the photograph out on to the table.

"Holy shit!"

The picture, taken from the church across the street, showed a group of people outside the entrance to Cabrini Hall. Ty recognized

Salvatore Positano, Massimo Gianfranco and several others of the Mafia elite. Standing next to Positano, smoking one of his Monte Cristo cigars, was CKCF TV President Victor Gordon.

"What the—?" he sputtered. "I can't believe it. Gordon! Son of a bitch!"

"Look like he's, 'ow you say? One of the boys?"

"But how? In what capacity? He's not even Italian. Far as I know, he's Jewish."

"*Un associé, n'est ce pas*? An associate."

"What's that mean?"

Gendron flagged a waiter.

"Two coffees, *s'il vous plaît*." He tapped a forefinger on the photograph. "Positano is smart guy, eh? The mob often recruits powerful businessmen. They don't 'ave to be Italian. They actually never join the Mafia. But, Gordon runs a TV station and that's an advantage."

"In what way?"

"A favor here. A favor there. Who knows?"

Ty's mind was racing. He thought of Polo's Restaurant and the many times he'd spotted Positano there. He remembered the time he had dinner with Elizabeth at The Hole, when the crime boss had sent drinks over to their table. Positano had waved at him, like he was an old friend.

"There's a guy who works in radio," he said. "Joe Maurizio. He used to get phone calls in master control from Gino Viscuso. Any Friday night, when Billy Sands was fighting out of town."

"There you go," Gendron nodded.

"Maurizio used to joke about it. Called it the Italian connection."

"If your president was a mob associate, the connection went a lot deeper than a few phone calls."

"I really don't get it, though. What possible use would Gordon be to a guy like Positano?"

"Think about it," Gendron said. "Air-time. Deals on commercials. Positano's into numerous legitimate businesses that need advertising. There's political influence. The way your news department covers the courts. City Hall. You name it."

Suddenly, Ty sat up straight in the booth.

"He tried to get Clyde Bertram to drop the story about the Sands fight."

"You mean, about Tubbs throwing the fight?"

"Exactly."

"Did Bertram agree?"

"Not on your life. But that's not to say there haven't been other occasions."

Gendron smacked his lips.

"Now, see, that's very interesting. Could be Gordon cashed in on the fight. Positano wouldn't have known anything about it."

"Dangerous game."

"About as dangerous as it gets."

Ty couldn't help but think of the lime-pit in Knowlton. He slid the photograph back into the envelope, thanked Gendron, and headed for the station.

Snow clouds hung low on the horizon as he swung Mobile 14 into the parking lot behind CKCF. His first priority was to consult with Jason Moore. Somehow, he felt sure the manila envelope he was carrying was the key to many doors. It was difficult to imagine what might be behind those doors and impossible to draw conclusions on his own.

Moore was still at lunch when Ty walked into the newsroom. He decided to show the photograph to Clyde Bertram, who was sorting through a pile of wire-copy in his office.

"Clyde, I need a few minutes."

Bertram glanced up, smiling. "Getting some positive feedback on our Mafia special."

Ty sat down next to the desk.

"That's good."

"So far," Clyde continued, "nothing but kudos from Toronto and Vancouver. Those are the big players on a local level. The network boys were damned happy as well. I wouldn't be surprised if the show gets nominated for an award."

"Uh-huh. Well, good."

Ty was too preoccupied with the business at hand to care about awards.

"Clyde, I picked up a photograph from Réal Gendron. It's a mind-blower."

"A photograph?"

"From Gendron's personal file. The night of the Mafia party at Cabrini Hall."

"Okay."

"Jason suggested I get in touch with him. We were hoping he might have something that would help us place Maria Claudio there on August 27th."

"And did he?"

"Not exactly. But this thing opens an entirely new can o' worms. Honestly, I don't know what to make of it."

He dropped the envelope on the desk and watched Bertram's reactions as he withdrew the photo. First, his ears turned bright red. Then, his eyes appeared as though they might explode from his head.

Chapter Thirty-Two

The stands were filled, with 33,172 fans. A tsunami of sound rolled through the Autostade and leapt across the St. Lawrence River. The field on November 30th was muddy. Ottawa's Bill Van Burkleo fumbled the ball in the first quarter. It was recovered by Saskatchewan's George Reed. Ron Lancaster passed to Alan Ford from the twenty-seven-yard line, giving Saskatchewan the game's first touchdown. Van Burkleo conceded a safety, adding to the Saskatchewan lead. Nine to nothing, Saskatchewan, at the end of the first quarter. CKAL radio announcer Dave Ferguson was doing the play-by-play.

"Doesn't look good for Ottawa heading into the second quarter here at the Autostade. The recent snow has made this field almost unplayable. The ball is greasy but the westerners seem to be handling it."

A second voice interjected. Larry Nichols was the color announcer.

"They are, Dave. But, y'know, it's been snowing in Saskatchewan for over a month now. They're just used to it."

A chuckle from Ferguson.

"Well, we'll just have to see how Ottawa fares in the next few minutes, Lar."

Ottawa began a touchdown drive in the second quarter.

"Russ Jackson is running the ball up the middle. It's good for eighteen yards and a first down."

Ottawa fans nearly brought the stadium down with their vocal enthusiasm.

"And Jackson is off again. A short run this time. He passes to Jay Roberts. Roberts is in the clear! He elbows his way past two Saskatchewan tacklers. It's a touchdown! A touchdown for Ottawa in this second quarter!"

Mud was key in the third. Saskatchewan was in perfect field position on a seventy-eight-yard kickoff return by Alan Ford.

"Ottawa had some momentum going as the second quarter came to an end. And there's the pass. It's fumbled! Reed drops the ball on the Ottawa thirty! It's recovered by Don Sutherin. Ottawa catches a major break."

Nichols chimed in.

"It seems mud is everybody's enemy."

"You got that right. Jackson goes back for the pass to Wayne Shaw. Shaw slips. He couldn't hold on to the ball, but he's tipped it to Ron Stewart. He's got it! Stewart is up against a virtual wall of blockers! He rolls to the right. And he's in the open! Look at him go! Running. Running. Saskatchewan can't catch him! Stewart scores. An eighty-yard run, folks! An incredible turn of events. Fourteen to eleven for Ottawa!"

A similar pattern unfolded in the fourth quarter.

"Jackson drops back, ready to pass. Oh my! He's driven to the ground by a teeth-rattling tackle! On to the soupy field goes Jackson. Where's the ball? Jackson pulls it off somehow. He's managed to flip it to Stewart. Stewart again, in the open! He's off and running! Saskatchewan didn't see this coming. They thought the play was over when Jackson was hit. Stewart is over the line. Another touchdown, Stewart's second, this time after a thirty-two yard run! Unbelievable!"

On November 30th, 1969, the Ottawa Rough Riders defeated the Saskatchewan Roughriders 29-11. It was the first time the City of Montreal had hosted a Grey Cup in thirty-eight years. The atmosphere was contagious. After the game, Montreal's Queen Elizabeth Hotel became party-central. No one seemed to care who'd won or lost. Most members of the Ottawa team departed for home, but Saskatchewan players and fans took over the hotel.

It was a long night of raucous celebrations. On the morning after, men in western boots and ten-gallon hats filled the breakfast counters and milled about the lobby. Many, in spite of regulations, still had alcoholic beverages in hand. The noise level was overwhelming and the festivities of another day were just getting underway.

Ty, Jason and Greg checked in at ten-thirty. Clyde Bertram hadn't been aware that the hotel would be the site of post-game madness. He was accustomed to using the Q.E., and thought they'd have peace and quiet to go over their notes. He didn't think twice about booking them in and Greg immediately got caught up in the revelry.

"Want a beer?" he asked the others.

Moore appeared startled by the suggestion.

"It's not even noon."

"I know. It might get us started. You know, prime the pump. Don't get me wrong. I'm just as worried about all this as you are. It's just, we keep hitting dead ends. Maybe a beer would help."

All three were carrying valises. Apart from a change of underwear and socks for a possible overnight stay, the luggage was crammed full of notepads, tape-recorders and other paraphernalia related to their investigation. Clyde Bertram had been adamant.

"Take every damn bit of it. Go over everything. Listen to every interview. Mobile 9 was driven by somebody that night. I want the sonofabitch!"

Ty walked toward the bank of elevators in the western end of the hotel lobby.

"Let's get this stuff up to the room. We can come back down if you really want a beer."

Moore pressed the button marked "up."

"Rather have a club sandwich and coffee."

"You health nuts," Greg muttered. He stepped aside as a very large man in a white cowboy hat and a buxom blonde woman emerged from the elevator. When the door closed, Ty smiled and said "Yee-haw."

The room on the fourth floor was nothing special. Clyde Bertram's secretary had ordered a double and a single-bed in case the task took them well into the night. Ty fluffed pillows on the single bed.

"I'll take this one. You jackasses can share the double."

He surveyed the sparse layout of the room.

"Nuthin' like it was for the John Lennon bed-in. He and Yoko had corner suite rooms on the 17th. Rooms 1738, 40 and 42. Room to breathe."

"Peace," said Moore. "Maybe we'll get this thing done and just go home."

Greg saw his opportunity for a beer slipping away.

"What about the brew? You can go eat if you want to. I'm gonna find a nice quiet bar-stool."

Moore scowled.

"Okay, okay. I think you've been unemployed for too long. You've lost the concept of deadlines."

Greg grinned widely.

"Jason, sometimes you can be a bit of an old woman and I wonder if I ever want to go back to work. If we're gonna solve this thing, we'll have to get the creative juices flowing. I prefer mine to have at least a four percent alcohol content."

The train from East Orange, New Jersey to Newark pulled out of Brick Church Station fifteen minutes behind schedule. Jackie Tubbs was always on time and he resented the delay. His training, since losing the middleweight championship in Montreal, depended on discipline. Tubbs' very life was based on disciplined behavior. Punctuality, in all situations, was a natural byproduct.

He left home at the usual time. Arlene and Jackie Jr. were finishing breakfast and the construction team was already hard at work on the last two units in his apartment building on South Munn Avenue. Now, as he sat on the train, he picked up a copy of the Newark *Star-Ledger*. He thought catching up on the latest news would kill time. Members of his entourage occupied separate seats.

Page one of the newspaper detailed another disastrous and bloody encounter between U.S. troops and Vietcong fighters outside some godforsaken village in Vietnam. It was the story on page three that caught his eye. The headline read "Montreal Mafia Vendetta." Tubbs' excitement grew as he read about the car bomb in Ste. Anne de Bellevue, Quebec. Carmen Acelino, the formidable trainer and corner man for Billy Sands, was dead.

"Acelino's death," the story continued, "was the latest of several incidents underlining an ongoing power struggle in the Montreal mob. On Saturday, the 18th, three men were murdered in Quebec's Eastern Townships region. They were identified as Gino Viscuso, a soldier in the crew of Mafia *capo* Tony Soccio, who is reputed to be a kingpin in the Salvatore Positano crime family. Viscuso's body and those of two Hells Angels bikers were recovered from a makeshift burial ground at Knowlton, Quebec. Speculation has it that Viscuso may have become a police informer."

Tubbs read on. The page three item referred to drug trafficking across the Canada-U.S. border, the RCMP raids in August and the possibility that Viscuso had been instrumental in tipping off the police. That, however, was not the information that held his attention.

"It's also fueled rumors," the article said, "that Viscuso and the two bikers were involved in a conspiracy to fix the outcome of the recent middleweight boxing championship at the Montreal Forum. Longtime champion Jackie Tubbs, of East Orange, New Jersey, lost the title on a split decision to Montreal's Billy Sands. *Star-Ledger* sources claim Viscuso might have acted, independent of the Positano organization, to threaten Tubbs and his family."

Jackie Tubbs rested the newspaper on his lap. As the train pulled into Newark, he felt certain that two things were about to happen. He'd be plagued by reporters at the gym and his organizers would demand a rematch with Billy Sands. And this time he would pulverize the bastard.

Chapter Thirty-three

The double bed in room 411 of the Queen Elizabeth Hotel was covered in debris. Jason suggested they re-examine events in order, from August 27th. On the left side of the bed, notes and tape-recorded interviews with CKCF staffers were carefully laid out. They'd studied the results of their roughly four-month investigation all day and there still seemed to be a daunting task ahead. Moore looked at his watch. It was shortly after the supper hour.

"If we do this sequentially, I think we'll be able to highlight the important discoveries without actually listening to all these tapes."

Ty made a kissing noise with his mouth.

"It'd take forever otherwise."

Greg sat in one of two upholstered chairs in the room, sipping on a Molson.

"What's the main focus? I mean, we're not going to resolve anything if we try to analyze all this stuff."

"Let's just discuss what we know," Moore replied. "Then, if we need to listen to another tape or review someone's notes, we'll do so. And the main focus, you silly bastard, is to get your job back."

"Okay," Ty said, "Maria Claudio gets attacked. Let's start with that."

Moore nodded.

"The witness sees the attacker drive off in a CKCF car. He's not clear what the guy looks like and he doesn't spot the mobile unit-number on the trunk."

"So, where's that get us?"

"It gets you and Greg, Keith, Tomlin and Brains into a police lineup."

Greg swallowed some beer.

"And she points at me."

"But your mother can't swear you didn't leave the house, because she was asleep."

"Right," Ty said. "And so we started interviewing everybody who had access to the keys in your office. We don't have to listen to these tapes to know that the interview with Dick Tomlin was suspicious, to say the least."

Moore picked up one of a dozen notepads on the bed.

"The timeline is what's important. Tomlin checked into the station just after midnight. Maggie Price was just leaving. We now know, from Maggie, that Vic Gordon had something going on in his office earlier that evening. Gordon's Chrysler was parked by his boat when Tomlin arrived. Maggie saw it. Tomlin says he didn't. Art Bradley had drinks in the Green Room around ten, which apparently was a continuation of the meeting in Gordon's office."

"But," Greg interjected, "Bradley said he saw Gordon only briefly in the Green Room. He left, and we have no information on whether he returned, because Bradley had to head back to news."

"Exactly. So now that we're sure Gordon was at the Mafia meeting at Cabrini Hall, the question is when did he actually leave the TV station?"

"I'm betting he never went back to the Green Room," Ty said.

Moore sat down on the edge of the bed.

"If that's the case, he could have left for Cabrini Hall just after Bradley saw him at ten."

"Or, he could have spent a couple hours giving some chick the infamous Gordon boat tour, and left later on."

Greg's face lit up.

"That would explain why the Chrysler was parked beside the boat."

"Yeah," Ty agreed. "Maybe he was still on the damn boat at midnight, when Maggie finished her shift and spotted the car and Tomlin signed in."

Moore rested his chin in one hand. He was holding the Dick Tomlin interview in the other.

"And we don't need to listen to this to know he was evasive about the keys. He says he knew nothing about the Chrysler, didn't see the boat, wasn't aware of the session in Gordon's office or the Green

Room party. He didn't even know about the Mafia meeting or the RCMP surveillance that night."

"Christ," Ty added, "according to him he didn't know about the attack on Maria Claudio until you told him he had to stand in the lineup."

"What does all this tell us?" Greg asked.

Moore was shaking his head.

"Let's add two and two. We've always assumed that Tomlin was covering for someone. What we didn't know, until we got the photograph from Gendron, is that Victor Gordon likes to hang out with gangsters." He paused, thinking. "Let's go with our guts here. What if the person Tomlin's protecting is Gordon himself?"

"Jesus!" Ty exclaimed. "That would explain almost everything. Gordon is screwing somebody on his boat between the Green Room at ten and midnight when Tomlin gets in. He leaves his Chrysler in the parking lot because—because why?"

Greg exploded out of his chair, spilling Molson ale on his chest.

"Fuck me! Gordon was driving Mobile 9! Tomlin gave him the keys!"

Moore was somewhat more cautious.

"All of this is possible but we can't prove it."

Ty's face reddened.

"All we can do is look at the evidence, Jason. And here's another radical thought. Who was Gordon fucking on the boat?"

"What's that got to do with anything?"

"Just this. Until today we've been able to place Mobile 9 at Cabrini Hall but not downtown where Claudio was attacked. We've been able to place Claudio downtown but we're all pretty damn sure she was at the Mafia meeting earlier. She's a Mafia lawyer, for chrissakes. So here's my radical thought. What if Maria Claudio was the woman Maggie heard in Gordon's office early that evening? What if *she* was Gordon's date on the boat?"

Greg was grinning ear to ear.

"They both had reasons to be at Cabrini Hall. So they drive over in Mobile 9, because a news car in the vicinity of a Mafia meeting wouldn't arouse any suspicion."

Moore was gradually coming around to the idea.

"Alright, alright. Suppose we look at the timing then. If Claudio was attacked at around one-thirty in the morning, and they didn't leave the station until just after midnight, they would have been able to stay only for a few minutes at Cabrini Hall before heading downtown."

Ty was almost jumping up and down with excitement.

"Gendron says she's got a high-end address down there. Maybe, on the way, they got into an argument or whatever. Gordon gets angry, gets violent and dumps her on that sidewalk. It would certainly explain Tomlin. We always thought he was lying about the keys. If this is how it went down, Victor Gordon took the news car and told Tomlin to keep his mouth shut."

"I hate to play devil's advocate," Moore said, "but we still can't prove any of this."

"So, we put our theories to the test."

"How?"

"We get Tomlin in the hot seat and scare the shit out of him. Clyde Bertram can go after Gordon. If we're right, and I'm ninety-nine point nine percent sure we are, our proof will be in their reactions."

"In the meantime," Greg was still smiling, "we've got a hotel room all paid for. We're not going to be able to do anything about this until we report back to Bertram tomorrow." He raised his beer above his head. "Let's party!"

Chapter Thirty-four

There was nothing extraordinary about the man sitting on a couch near the hotel's registration desk. He was clean-shaven and smartly dressed, but his face was unremarkable. Anyone spotting him on the couch, however, couldn't say the same about his eyes. They stared intently at the hotel's bank of elevators and they were not the eyes of a peaceful man. They were very black and utterly void of emotion.

Grey Cup celebrations had swept the entire lobby, spreading like an ocean wave through the suites, conference rooms and corridors upstairs. Individual parties were taking place all over the hotel. In spite of efforts by the staff to control the revelers, hookers wandered in off Dorchester Boulevard. Drunken cowboys whooped and hollered. Saskatchewan players, who seemed to have forgotten they'd lost the game, signed autographs and slugged down huge quantities of beer and spirits.

The man watched. When Jason Moore, Ty Davis and Greg Peterson emerged from one of the elevators, he slowly stood up and followed them.

"There's a live band in the ballroom," Greg said enthusiastically. "What say we grab a table?"

"Gotta call Liz," Ty announced. He strolled over to some pay phones along a wall near the elevators. "I'll join you in a few minutes."

Moore looked at his watch.

"Hotel room or not, Greg, I've gotta work tomorrow. I'm not planning a late night."

"Yeah, well we need to raise a glass or two. And I'm buying the first round. You guys have no idea how grateful I am. It really feels like we're near the end of this thing."

The ballroom, off the hotel's main lobby, was packed. A jazz band was pounding out a Miles Davis number. Bars had been set up in three corners of the huge room. Greg walked towards one of them.

"Get us a table, Jason. What're you drinking?"

"Glass of red wine. I'll be over there." He pointed to a couple of empty tables, far enough away from the band to enjoy the music and still be able to have a conversation.

"Glass of red," Greg told the bartender. "And a Molson for me and a Labatt 50 for another guy I'm with."

The barkeep smiled and served up the order. Greg paid, carried the drinks through the crowd and sat down with Moore. Ty eventually came through the doors, spotted them and walked over.

"Liz says to say hello."

Both Greg and Moore said "Hello Liz," then lapsed into silence, sipping their drinks and listening to the music.

The man moved in. He waited until they were seated, sauntered over and sat down at the table like an invited friend.

"You boys been doin' some homework," he said.

Moore was the first to speak. All three were flabbergasted.

"Can we help you?"

The man's face was unreadable.

"I take it you're putting the pieces together."

"Pieces?"

"So you can bring them to your boss, Clyde Bertram."

Ty suddenly felt a mixture of anger and fear.

"Just who the hell are you, anyway?"

"Someone like you, who has to report to his boss."

"Who would that be?"

The man smiled, sardonically.

"Let's just say, he's somebody you want to pay attention to."

Images of his savage beating on Querbes Avenue flashed through Greg's mind. He felt certain this could lead to more of the same.

"I think we know who he is. Why are you here? What's his interest in what we're doing?"

"Oh, he's got his ear to the ground on many things. Like your recent television reports, Mr. Davis. Most insightful."

Ty relaxed his shoulders, placed his elbows on the table and leaned in face-to-face with the stranger.

"Look. Exactly what do you want?"

"It's really very simple. My boss has nothing against any of you. But, he has a particular interest in your boss, that is, your boss's boss."

"I bet he has."

"No need for impertinence, young man. For your own good, for the good of your families—"

"You sonofabitch!" Greg exclaimed.

"Now, now, young man. Just listen to what I have to say. No one wants to harm your families. Bottom line is, you must stop your snooping. Everything *you* know, my boss knows. He likes to take care of his own business. And, Mr. Peterson, he offers assurances your little legal problem will evaporate. But, no more investigations. Understand?"

Ty was shaking with anger.

"Be specific. We stop asking questions and you do what?"

"My employer is very thorough, Mr. Davis. Suffice it to say that a certain lawyer has dishonored him. He has that matter in hand. The lawyer will have second thoughts about that police lineup last summer. As for the individual who was actually involved with the lawyer, it's come to my boss's attention that he's been extremely greedy. I refer, of course, to a recent boxing event."

"I suppose your employer has that matter in hand as well?"

"How very astute of you. And that's why I joined your table this evening. Your part in this is at an end. *Capisce*?"

"You're threatening us."

"That's a big word."

"So what should we do now?"

"Nothing, Mr. Davis. Nothing at all."

The man stood up, straightened his suit-jacket and disappeared into the crowd.

Chapter Thirty-five

The city was lit up like a Christmas tree. Store windows sparkled with a seasonal glow. Strings of color decorated hydro poles and balconies and people in the streets seemed more cheerful than usual. Old St. Nick was due in less than three weeks, but no visions of sugarplums danced in Ty's head as he maneuvered through late evening traffic.

"We've got to tell somebody," Moore had said.

The trio had returned to Room 411 shortly after eight, intending to urgently discuss their situation. The room had been tossed. Valises had been opened and searched. All materials related to their investigation were gone. Greg felt he was going to be sick.

"He said do nothing, guys. Remember, if they know my mother's address they also know yours. These people don't fool around. We have to think about this."

Ty was still angry.

"That bastard had us by the balls. I hate this. Now everything's gone. The tapes. The notes. Dates, names, everything."

"But it's all in our heads," Moore pointed out. "Look, I'm not suggesting we put our families at risk. I'm only saying we should do what we planned to do in the first place."

"What exactly?" Greg demanded to know.

"Talk to Clyde. Tell him what we know, or what we think we know. We don't need the tapes or the notes for that. I'm sure he'll realize the danger we're all in. At least we'll have completed what we've been doing all these months."

"Let's get out of here," Ty replied. "Let's just check out and go home. I'm not leaving Liz and the kids alone."

Moore was already stuffing things back into his valise.

"For sure. Greg, I'll drive you home on my way to St. Laurent. I'm going to get hold of Bertram by phone as soon as I get to my place. I'll tell him what's happened. Get his reaction and then I'll call you guys. Alright?"

Greg sat down hard in one of the chairs. He wasn't at all sure that was alright.

"What if Bertram goes off half-cocked? What if he decides to call the cops? It's our necks, not his."

"Clyde has to know," Moore replied, "that these people don't just make idle threats. He won't do anything rash. Count on it."

Now, as Ty drove Mobile 14 towards NDG, through the Christmas lights of Westmount, he could think of only one thing. His family was alone on Oxford Avenue.

Clyde Bertram knew about threats. Moore pulled into his own driveway in Ville St. Laurent a little after nine-thirty and immediately went to the telephone. When he told Bertram what they had concluded and about the dire warning they had received, he knew exactly what he had to do. It was the only morally responsible thing, in spite of the risk. He had to let Victor Gordon know that his life might be in danger. He knew the telephone number off by heart. It rang six times before Gordon's wife, Olivia, picked up the receiver. Her right leg and arm had been affected by a stroke and she used a walker to get around.

"H-hello."

"Mrs. Gordon," Bertram said. "Sorry to disturb you. It's Clyde Bertram."

"Yes, Clyde. Is there some kind of trouble at work?"

"You could say that, Mrs. Gordon. Is your husband around?"

"He's been working in his greenhouse since we had supper. It was a late supper, but he's been out there for over an hour."

Bertram hesitated.

"I hate to ask you to go get him."

"Oh, that's alright. I don't have to. We have an intercom here in the den."

"Great. Would you mind asking him to come to the phone? It's a matter of some urgency."

"Not at all. Just a moment."

He heard her put the phone down, followed by the sounds of her walker being dragged across the den floor.

"Dear, are you there?"

Silence from the greenhouse.

"Victor, are you still out there?" No response.

Bertram listened as the walker scraped its way back to the telephone.

"Hello, Clyde. He doesn't seem to be answering. I don't know why. I'm pretty sure the intercom works. I spoke to him not half an hour ago."

Bertram felt equally sure there was nothing wrong with the intercom. A chill ran up his spine.

"Mrs. Gordon," he said, "I don't want you to try to go out there. I don't want to alarm you in any way, but I think perhaps I'm going to ask your local police to check the greenhouse."

"Police! My goodness! You don't think—"

He tried to sound reassuring.

"I'm not sure there's any need to be concerned. Maybe he just stepped out to smoke. Does he smoke those Monte Cristos in the greenhouse?"

"All the time. I've told him I didn't think the plants would appreciate it, but he's a determined man. He does pretty much whatever he wants."

Bertram wanted to say that was certainly the way he behaved at the station.

"Fine. Look, don't worry. It's just that I need to speak with him. You don't mind if I call the police?"

"If you feel it's necessary, Clyde. It's going on ten o'clock. He should have come back to the house by now."

Beads of perspiration had popped out on his forehead. He wouldn't involve the police in anything but a routine call. The man at the hotel had said, "Do nothing. Nothing at all."

"Here's what, Mrs. Gordon. I'm going to hang up now. I'll contact the Pointe Claire police. As soon as they've checked the greenhouse and reported back to you, could you call me?"

"Yes, I can do that."

"Good. Do you have a pen or pencil handy?"

"Yes."

"Here's my number."

* * *

Lake St. Louis appeared like rippled, black silk. Easterly currents prevented a freeze, sometimes until late January or early February. On this first night of December, cold waters lapped at the shoreline property. Pointe Claire Police Constable Sean Gray was just ending his shift when the desk sergeant asked him to put in an hour's overtime.

"Victor Gordon's home. Bayside off the Lakeshore Road. Had a call from CKCF TV's news director who works for this guy. Olivia Gordon is concerned. Apparently her husband's been out in his greenhouse too long, or some such nonsense. Shouldn't take you more than a few minutes to have a look-see."

Gray avoided immediate contact with Olivia Gordon. The residence was surrounded by a fieldstone fence. He drove through a wrought-iron gate, passing the Tudor-style home and parking near a four-car garage at the rear. At least two acres of lawns—still looking manicured through the snow—sloped downward to the edge of the lake. He could see a light on in the greenhouse, which was located about midway between the house and the water. Gray fished a flashlight out of the glove compartment.

"Rich bastard," he said aloud. "Prob'ly drinkin' out here. Avoidin' the wife."

He was about to use the flashlight when someone inside the house hit a switch. Suddenly a red-tiled path was illuminated. Leafless trees marking the property's western boundary leaned in, the branches drumming out a staccato rhythm in a stiff breeze off Lake St. Louis. Gray turned around and faced the house. Olivia Gordon stood behind a huge, picture window, straining to see what he was doing. She'd obviously seen him drive in.

"Yeah, yeah," he muttered, resenting the overtime and the assignment in general. His own family was of working-class British stock. His father had spent a lifetime as a factory laborer in Manchester and his mother had taken in laundry to supplement their meager income. He'd immigrated to Canada in his late teens and would never have this kind of money. He had a deep-seated bias against anyone who did.

Carefully groomed floral borders flanked the pathway. As he drew near the greenhouse, Gray shouted into the wind.

"Mr. Gordon. Mi-i-ster-r-r Gor-rdon-n."

Only the wind and the strumming of tree branches replied. He moved to the entranceway. By this time he'd begun to think maybe this would take longer than a few minutes. Maybe this guy'd had a heart attack or something.

"Mis-s-t-er-r Gor-rdo-on."

He couldn't see anything untoward outside the structure, so he pulled open the door and cautiously stepped inside. What he saw felt like a physical punch to the diaphragm. He could scarcely breathe. Victor Gordon's body hung like a broken doll. His head was thrust through the greenhouse glass on one side of the building. His neck had been sliced, almost to the point of decapitation. There was blood everywhere. Sean Gray returned to the police cruiser at a full run.

He would report what appeared to be a grisly accident on Lakeshore Road.

Chapter Thirty-six

A collective sense of shock descended on CKCF personnel Wednesday morning, leapfrogging like a California wildfire from the news department to all levels of the TV station. Clyde Bertram arrived at six forty-five and began making phone calls to department heads. Jason Moore, who normally began his day at eight, came in an hour early. Bertram was wearing a grim expression.

"It's gone to the coroner's office. They'll poke around of course. There'll be an autopsy, but the police are apparently convinced Vic slipped and fell. I want you to get on the blower to some of your contacts, Jason. See what you can find out about the police investigation. I want to know if there was even the slightest evidence of foul play."

"Clyde, you and I both know that Gordon didn't just fall."

Bertram's face was very pale. It was the first time Moore had ever seen him actually frightened.

"This was professional," he said. "But, Jason, I need to know every last detail of the investigation. Any signs of struggle. Residue under Vic's fingernails. Blood patterns. Anything that might point to defensive action on his part. The coroner's report will probably deal primarily with cause of death."

"Let's face it, Clyde, they're not going to find anything suspicious. As you say, it was a professional job. We're looking at an eventual ruling of accidental."

"And that's all we can go with on the air."

Moore pinched his lips together. Anger burned just beneath the surface.

"Clyde, did it occur to you last night that your call to Mrs. Gordon put us all at risk? I mean, Ty, Greg and me? What if you'd managed to head off the killer? Positano would have known we warned Vic."

"What choice was there?"

"I dunno, Clyde. I dunno."

Moore slowly turned to leave Bertram's office.

"I'm certainly sorry about what happened to Vic. At the same time, I wonder how you'd be feeling this morning if it happened to any of us."

Bertram didn't reply. He suddenly looked very tired and very old.

When Greg Peterson woke up, he had to remind himself that it hadn't all been a dream. The empty eyes of the stranger in the hotel bored into his conscious mind as he shook off sleep and faced the day. Greg didn't know whether to feel happy that his legal ordeal might soon be over, or intimidated by the stranger's threats. He heard noises in the kitchen and knew his mother would be at the breakfast table, sipping her morning tea and munching on one of her scones. He forced himself off the edge of his bed and began dressing. If nothing else, he would make sure his mother knew every detail of the previous evening.

"For your own good. For the good of your families." He played back the stranger's voice in his head. Then he thought of Suzie.

"God! Suzie!" he exclaimed under his breath. It hadn't occurred to him, until now, that the mob would know about her. What if something happened to her? He'd call Ottawa. She'd have to know about everything. As he walked into the kitchen, the telephone was ringing. It was Jason Moore on the line.

"You up and running?"

"Barely."

"Okay. Maybe you'd better sit down for this."

"I haven't even had my first cup of coffee."

"Sit down, anyway."

"What? What now?"

Moore let a couple of seconds pass.

"Are you sitting down?"

"Christ, Jason, I'm sitting down as we speak. What's going on?"

"It's Victor Gordon. He's dead."

Greg closed his eyes. The stranger stared back at him out of the abyss.

"Dead! How?"

As Moore recounted the events of the night, Greg's mind was racing.

"What do we do now? What's Bertram have to say for himself?"

"He wants you to come into the station. Wants to talk to both of us."

"I'm sure he does. He could've got *us* killed y'know."

"I know and he knows."

"Well, good for him."

Moore sighed.

"Anyway, when can you make it in?"

"Gimme an hour."

He hung up the phone, smiled at his mother and began dialing the number for Suzie Waldon.

The hours passed slowly for Ty Davis. No matter how hard he tried to sleep, he couldn't stop going over and over the situation. If they did nothing, Victor Gordon was in deadly peril. If they warned him, odds were very good that Salvatore Positano would come after them. Ty watched Liz as she slept. He listened to her rhythmic breathing and to the sounds outside their bedroom window.

A wind rattled old boards in the sheds behind the flat. Somewhere, a tomcat yowled at the night. He thought of waking Liz and telling her how much he loved her; how much he needed her. Instead, he just watched as her chest rose and fell in peaceful, blissful sleep. What could he do to protect her and the children? What could anyone do against the insidious scheming of the Mafia? It was shortly after seven when Jason telephoned.

Clyde Bertram paced back and forth in his office. His face was flushed and he waved his arms as he spoke.

"No one should be able to muzzle a news-op. No one!"

Ty, Jason and Greg sat in chairs opposite Bertram's desk. They listened to the tirade, each of them weighing their thoughts carefully before verbalizing them. Ty was first to interrupt.

"Clyde, they already have."

"Have what?" Bertram demanded to know.

"Muzzled us. Nobody knows what happened at the Queen Elizabeth Hotel but the four of us, and we can't tell anybody else."

"Hell we can't! What are we? We're a professional news team. Granted, we'll have to wait until we know a little more about Vic's death, but we're journalists. We owe it to Vic. We owe it to our viewers."

"Pardon me," Moore said, suddenly furious, "but fuck our viewers! We've been warned off, Clyde. Now, I don't have children like Ty or a mother and girlfriend like Greg, but I do value my own life. Fuck our viewers!"

Bertram's mouth hung open in astonishment.

"I'm not forgetting any of that. Alright, let me hear what you think our responsibility should be. Ty, what about you?"

"To our families," Ty asserted. "If, in its own good time, the official investigation turns up evidence that Vic was murdered, then we can run with it. If not, we go with the party line. I for one am no longer interested in conducting an independent inquiry, beyond the usual questions to the authorities."

"Is that the way you all feel?"

Greg shifted nervously in his chair.

"You didn't see this guy, Clyde. He was the real deal. Slit your throat as soon as look at ya. It's certainly the way I feel."

"Ditto," said Moore.

For what seemed a long time, Bertram stared at them. When he finally spoke, his voice lacked the usual self-assuredness.

"Alright. Point taken. Our suspicions stay in this office."

He paused again, a combination of resignation and humility radiating from his eyes.

"One thing I want you to know. If I had been successful in warning Vic last night, I would have notified each of you. I'm pigheaded sometimes, but I'm not a fool."

Chapter Thirty-seven

Coroner Guy David's report of Monday, December 7th contained four principal recommendations. It read:

In finding the death of Mr. Victor Gordon on the evening of Tuesday, December 1st, 1969, to have been the result of an unfortunate accident, this office has issued the following four recommendations. One: that the manufacturers of pre-fabricated greenhouses ensure a non-slippery floor surface. Two: that glass, installed in said greenhouses for the purpose of enhancing plant-growth benefits of UV rays, be shatter resistant, i.e., motor vehicle windshields. Three: that said shatter resistant glass reach a height of not less than seven feet, in order to prevent mishaps of this nature. Four: that said greenhouses be equipped with connections for proper drainage, to counter potentially slippery surface areas.

The document bore an official stamp. As far as the coroner was concerned, the case was closed.

"Lies have a way of catching up with you."
RCMP Corporal Normand Francoeur was on the phone with Jason Moore.
"In Maria Claudio's case, it's a complicated web."
Moore was scarfing down a slightly stale toasted sandwich. Francoeur had caught him on his lunch break.
"She's in trouble, then?"
"That's an understatement. By the way, this is off the record, Jason."
"Understood."

"To begin with, she could eventually face disbarment. Even prison. It seems a certain Superior Court judge is having second thoughts about some of his rulings."

"Claudio's involved?"

"Up to her neck. The judge is in a tight spot. Remember the court clerk I told you about, the one keeping track of meetings in the judge's chambers and so on?"

"Yeah, I remember."

"Claudio's been in and out of those meetings like a horse to a watering hole."

"And?"

"And every time, the clerk has filled us in. Names. Dates. Everything. We managed to obtain access to the judge's financial records, without his knowledge of course. It seems these meetings with Claudio usually coincide with a sizeable deposit in His Worship's bank account."

"What's Claudio get in return?"

"Another little coincidence. The deposits are always made shortly after she's represented one of her shady clients in the judge's courtroom."

"And they're back on the street," Moore concluded.

Francoeur laughed.

"Most of the time. Anyway, all of this was circumstantial, but when we laid it out for the judge he had what you might call," another chuckle, "a crisis of conscience."

"Sure he did. So his epiphany comes back and bites Claudio on the ass."

"Hasn't yet. But it will."

Moore had a sudden thought.

"Got a favor to ask, Normand."

"Yeah? Well I owe you one. Those jokers we arrested after the Knowlton incident will be going away for a long time. The film nailed it."

"Glad to hear it. We're planning a follow up on that case. Look, here's the favor. You've spoken to me off the record about Claudio and the judge. Would you be willing to have a confidential tête-à-tête, cop to cop, with a certain Montreal homicide sergeant?"

"The guy who's after Peterson?"

"One and the same."

"And tell him what?"

"Basically what you just told me. His name is Detective Sergeant Pierre Maillot. I have the number in my wallet."

Whether it trickled down from the Mafia hierarchy or was a direct result of Francoeur's phone call, Greg Peterson didn't know and didn't care. The effect was the same. Montreal Police Detective-Sergeant Pierre Maillot finally backed off. The August lineup on Gosford Street would enter the realm of the forgotten.

Suzie Waldon drove in from Ottawa on the fifteenth. She'd banked a two-week summer vacation in order to spend the Christmas holidays in Park Ex. The year 1969 was slipping away. Greg and his mother looked forward to ushering it out.

The photo studio in Old Montreal became a joint venture. Enough income was generated from weekend fashion shoots, commercial product stills and the occasional wedding to allow Greg to buy into the operation Suzie had so generously financed.

"Keep the money," she told him. "I'll be a partner with controlling interest until the place pays for itself. Then we'll just be equal shareholders."

It became a moot point, when CKCF operations chief Hal Nichols had to eat crow and reinstate Greg complete with nearly four months of back pay. Greg's injured hand still ached from time to time, reminding him of the beating on Querbes Avenue. There was, however, no permanent damage.

New York crime boss Frank Ragusa was sentenced to life in prison for his role in a series of murders in the 'fifties. Alphonse Scarpa, the whistle-blower, disappeared forever into the shadows of witness protection.

The Salvatore Positano *borgata* never fully recovered from the death of Massimo Gianfranco and the eventual conviction of two of Tony Soccio's crew in the Knowlton killings. Positano was growing old. With no heir apparent, the Sicilian wing of the mob made rapid inroads into a new style of underworld enterprise. Rocco Panepinto wore the crown of criminal power in Montreal.

Maria Claudio, now discredited in Positano's fatherly eye and shunned by the mob's Calabrian faction, faced formal charges in a

Mafia plot to corrupt the courts. Two judges were forced to resign from the bench in disgrace. Several cases involving Claudio's former clients were reopened. She never recovered her underworld status and ultimately lost her license to practice law.

Ty Davis, Greg Peterson, Jason Moore and Clyde Bertram had one last meeting to discuss the death of Victor Gordon. They agreed the murder theory was something that could, or should not, be pursued by Flash News. The risk was too great. Bertram, however, had one last mission to accomplish in that regard. He fired his overnight police reporter, Dick Tomlin.

Ty, Liz, Catherine and Robin returned to a normal routine of family life. Happiness arrived and departed, only to reenter their lives again according to its own, unpredictable nature. Liz gave up drinking altogether. Eventually, therapy for her postpartum depression was no longer necessary.

Ty collected fifty dollars from sports director Walt Taylor in the wake of Ottawa's Grey Cup victory. In passing, Taylor informed him there'd be a rematch in June between Billy Sands and New Jersey's Jackie Tubbs.

"I'm not usually a betting man," Ty grinned at Taylor, "but my money's going to be on Tubbs."

Now, he sat at his typewriter in the news department. He felt frustrated that Salvatore Positano had gotten away with the Gordon murder. He rubbed his eyes. Bertram's cigar smoke permeated the newsroom atmosphere. Suddenly, he made a decision. He picked up his phone and dialed the number for *La Voix*. When their switchboard operator answered, he asked to speak with Réal Gendron. The crime reporter came on with a cheerful greeting.

"*Allo*, my frien'."

Ty sat back in his chair.

"Réal," he said. "Have I got a story for you."